HOW TO WRITE A NOVEL

Melanie Sumner, a recipient of the Whiting Writers' Award and a fellowship from the National Endowment for the Arts, is the author of *The Ghost of Milagro Creek*, *The School of Beauty and Charm*, and *Polite Society*. Her fiction has been published in *The New Yorker*, *Harper's Magazine*, and *Seventeen*. Previous awards include the New Mexico Book Award, the Maria Thomas Fiction Award for Peace Corps volunteers, and the regional pick for *Granta*'s Best of Young American Novelists. Sumner graduated from the University of North Carolina at Chapel Hill and earned her MFA from Boston University. Currently, she lives in Georgia and teaches at Kennesaw State University.

www.melanie-sumner.com

HOW
TO
WRITE
A NOVEL

HOW
TO
WRITE
A NOVEL

A Novel

Melanie Sumner

VINTAGE CONTEMPORARIES

VINTAGE BOOKS

A DIVISION OF PENGUIN RANDOM HOUSE LLC

NEW YORK

A VINTAGE CONTEMPORARIES ORIGINAL, AUGUST 2015

Copyright © 2015 by Melanie Sumner

All rights reserved. Published in the United States by
Vintage Books, a division of Penguin Random House LLC, New York,
and distributed in Canada by Random House of Canada,
a division of Penguin Random House Ltd., Toronto.

Vintage is a registered trademark and Vintage Contemporaries
and colophon are trademarks of Penguin Random House LLC.

The Library of Congress Cataloging-in-Publication Data
Sumner, Melanie.
How to write a novel : a novel / Melanie Sumner.
pages ; cm
I. Title.
PS3569.U46H69 2015   813'.54—dc23   2014042613

Vintage Books Trade Paperback ISBN: 978-1-101-87347-2
eBook ISBN: 978-1-101-87348-9

AUG 4 2015

Illustrations courtesy of Z. P. Marr
Book design by Heather Kelly

www.vintagebooks.com

Printed in the United States of America
10 9 8 7 6 5 4 3 2 1

To the godparents,
Brian Sumner (1961–2013) and Leslee Sumner,
and, of course! Zoë and Rider

HOW
TO
WRITE
A NOVEL

PROLOGUE

I'm skipping the prologue because I don't know anyone who reads prologues except my mother. Hi, Merm!

INTRODUCTION

Prologue skippers may be inclined to skip introductions as well, but my editors have suggested that this novel contains a minor flaw, which I might want to fix before it goes up for the Pulitzer Prize. The problem, as they see it, is that no 12.5-year-old could write this story. Allow me to propose that as a fictional character, I exist in the fourth dimension of reality, in which space and time have collapsed into an instantaneous and infinite experience that is itself, in accordance with Einstein's theory of relativity ($E = mc^2$), nothing more than an illusion.

Or I could be lying about my age.

EXPOSITION

For my 12.5th birthday, my mom gave me a book called *Write a
Novel in Thirty Days!* Subliminally, of course, Diane (that's my
mom) wants to write a novel herself, but she doesn't have a spare
thirty days. Already, you can see our family dynamic. I'm supposed to talk to Dr. Victoria Dhang, MS, LPC, about how I have
to do practically everything around here, but Diane conveniently
forgets to make the appointment.

"You're not that bad," she'll say, looking me over like I'm a
jacket that's a little tight in the shoulders and frayed at the cuffs but
good for another year. Therapy money goes to my little brother,
Max, who merits weekly counseling due to his "unique sensitivity
to the world," aka, dude hits himself!

Since there's no man in the house, Diane and I have our hands
full co-parenting Max. Every Tuesday afternoon, we take him to
the office of Dr. Dhang to work on his issues. "Dang, Max," I say.
"Is it already Tuesday again?" He scowls at me, which makes him
look almost handsome. He's big for an eight-year-old, with a teddy
bear face and a Play-Doh belly. When he pokes his finger in his
belly or counts the bruises on his knees, he gets a curious look

in his eyes, like someone just gave him this body for Christmas. Definitely a new soul.

I am an old soul, which is possibly why my parents named me Aristotle, Aris for short. Yes, I'm a girl. What were they thinking! Well, they were hunkered down in this shack in Alaska, living off a bag of dried beans, suffering from light deprivation, and this baby (*moi!*) arrived. In my baby pictures, you'll see my bald head sticking up over the side of the empty chicken crate that worked for a crib. They had, like, no money. My father, the wild Joe Thibodeau from Houma, Louisiana, was a saxophone player. I have his olive skin, wavy hair, red lips, and violet eyes.

I'm short. I can reach the coffeepot on the kitchen counter and pour myself a cup, but I have to swing up on the cabinet to get the sugar from the back corner of the shelf where Diane hides it from herself. You probably want to know what Diane looks like, but she says descriptions aren't my strong point, so I may not give her one. She told me to stop giving my characters violet eyes and making everybody gorgeous. Excuse me? It's my novel.

Sometimes Diane thinks she knows everything about writing because she published a short story before she became an adjunct English professor at Kanuga Christian College. The sign in front of the college reads Transforming Lives Through Christ, which sounds like a good idea, but it hasn't happened yet. Diane's story was called "Why I Love Jesus." It was about this thirteen-year-old girl who went on a youth retreat with the First Baptist Church and didn't get saved. The last scene is pretty good—the youths are all sitting in a circle around a fire, going up one by one to answer the call to rededicate their lives to Jesus, even though they don't give a damn. The preacher calls and calls, but the girl, who is really Diane, doesn't come. She sits out there in the dark by herself.

Diane is forty-three now, short and either curvy or chubby, depending on her mood, with a button nose and blondish bangs that are always falling in her face. You can tell she's a Montgomery by her recessive-gene green eyes and the way she gives the Montgomery handshake. Papa Montgomery teaches the handshake to all of his descendants. It requires direct eye contact, a smile, and a firm grip. It's how we show our character, how we do business, how we make friends. It's how we make our way in a dog-eat-dog world where time is money and nothing in life is certain but death. The Montgomery handshake is proof that we don't have secrets.

"Men originally shook hands to show each other that they didn't have weapons," Papa told me once.

"What about women?" I asked him.

"Well," he said. He got a faraway look in his eyes as he patted a strand of white hair over the bald spot on top of his head. "I guess women could have weapons too," he said finally. Then he grinned. Papa was old before braces came out, so his teeth are slightly crooked, just enough to make him look like he can tell a good joke.

Grandma is the only Montgomery who doesn't have a handshake, but ladies in the South don't shake hands. Instead, they fold their cool fingers over yours and press ever so gently, leaning in close until you smell breath mints and the dab of eau de toilette behind each ear. Then they say something awful. A few days after Joe died, Grandma knelt beside Diane's bed and folded her fingers over her hand. After looking into her eyes for a moment, she whispered, "Why didn't he ever have a better job?"

Papa and Grandma are very interested in people's jobs. If I make a new friend, they immediately ask, "What do his/her parents *do*?" When they ask Diane what her friends *do*, she'll say something like, "Viola likes to drink Earl Grey tea and watch the hummingbirds," or "Penn does crossword puzzles." This upsets them. Sometimes she says, "I don't know." Then the grandparents gape at her.

"You don't *know*?" Papa will ask. "You don't know what his/her job is? Does he/she *have* a job? How can you not know this?" Papa managed Southern Board before it merged with Southern Paper and started smelling bad. He kept his job for thirty-five years even though he didn't like it.

Diane says this is tragic.

"Whatever you do," Papa tells her, "don't lose *your* job." Diane is the only Montgomery to ever lose a job. At fifteen, she was dismissed from the Avon sales force for convincing women that they were more beautiful without cosmetics. When she moved to Alaska with Joe, she worked with him at a fish-processing plant until it closed for some weird reason. That winter, they made halibut enchiladas and hiked around on snowshoes looking at eagles and bighorn sheep, with me bundled into a baby sling on Joe's chest. He wore a coyote fur–lined hat, with earmuffs that swiveled up and down over his ears. He called it his mad bomber hat, and sometimes he would yell, "Mad bomber!" and dive into a snowbank with me. I remember the way his voice growled softly in my ear just before a jump, asking me if I was ready, how his arms tightened around me. We went deep into the snowbanks, down and down and down. Sometimes I held on to the furry earmuffs as we climbed out, my hands loose in the mittens attached to my sleeves with string. Our breath steamed when we climbed out into the sky that was always night. This is what he wrote inside the cover of our photo album: *YOU SHOULD NEVER SAY SHOULD.*

Out there, Diane says, the land is so beautiful it's sometimes terrifying. It's so big you can't forget God, even for a minute. Another human being becomes a rare and interesting animal. She gets quiet, looks at her hands. "Buy life insurance," she says.

Joe died in a car wreck on the Richardson Highway. I was four years old, Max was in the oven, and Diane was broke, so Papa and Grandma took us under their wing. When we moved to Kanuga,[1] Georgia, I was transferred from one of the last wild places on earth to a two-Walmart, no-Target town fueled by fast food and tethered to heaven by a church on every corner. All I have left of Joe are a few pictures, my DNA, and the mad bomber hat.

In case you were wondering, yes, it is extremely awkward

---

1 Pronounced Ka-NOOG-aah, like a sneeze.

to have a dead father. All of my classmates at the Lab (Lavender Mountain Laboratory School, Grades Pre-K–8) have a complete set of parents, except for Anders Anderson, but he's a minor character in my novel, so I'm not wasting first-chapter space on him. *Write a Novel in Thirty Days!* says that the first chapter is prime real estate. Believe me, if I let Anders hang out in the first chapter, you'd be gone. My best friend, Kate Harrington, has a divorced dad. She only sees him every third Thursday, but still, she has him. Diane says our family is like a three-legged dog and we get around just fine. I tell her that people who get around just fine don't become writers.

A lot of people say they want to be writers, but they don't write. They either lack the necessary misery, have an overly critical English teacher (hello, Mrs. Waller!), or just aren't wired for it. I'm not worried. I've had movies running in my head as long as I can remember—it's genetic. When we were little, riding along in the car, Diane would say:

"Aris, I only put one chopstick in your lunchbox today because I couldn't find the other one, but you can eat sushi with your hands if you wash them."

I'd say, "Okay, thanks, Merm. I have a movie in my head now. Please don't talk to me."

Then Max would repeat, "Ihaveamovieinmyheadnowplease donttalktome." He doesn't talk quite so fast now that Dr. Dhang has put him on speed, which, ironically, slows down hyper kids, but he's not exactly coherent. Diane always has at least three movies going on in her head. This is why our friends wave and honk their horns at us on the road and practically drive onto the hood of our car, and she doesn't see them.

She's like, "Did we know them?" Kanuga isn't so small that we all know one another, but everybody looks *very* familiar. Most people go ahead and wave.

We are different from most people in Kanuga.

WAYS WE ARE DIFFERENT

- Max and I have been eating with chopsticks since we were babies, even though we are of English/Scottish/French/Cajun descent.

- We aren't Republicans even though we are white.

- In addition to the medical kit, baby wipes, bottles of water, and goldfish crackers that all mothers keep in the car for emergencies, Diane stashes a machete in the back of our car. She has never explained why.

- We don't have a football team. Or a TV to watch it on.

- We aren't fundamentalist Christians. This is a very touchy subject in Kanuga. Anders Anderson told me I was going to hell because I didn't go to church. I said any place without him was fine with me. Then he said my father wasn't in heaven, since he didn't go to church.

During our Sunday Night Meeting, when we sit around the table with cups of coffee and clipboards discussing our goals for the upcoming week and the rest of our lives as a family, I asked Diane if Joe was in hell.

"No," she said. "Your father went to hell before he died."

Max, who had been tilting his chair back on two legs, let it fall forward. "You can *visit* hell?"

"The chair stays on four legs," said Diane. "Aris, who told you that your father was in hell?"

"I dunno," I said, wishing I hadn't mentioned it.

"Who?"

"I don't remember." Our dogs were flattened against the French doors, quivering as they watched a squirrel climb a tree. Lucky, the paranoid alpha with a Mensa IQ, stood up on her hind legs and tapped on the glass of one of the French doors with the nails of her right paw. Hiroshima, the cute one, body-slammed the door, barking spastically to overcome an inferiority complex. I got up to let them out.

"Aris," she said, in *that* voice. Tendrils of smoke were curling out of her ears.[2] "Sit back down here and tell me."

"Uh, maybe Anders?"

"Which one is Anders?"

I have had the same eight classmates at the Lab since pre-K, but Diane still can't tell them apart.

"I saw a burn mark on Dad once," said Max. When no one responded, he tilted his chair back again.

"Your father died before you were born, honey," said Diane. She looked at him. "Max, leave that chair alone."

"I'm practicing chair tilting for the talent show at school," said Max. "Everyone has to have a talent."

Max has been searching for his talent for quite some time. Bypassing the more conventional art forms (too much competition), he has tried squirting milk out of his nose for long distances, training snails to swim (that was a sad one), and squeezing himself through a tennis racket. We're still searching.

"You're going to break your neck," said Diane, "and we do not have health insurance." When the dogs had finished their squirrel hunt, they announced themselves at the door, and I got up to let them back inside.

Diane turned back to me. "Aris, do I know Anders?"

"Anders Anderson. The other single-parent kid. Dirt-brown hair, kind of skinny, walks like a hedgehog."

"Oh, *him*," Diane said. "The one whose mother left?"

She closed her eyes and began to pray. Diane's spiritual beliefs are too complicated to go into here, but I knew she was praying her resentment prayer. I read her lips as she prayed silently, *Great*

2   A writer gets one hyperbole per novel.

Spirit, Great Friend, Mahaya, may that little shit Anders Anderson and his parents have peace, prosperity, and a greater love than they have ever known. Amen.

When she had finished her prayer, she scribbled something on her clipboard. Then she announced that we were getting a religion and a football team.

A grocery-store daisy in the vase on the table wilted right before my eyes—I'm not kidding. My dad does stuff like that now that he's a ghost; he still wants to have a say in family affairs. I don't remember when I first realized that Joe's spirit was in our house after he died; it seems like he never quite left. I'd see things out of the corner of my eye—flickers of light in the living room, like the faint green glow of lightning bugs, the coffee brewing even when Diane forgot to turn the switch on, a hand adjusting the covers around my shoulders as I fell asleep.

"We're going to be normal!" cheered Max. In his excitement, he leaned his chair back too far and hit the floor with a smack.

One week later, we were Episcopalians at St. Michael's Church, wearing red and black *Go Dawgs* shirts. Most Southern Baptists can't quite put their finger on Episcopalian. Clearly I'm not one of *them*, and I'm not even a Methodist, which is just an uppity Baptist anyway. I'm dangerously close to Catholic, even smelling faintly of incense on some Sundays, but I don't worship statues. So they just look at my Georgia Bulldogs shirt and say the magic words of belonging—"Go Dawgs."

It was one of Diane's better plans, but it didn't work. You can't be a football fan without cable, and on most Sunday mornings we didn't feel like getting out of our pajamas. I knew how these small failures nibbled at Diane's self-esteem. On bad days, she couldn't get out of bed. Then I'd make popcorn for breakfast and take Max outside so he couldn't hear her crying.

Diane says that a woman makes a big mistake when she tries to solve her problems by latching on to a man, but I thought she should give it a go. Joe couldn't be replaced, at least not the way I thought he could when I was five and asked Diane to go to Walmart and get me a new father.

"You don't want the kind they sell there," she said. That was probably the only laugh I got out of her for two years after Joe's death. All the same, remarriage was on my agenda for getting the family back on its feet. When I outlined my plan to Diane, she said, "This takes time, honey, and some things are just out of our control."

"Right," I said. I didn't want to discourage her, but I knew that we had to do something soon. Luckily, it only takes thirty days to write a novel. I figured I'd knock one out, make a wad of cash, and get famous. That would draw some attention to our situation.

The first exercise in *Write a Novel in Thirty Days!*, after you skip the yadda yadda yadda about having the courage to write, is to create the setting of your story. When I settled down to answer Question #1, Where does this scene take place?, I was stumped. Everything takes place in my head. I have no idea what my head looks like. I decided to tell someone that I was writing a novel, in case I needed help beyond the scope of *Write a Novel in Thirty Days!* Of course, Diane and Max knew, and I had already told Kate, who has BFF[3] rights to all classified information, but I needed professional feedback, so I selected Ms. Chu, our librarian at the Lab.

My opportunity to broach the subject came on a Tuesday during library hour when Ms. Chu appeared, shadowlike, beside the table I shared with Kate. Ms. Chu's first name is Mandy. She is tall and skinny, with glossy black hair that swings across her cheek. She has acne in her T-zone, which is where mine is coming out, and even though she's twenty or thirty years old, she has braces. That day she was wearing a white blouse and a gray skirt that flowed around her like water. Around her neck hung a tiny ball of crystal on a silver chain.

"Do you need any help, Aris?" she whispered, because Ms.

3   Best friends forever.

Chu always whispers. If you spend most of your time in a library, it becomes a habit.

"Well, actually," I whispered, "I need some advice. I'm writing a novel?"

She nodded, lightly touching the crystal around her neck. Out of nowhere, Anders Anderson materialized and plunked himself down in the chair beside me. I shifted my shoulders to exclude him from the conversation and continued.

"I've got all the characters going," I said, "but I have trouble with settings. I forget all about settings."

"I hope this isn't a love story," said Anders. "Am I in it?"

"Maybe," I mused, watching the light refract from Ms. Chu's crystal, "it's because I skip settings when I'm reading? Actually, I skim. Skim settings and descriptions."

"Is there something disturbing in your novel?" she asked.

"No, of course not," I said.

Ms. Chu looked disappointed. "There must be something disturbing in your story," she said. "Some parts should be painful to write. Sometimes you'll feel like you are bleeding the words onto the page."

"Right," I said, but I was worried. The author of *Write a Novel in Thirty Days!* had not mentioned blood. What if I had the wrong book on novel writing? I asked Ms. Chu about this, but she discouraged me from reading more writing advice.

"One how-to book is plenty," she said. Then she disappeared into a secret chamber behind her desk where she keeps new books that haven't been cataloged. In a few minutes, she emerged and handed me a small brown volume: *Songs of Innocence and of Experience*, by William Blake.

"When I need advice, I read poetry," she said.

"Thank you," I said, and cracked the cover of the book to hide my disappointment. I had skimmed enough of Blake in Mrs. Waller's class to know that pastoral poetry about lambs and cherub-children wasn't going to help me write a disturbing novel.

"Just write a poem," said Anders. "It takes too long to write a novel, and who really reads them?"

"I do," said Kate. She sat up very straight in her chair and quoted her favorite writer, Jane Austen. "'The person, be it gentleman or lady, who has not pleasure in a good novel, must be intolerably stupid.'"

Kate looks like a character in an Austen novel. She's a blue-eyed ginger who has worn sunscreen since the day she was born, so her skin is pale even in the summer. She enunciates her words so clearly that Kanugians sometimes suggest, "You ain't from around here," but she is. "I am a nerd," she tells people proudly. To prove it, she has clipped a small bottle of hand sanitizer to her backpack.

Ms. Chu led Kate to the shelves to find a Jane Austen novel Kate hadn't already devoured. While Anders created a missile with a pencil, a rubber band, and an eraser, I sniffed the wonderful new-book smell of *Songs of Innocence and of Experience*. I was skipping the prologue, of course, but an interesting quote caught my eye: "The difference between a bad artist and a good one is: the bad artist seems to copy a great deal; the good one really does." As I considered this, a pencil-missile pinged the cover of the book I had erected between myself and Anders. When I glared at him, he laughed triumphantly.

"Heard from Billy lately?" he asked. Wrapping his arms around himself to suggest a couple making out, he emitted vulgar kissing sounds.

I sighed. How did this emotional retrograde sneak into the first chapter of my novel? In any case, I will now have to share with you, dear reader, the sad news that my fiancé, Billy Starr III, moved to Boston last summer after his mother, a professor at KCC, was fired for staging a proabortion demonstration. Diane says that professors aren't fired—that word is too plebian for academia. Instead, they are "denied tenure." Whatever you call it, my fiancé was picked up like a suitcase and transported to another state.

I hate it when people go on about their long-distance

relationship—you start to wonder if they're making it all up—so I'll refrain. Let me just say that Billy Starr III once sat in this same seat that Anders now occupied. His library voice was a sweet, low growl, meant for my ears only as he leaned forward to gaze meaningfully into my eyes. Most of the time I didn't care (not that much) that he was talking about baseball or basketball. Sometimes his hand brushed against mine, and then, like two repressed fools in a Jane Austen novel, we blushed.

"Billy is fine," I told Anders. "I'll tell him you said hello." Ha, right. Last year, when Billy announced, with sorrowful blue eyes, that he was leaving the Lab, Anders asked him if he could have his girlfriend. EXCUSE ME? Am I a locker to be passed on to the next student? When I heard about this conversation, I sat Anders down and spent an hour explaining the absurd injustice of treating females like chattel. I thought he might have come across the word "chattel" in his frequent Bible reading and hoped this would strengthen my argument, but he didn't hear a single word. When I finished my lecture, he only asked me to sit beside him at lunch.

"The average amount of time it takes for a long-distance relationship to break up is 4.5 months," Anders said now.

He waved five fingers at me—yes, Billy had been gone for five months. Thankfully, the bell rang, and he loped out the door like his ass was on fire.

As I walked out of the library, I happened to pick up a catalog for Lavender Mountain Laboratory School. Holy moly! There, on the front page, was the setting I needed to steal for my novel.

The Lavender Mountain Laboratory School, affectionately called "The Lab" by students and families, is a private co-educational day school nestled in the foothills of northwest Georgia. Our campus stretches across four hundred acres of field and forest at the base of Kanuga's beautiful Lavender Mountain. On the LMLS campus, you will find modern

convenience and the latest technology housed in rustic cab-
ins constructed of local pine and native stone. White-tailed
deer graze alongside cobbled paths connecting our main
learning centers with a state-of-the-art gymnasium and a
media center that houses an impressive collection of clas-
sic and contemporary works in print and digital archives.
Ducks, geese, and swans dot the ponds scattered through-
out the campus, where students are encouraged to engage
in outdoor, hands-on learning with our interactive science,
math, language arts, and fine arts departments. The faculty
is composed of dedicated, highly skilled professionals who
are devoted to helping our students achieve their academic,
social, and spiritual potential.[4]

In the margin, someone (a student? parent? teacher?) had
scrawled, "oh PULEESE."

I was ready for the next exercise in *Write a Novel in Thirty
Days!,* Choose a Protagonist and Uncover Her Motivation. The
first part was a no-brainer. If you can't be the heroine of your own
novel, why bother? Diane agrees that I make an exciting protagonist, but deep down, she was hoping to have the starring role in my
novel. Her theory: If Mama ain't happy, ain't nobody happy.

Sorry, Diane! So I'm the protagonist, and my motivation is . . .
To be perfectly honest,[5] I'm not a very motivated person. Teachers
are always checking off "Lacks Motivation" on my Lab report.
Diane likes to remind me that I rank in the top one percent in the
nation on standardized test scores, so I should be able to pass Algebra or whatever. I agree that the dichotomy here is disturbing, but
just the thought of picking up my room or factoring a trinomial
makes me really, *really* tired. Sometimes after a day of thinking

4   Skim recommended.
5   My English teacher, Mrs. Waller, takes off a point for that phrase because she says
only dishonest people use it.

about doing some kind of work, my arms and legs ache so much I think they might fall off. Diane says these are growing pains. Normally, a protagonist in so much pain would *never* get a motivation, and the novel would go kaput, but something unexpected happened.

Write a Novel in Thirty Days! says that your book must have a conflict. Something has to happen that changes the world the characters inhabit. Since nothing happens in Kanuga, I was afraid this might be a problem, but when I thought about all the library books Ms. Chu has loaned me, and all the yarns I hear at church, I realized that great literature often begins with a flood.

Our flood happened on a Sunday when I was supposed to acolyte at St. Michael's. Diane had signed me up to be an acolyte in hopes that my sacred duty would compel her to get us to church. At the time, Billy was in town, and he was an acolyte, so of course I agreed. Gradually, however, we lapsed back into our heathen habits.

This Sunday, Diane had again woken up with the alarm clock in her fist. She staggered down the hall in Joe's old flannel bathrobe with her slippers on the wrong feet, yelling, "Get up! We're late!" With her left hand she banged on my bedroom door, and with her right hand she banged on Max's door. It's a real gift she has, the double-fisted knock, but I've never mentioned it to her because she doesn't have a sense of humor until she's had two cups of coffee. In fact, if we say anything to her at this time, other than "Yes, ma'am," she wails, "I haven't had my coffee yet!" Translated: *My name is Diane, and I am a caffeine fiend. I am incoherent, completely dysfunctional, and probably dangerous.* We never come out of our rooms until she has poured her coffee and taken it back to the brown leather chair in the corner of her room, where she chugs it down while she talks to God about the day at hand.

However, on this morning, the fated February first, both Diane and God had gone back to sleep. Max was in the shower, and he wasn't howling, so apparently he hadn't confused the "H" knob with the "C" knob.

After pouring myself a cup of java, I pulled out the stack of papers Diane had been meaning to grade. Difficulty getting out of bed in the morning is a sign of depression, and I didn't want Diane to slip into the blues and fall behind on her work. So far, she had only commented on one paper.

Charles Hutchins
English 1102

> I am throwing the grading rubric out for this paper and giving you an A because, despite minor flaws, you reveal something profound. A+ A+ A+

The Most Important Person in My Life:
Mrs. Octavia Hutchins

~~To begin with, we live in a society and all of us are influenced by others who might be constantly changing us for better or worse. There are a lot of people who help us form our personalities and become who we are. I believe that my mother is the most significant person in my life in this regard. I call her Mama.~~

> Cut

Mama is a big woman with arms that are strong enough to do justice to a child's bottom if that is needed, and fat enough to feel soft and warm when she hugs you. Before she bought colored contact lenses, her eyes were brown, and they got big and dark when she was mad.

> The story begins here.

If I back talk her, she'll say, "Excuse me? To *whom* are you talking?" I am the first one in our family to go to college, and she was the first one in her family to graduate from high school. She wanted to be a teacher, but my father convinced her to marry him and bury her dreams. He resented her education, especially if he had a hangover.

One morning, he almost killed me. She had made us fried eggs with bacon, biscuits, and gravy. I must have been pretty small because she was still cutting my biscuit for me. She glanced over at my father and said, "Marvin, please chew with your mouth closed."

He looked at her slant-eyed. "You the smart one in the family," he said. I knew what was coming. I wished we could hide in the mornings, but she taught me you can't hide from life. You look life in the face.

"You so smart. Ain't your mama smart? She talkety-talk and I workety-work? Fuck that shit." He stood up, unbuckled his belt, and whipped it out of his pants. I watched as it made the familiar loop in his hand. I hated him for making us afraid. I wanted to slide under the table, but I had to protect my mother, so I grabbed his arm.

When he flung me across the room, my head hit the edge of the refrigerator. I remember seeing the linoleum up close, and her screams. "He's hurt!" she yelled. "Charles is hurt! Stop! He's not moving!" My father kept beating her with the belt. Over her screams, I heard this hiss, slap, hiss, slap, hiss, slap. Then nothingness started falling into my head, all cool and sweet, and I disappeared for a while.

Later, after my father left us, I had to wear his clothes. Mama got a second job, but we still didn't have money for new clothes. Marvin's clothes were big for me, even after she cut them down. The kids at school called me Big Foot because of the shoes.

Mama said it didn't matter what those fools called me. She said, "You are there to learn. Learn it all. When you get a scholarship to college, I'm going to make all this up to you." At night sometimes I could hear her praying for me through her bedroom door.

I received a full scholarship to Kanuga Community College, paying room and board, books, and full tuition plus a stipend. Mama would not let me give her any money. Instead, she gave me the money she had put away, year after year, to help pay for my education.

"You buy something for yourself," she said. "Buy something that makes you proud of your accomplishment."

She is an amazing woman!

When I pulled up in front of the house in a black BMW: all-wheel drive, 400 horsepower, she came out on the porch and started crying. Then she went back inside and changed her clothes. That day I drove her to the optical shop to get fitted for colored contact lenses. The ones she chose were purple. I can't say that I liked the new color, but I got used to it.

"What do you think?" she asked me.

"Very striking," I told her. What was really beautiful to me was her smile. To conclude, I consider that I am a lucky person to have Mrs. Octavia Hutchins for my mother.

I LOVE THIS GUY!!!!

I agree.

Wow, I thought, putting Charles's paper back in the pile, *this guy has a story.* Most of Diane's students write papers like this: *Hello. This essay is a bag over my head. I'm not here. Give me an A. That's five hundred words. The end.* I looked over Diane's comments again. Was she giving him enough encouragement? Writers need a lot of love. When I had a chance, I decided, I would add my own comments to Charles's story. At the moment, however, I needed some fresh air to clear my head. I put on Joe's mad bomber hat and was headed outside when Max screamed.

It was the kind of scream you feel in your own throat. My heart went blip, and for a second I couldn't breathe. Diane says that mothers feel the burn when a baby touches a hot stove. As a co-parent, when I heard that scream, I felt something wet all over me, like blood. Crazy thoughts flashed through my mind. He'd drunk nail polish remover. Swallowed a razor blade. Impaled himself on the shower curtain rod.

"I'm coming!" I yelled, careering through the living room and hitting the hallway at full speed. I skidded to a stop on the wet floor. Water was overflowing the bathroom sink and had started running into the hall. Max was in the middle of it all, ankle deep, buck naked, a blow-dryer in his hand.

"Turn it off!" I yelled. "Max! Turn it off right now!"

"I can't! The handle came off!"

"No, the dryer! You're going to be electrocuted, you idiot!"

"Help!" he cried, clenching the dryer with both fists. "Somebody! Please! Help me!"

"Oh fuck," I said, splashing toward him, ready to die. Then I saw the electrical cord from the blow-dryer lying on the sink, unplugged. Beneath the sound of sobbing and rushing water, the tinkle of Diane's alarm signaled the end of meditation.

"Turn that water off!" she yelled from behind her locked bedroom door. "Our water bill was fifty-eight dollars last month!"

"You said a bad word," Max informed me with one eyebrow raised.

"No, I didn't. That was your imagination. What did you do? Why is water pouring out of the sink?"

"I didn't touch it!" He stood with his feet planted wide and his face set in defiance. The doctor says that Max might grow to over six feet. Already, football coaches look him over with a gleam in their eyes. With Diane's hand-me-down short genes, I'll be lucky to clear five, but for now, I rule.

"Tell the truth, Max."

"I did it!" he sobbed. "It's all my fault. I'm stupid! I'm so stupid! I'm an idiot!"

Enter Diane. A regal five-foot-two in her old blue bathrobe. As tradition dictates, she glared at me, her firstborn. Whatever the youngest child is guilty of should have been stopped by the elder one.

"What is going on in here?"

"Use your nice voice," said Max. "Not that one."

"Are you drying your hair with water on the floor?" asked Diane. "Honey! You'll be electrocuted."

"He doesn't dry his hair, Diane," I said. "His towel is wadded up somewhere in his room, so he blow-dries his *body*."

This gave her pause.

"He is weird," I explained.

Max shot me a death glare, then covered his genitals with his hands and said quietly, "Mom, this may not be the right time to tell you this."

"Tell me."

"I can't. You'll get mad. It will be too much on your plate."

"Max, tell me why the bathroom is flooding!"

"It's not that," he said as the puddle grew around our feet. "It's something else." He took a deep breath. "Aris dropped the F-bomb."

"Goddammit!" she screamed. "Get off that wet floor and turn the water off, now!"

"I knew you'd get mad," Max whimpered. Then he tilted his head back and wailed. "It came off in my hand!"

I imagined my end of the banner sagging down at the eleven o'clock service as the acolytes at St. Michael's carried on without me, again. When Diane told Max to bring her a screwdriver and he showed up with a wrench, I realized that we'd have to call Penn.

OMG! I forgot to introduce Penn! Reader, meet Penn MacGuf-fin: family friend (currently without benefits), handyman, nanny. He says he prefers the term "PMI" (positive male influence) to "nanny." Diane says that sounds more affordable. Penn is a possible catch for ole Diane. He's old too—thirty or forty or something— and bald under his baseball cap, but he has muscles, gray eyes, and seriously cute ears. He says that's because his grandmother is a full-blooded Cherokee, and all Cherokees have cute ears. He told us that "kanuga" means "briars" in Cherokee, and Chutiksee, the name of our county, comes from the word "*dudun'leksun'yi*," which means "where its legs were broken off."

Obviously, it's hard to find a date in Where Its Legs Were Bro-ken Off. You have to look long, hard, and far. Since I've already picked my husband out, I don't have to bother with dating, but Diane hops on and off Match.com. When she's off the site, she stops getting pedicures and tells me about her childhood dream of becoming a nun.

"We used to drive by a convent on Lookout Mountain, on the way to see my grandparents in Kentucky," she tells me. "I'd look up through the trees at those steep slate roofs and feel like that was my home." She describes her imaginary self, gliding over the polished stone walkways of porticos, through shadowy passages lit by flickering gas lanterns, and out into sunny, well-tended gardens. She gets to read for most of the day, and she eats loaves of freshly baked French bread with local goat cheese and sips mugs of steaming café au lait. She is married to God.

Grandma and Papa say there has never been a convent on Lookout Mountain.

"Let's call Penn," I said when the wrench fell apart in Diane's hand.

"I've got this," she said. She tried a pair of pliers. By this time, her sleeves were soaked. Water swished around her ankles.

"We should turn the main line off," said Max, but he whispered it, not wanting to make her mad.

"She doesn't remember how," I whispered back.

Diane isn't stupid. She really isn't. It's just that when a woman has a baby, something happens to her brain. When she had me, after sixteen hours of unmedicated labor, a gap opened up between her front teeth, her feet grew from a size eight to an eight and a half, and she shot a few brain circuits. She said you have to make certain concessions to women after childbirth, the way you do to veterans of wars. When she explained all this to me, I doubled the effect to include the damage of Max, and there you have it.

"Call Papa," said Diane with forced calm. "Tell him that everything is fine"—she paused to wring out her sleeves—"but we'd like him to stop by for a few minutes."

"They've gone to see Elvis," I reminded her. "But don't freak," I said, because Diane was digging frantically in her pockets for a piece of nicotine gum and starting to get that look on her face. "I'll call Penn."

Diane met Penn at an AA meeting. I've never seen either one of them drunk; in fact, I've never seen anyone drink alcohol except at communion, but if Diane drank booze the way she chews nicotine gum, she once had a problem. Her nicotine-gum addiction affects every member of the family, even the dogs. It gets in their hair. Sometimes they go through the trash and rechew the pieces that still have a little squirt of nicotine in them, and then they get all weird. I'm like, *Diane, the dogs are high again.*

Time and time again, she has *promised* to quit. Sometimes she tries. She'll go for maybe two days without her drug, crying and walking around like a zombie. During this special time, Max and I are not allowed to fight or ask for money or express ourselves, lest we send her back to the fires of addiction. Then, suddenly, she's at it again. She's driving down the road grinning and smacking the gum hell-for-leather, making a nasty wad of the chewed pieces on the dashboard and risking our lives to tear back into the childproof package for the next piece.

Now, as she bit into the gum, the wrinkle on her forehead smoothed out, and she almost smiled.

"We don't need to call Penn," she said. "We aren't helpless females."

"I'm not female," said Max, but we ignored him; the poor kid was four before Diane and I realized that we had taught him how to pee like a girl.

Diane turned the other handle on the sink, and it came off in her hand. "We'll call a plumber."

"Plumbers go fishing on Sundays," I said.

"Hush," she said. "This is serious. Where's my phone?"

I started to suggest calling one of Diane's students but thought better of it. Diane is a popular teacher. Last semester, her favorite students came over on Sunday afternoons to eat chocolate chip pancakes, talk about novels, and jump on the trampoline. One girl even lost her virginity in Diane's bed when no one was looking. That's when the dean told Diane to cool it. "If you were a permanent faculty member, this behavior would result in severe consequences," he wrote in a letter with CONFIDENTIAL stamped across the envelope in red ink. Dr. Dhang has told Diane not to discuss adult matters with us, but Max and I are such good listeners that it's always a temptation.

"That sucks," said Max when Diane had read the letter aloud. He scrunched up his face and balled his fist. "I'll beat that damn's face in!"

"'Damn' is an adjective, not a noun," I said, but he was in boxing mode and didn't hear. He knocked over a couple of chairs, then stopped, a look of horror spreading over his face.

"Mom! Are you going to get fired?" he asked.

Diane said that adjuncts never get fired. "We're not worth the paperwork," she said. All the same, we stopped having students over on Sundays.

Now Diane's cellphone floated past my ankles. Max let out a whoop and yelled, "I found it!"

I went in my room and called the plumber.

"He ain't here," said his wife.

"Do you know when he'll be back?"

"Well," she said. "It's Sunday."

She let this sink in.

"Yes, ma'am," I said; then neither one of us spoke for a while. I listened to her light a cigarette and exhale deeply.

"I wanted him to go to church," she continued, "but he done gone and went fishing on me."

"Do you think he'll be back in a couple of hours?"

"There ain't no telling," she said firmly.

In the hallway, Diane was freaking out. "Those aren't *rags*, Max. Those are *towels*! Those are my *guest towels*."

"We don't have guests," said Max.

Penn is the closest thing we have to a guest, and he doesn't use towels. When I explained to Diane that the plumber had gone fishing, she broke down and told me to call Papa on his cellphone.

"Don't talk to Grandma," she warned me. "Ask him how to turn off the main line. He told me once, but I forgot." She smacked her gum thoughtfully. "Tell him we have a small leak."

"All righty, then," I said in the cheerful voice I use when everything has gone to hell. I shut the door to my room and moved my bear, Zimmerman, from my bed to a high shelf. I put the mad bomber hat and my laptop up there too. Then I texted Penn:

DISASTER! WE ARE IN A FLOOD. SOS.

I waited. One Mississippi, two Mississippi, three . . . No response. Penn doesn't keep close tabs on his phone. Either he has misplaced it or some chick is trying to get a scope on him. Diane says he doesn't like control.

Papa, on the other hand, loves control. He answered his phone immediately, as he always does, but it took me a while to get any information from him because he had to verify that something so ridiculous could happen to people who are related to him.

"The faucet came off? It just came off? In Max's hand? How did that happen? What was he doing?"

"Nothing."

"He had to be doing *something*."

You could hear Grandma in the background demanding to know what was going on.

"Y'all must have been clowning around in there," he said. "Water faucets don't just come off in your hand."

"It wasn't really the faucet. It was the handle-thingy."

"The what?"

"I don't know. I was going outside."

"Outside? What were you doing outside?"

"Nothing."

"You had to be doing *something*."

Eventually, Papa gave up. To regain his territory, he began to explain that in all of his eighty years on this earth, he had never had a sink handle just come off in his hand. In fact, he had never heard of such a thing. Was I *sure* this is what happened? You have to let these inquiries run their course with Papa. Over his shoulder, Grandma was going, "Nah nah nah nah."

"Was it the hot or cold water?" he asked.

"Cold."

"Well, that's a blessing. If it were hot water, you'd have a real problem on your hands." He sighed. He told Grandma to be quiet for a minute; he was trying to think. Finally, he began his careful instructions. "Tell your mother to open the cabinet under the sink and reach in there and feel around for the nozzle and turn it to the right. I've shown this to her ten times."

"Okay-doe-kay," I said. I waded down the hall and relayed this to Diane, who was kneeling in front of the cabinet with the robe bunched around her hips to keep the hem dry.

"If you will *wait* one minute," Papa was telling Grandma.

"I'm part of this family too," she said. "Don't shut me out. Is the toilet running over?"

I covered the phone with my hand and told Diane that Penn might drop by. Penn is really the best option for Diane, but I don't mind waiting for them to figure it out. From the few forays she has made into the world of romance, I can tell you that introducing some dating disaster as "my mother's boyfriend" is extremely awkward. Of course, if the relationship with Penn didn't work out, we'd be left without a PMI. For example, if the bathroom flooded and Papa and Grandma were headed to Graceland on a bus with other old people from the First Baptist Church, we would have no one to call. We would probably drown.

Papa asked if Diane had found the nozzle yet.

"She's looking for it," I said.

"Turn it to the *right*," Papa said.

"To the *right*, Diane," I said.

"Gotcha," she said. Neither one of us actually knows left from right. We're creative like that.

"There's so much shit in this cabinet, I can't reach the wall," she said.

"What?" asked Grandma, who had somehow gotten the phone. "What did Diane say?"

"Fuck," said Diane.

"She said she's almost got it, Grandma. Are y'all having fun on the bus?"

Disturbing fact #1: Grandma crushes on dead Elvis.

Disturbing fact #2: The First Baptist Church of Kanuga encourages this.

Grandma said that no, she was not having fun on the bus. I put her on speakerphone while I made some breakfast.

Suddenly, Max charged down the hall, yelling, "Main line, main line! Mayday! We're going down!" He slipped on the wet floor, crashed, and yelled that the bathroom sink was throwing up.

"I'll call you back," I told Grandma.

Don't ask me how it happened, but another pipe-thing had broken. A geyser erupted and shot off the cabinet door. All this stuff was floating down the hall—junk like shampoo bottles, toothbrushes, and toy boats, along with some of Max's collectibles, including his Dum Dum wrapper collection and a red ballet shoe he had stolen from me years ago. A tae kwon do medal of participation swirled around my feet.

Max and Diane went to the front yard looking for the main line, while I put my hand in the cabinet to see if I could find the knob and turn it to the right. I tried both directions. The heavier items had not floated out yet. I discovered a jar of old Halloween candy and, wrapped up tight in a plastic bag, a stack of Diane's journals.

Diane had warned me never to read anyone's journal. She said that journal reading was like egg sucking with dogs. Once a dog gets a taste of egg sucking, he'll be in every henhouse in the county. Eventually, she explained, that dog will have to be shot.

I opened the bag and counted seven of them, gray and worn around the edges, some with covers coming apart, only slightly damp. A shiver ran down my spine as I pulled the first one out. It had been patched with Scotch tape and then duct tape. When I opened it, a loose page fell out; I placed it back, carefully, between the other pages.

Suddenly, the spirit of my dad descended upon me and said, "Aris, put that back right now." Joe does what he can to help Diane with the parenting.

"In a minute," I said. In the hallway, Lucky and Hiroshima were barking their special *Penn is here* bark.

The Ghost of Dad said, "I mean it, Aris. Don't read those."

"Just a *minute*," I said. Then, with a sick, excited feeling in my stomach, I read the first entry, where Diane had made a list of goals.

MY GOALS

1. Lose ten pounds, lower my cholesterol, and increase my muscle tone.

2. Achieve financial clarity and stability by following a monthly action plan.

3. Quit nicotine gum!

4. Organize my teaching materials and follow a schedule of efficient, effective, creative design.

5. Write a novel.

6. Move out west.

7. Follow a meditation routine and attend one AA meeting a week and one church service each month.

8. Orchestrate a stable, peaceful, joyful family life while training my children to be healthy, responsible, and respectful.

On the next page, she wrote a quote from some chick named Evelyn Waugh. "My children weary me. I can only see them as defective adults." Thanks a lot, Evelyn; that makes me feel really magical. Beneath the quote, Diane had made another list.

THINGS THAT RAISED MY BLOOD PRESSURE TODAY

1. The shaggy brown dog the kids brought home. No, we are not keeping it. You don't walk or feed the two dogs we have unless I nag you. Do you know what our vet bill was last month? They couldn't care less about the bill. It's their job to argue and plead until I lose my patience. Then they feel sorry for themselves. Then they go back to feeling sorry for the dog.

2. Dinner. I wrestled with phyllo dough for an hour to feed them a trans-fat-free vegetable potpie. Do they care about the rising incidence of type 2 diabetes in children? They picked at it, lying with pretty smiles so I wouldn't put a moratorium on candy during the evening movie. The smiles endeared me, pulling me back into that hopeless love even as I faced the dirty kitchen, too tired to say, "Cleaning off the table means taking the glasses off too." They slipped away. I cleaned the kitchen by myself, then got everyone in the car. I emptied my wallet on *Gnomeo & Juliet.*

3. *Gnomeo & Juliet.* Please, *God, let it be over,* I started praying after the opening scene. It's a British form of cruelty to make people look at animated ceramic garden gnomes for two hours. The kids got upset when they saw me looking at my watch. In the car they asked when we can see it again.

4. The handsome man in the parking lot who said hello to me.

"What are you doing with my journals?"

Diane was standing in the doorway, still in the bathrobe, looking mad as h-e-double-hockey-sticks.

"She's not doing anything," said Max, wading up behind her. "She's saving your journals from the water, Mom. Aren't you, Aris? She doesn't want them to get all wet and ruined."

Diane and I stared at each other.

"Don't be mad, Mom," Max said. "Okay? Everybody, just be happy." He gave us both this insane smile.

"You are reading my journal," Diane said coldly, perfectly still as the water gushed all around.

Max wedged himself between us. "We are having a cat's trophy here," he announced, "and I think everybody should just stay calm."

"I don't read *your* journals," said Diane.

"Ommmmmm," said Max, holding his hands in the shape of an egg the way Diane does when she meditates.

"I don't put my journals in the bathroom," I said. Oops. WRONG THING TO SAY. Where did that suicidal impulse come from? The spirit of Dad threw up his hands.

"What?" she said in her ice-queen voice. "What did you say?"

A stillness fell around us, the way it does just before a tornado, when the leaves on the trees stop twisting, the birds disappear, and the sky glows green.

"Give them here!" she shrieked. "All of them! Now! Because there is nowhere else to put them! Because this house is so jam-packed full of junk I can't breathe. I have zero privacy! I can't have a life with you two—"

Max couldn't take it anymore. He slapped himself hard in the face. "It's all my fault!" he screamed. "I broke the sink! I did it! You hate me, both of you!"

"Max!" Diane set her mouth in a hard line, but her eyes were panicked. "Don't start that. You are not allowed to hit yourself. Remember what Dr. Dhang told you. Max! Breathe." She began taking slow, deep, exaggerated breaths, as if she could breathe for him.

"I'm going to kill myself!" he cried.

I don't know what would have happened if Penn hadn't shown up at that moment.

"Howdy!" he called from the front door. "How come nobody invited me to the pool party?"

"Mom's mad," Max explained. He was breathing again.

"Imagine that," said Penn, lifting his feet carefully so as not to splash the walls he had painted last summer. "If you two ladies will step out of the bathroom for a moment, I'll reach under there and turn that thing off before somebody drowns in here."

Relieved, Diane scooted into the hall. As much as she hates to call Penn and ask him for help, she's delighted when he shows up.

As Penn worked under the sink, I watched the muscles move under his T-shirt. He buys his shirts at the Salvation Army thrift store. This one had *Employee of the Month* printed across the back. I'm not a pervert or anything, but Penn has really broad shoulders. When he's cutting the grass and he takes off his jacket, he hangs it over one shoulder. If my fiancé, Billy, tried that, the jacket would fall right off. Billy is gorgeous, and I would never cheat on him, but I'm just saying.

Diane was coming back from the kitchen with a plastic garbage bag. "Where did we get all this junk?"

"Planned obsolescence is one of the finer tools of capitalism," said Penn, his head still stuck in the cabinet. "Reduce time between repeat purchases. Practice inferior workmanship. Change the color." He pulled his head out of the cabinet. "Seen any avocado-green kitchen appliances lately?"

"Grandma painted hers," said Max.

"They grew up in the Depression," said Diane. "They don't throw anything away."

I kept a sharp lookout for the stack of gray notebooks, but no luck. Diane could be dangerous on these rampages.

"My tae kwon do medal!" cried Max, grabbing her arm as she shoved the medal into her plastic bag. "I love that medal. Don't throw it out!"

I don't even know how Max got the participation medal, because he did not participate. When he was supposed to *choon bee* and belt out "Yah," he covered his eyes and screamed, "Mama!"

"Chariot!" Master Seo would roar, facing him with his lethal-weapon body, but he couldn't hold Max's attention. "You mama's boy?" he demanded.

Then Max would scream, "Mama!"

"Just take a picture of the medal," Diane said, but he had already pulled it out of the bag and was trotting back to his room. Diane shook her head and started muttering about how we have too much stuff, how our stuff owns us, how nice it would be—

"Don't go on a cleaning binge," I warned her. "Remember what happened last time."

"I know, I know," she said, brushing me off with a wave of her hand as she headed toward her room. "I'm only going to sort—I promise. I'll start with my sock drawer."

"You have OCD," I reminded her. "It starts with just one sock . . ."

An intervention was called for, but Penn pulled his head from under the sink.

"Look here, Aris. I want to show you what to do if this ever happens again." I knelt down beside him and pretended to look under the sink. "See that knob? You turn it to the right."

"Right," I said. On the floor, eye level with Penn, I recognized the opportunity to encourage his romantic leanings toward Diane. Even if he didn't have these leanings, they could be encouraged.

Looking down, I sighed wearily. Then I did it again, a little louder.

"What's up?" Penn asked.

"Diane is on Match.com again."

"Is she, now?" He tapped a pipe with a wrench to hear the sound of it. "Finding anybody wonderful?"

"Mostly the same losers who were on there last year. I recognized Bearhug64 and Lonely911."

"I remember him. He sees the glass as half-full, not half-empty. Seeks a Christian lady, but you can leave your baggage at the door?" He stood up and smiled. "Or was that somebody else? They all seem so much alike after a while."

"I keep telling her. Then she says, 'I used to look at Barbies with you and say the same thing.'"

He laughed. "Come on. Let's go out on the back porch and have a smoke."

Outside, I climbed onto the railing and sat with my feet in front of me, leaning back against the wall of the house. This seat is more comfortable than it sounds. Then I let out another dramatic sigh, hoping Penn wouldn't change the subject the way he does sometimes.

"It's such a challenge to find your soul mate in Where Its Legs Were Broken Off," I said.

"You ain't wrong." He tightened the rope he uses to hold up his jeans, then pulled a package of Bugler tobacco from his back pocket and rolled a cigarette. Despite the fact that Penn is unemployed and lives with his mother, he's a chick magnet. Diane and I only catch glimpses of these girls, the back of a shiny blond head in his truck, a soprano coming through the speaker on his phone. They don't last long because Penn uses the zigzag method on them. Penn likes women, but he doesn't like relationships. We can't imagine what he does when he goes out with a girl, because he doesn't eat or sleep or touch people. Once, Max asked him if he was an alien. Then Penn said, "Now I'll have to kill you."

"It's harder for a widow to date," I said with another sigh. "Diane doesn't have an ex-husband to keep the children every other weekend, and so many men don't want the burden of another man's offspring."

Penn exhaled over his shoulder, keeping the smoke away from me.

"Remember Arnold?" I asked. "From two years ago?"

"The one who graduated from high school? No, wait a second. He's the one with man boobs. Sorry."

Arnold materialized from Match.com in January, an after-Christmas sale item. Arnold liked everything about Diane except for the fact that she had two children under the age of twenty, but he didn't tell her that until she had made him dinner for a year. "I know he's not pretty," she said, "but I think he looks a little like Harvey Keitel in *The Piano*." Arnold was butt-ugly. When she brought him to the talent show at the Lab, I had to go around introducing him as "my mother's boyfriend." Which sounds so wrong.

"Just say, 'my mother's friend,'" Diane suggested. Ms. Chu once gave me a copy of a story called "Where Are You Going, Where Have You Been?," which is hilarious if you haven't read it, so I started calling him Arnold Friend, after the freakish guy in the story. Now Kate and I refer to any mother's boyfriend as "Mr. Friend."

Penn pulled a folded *New York Times* crossword puzzle out of his back pocket and started to work on it with a stub of pencil. Apparently, he was finished discussing Diane's love life. I briefly considered giving up on him as future father material. Of course, I had never come out and asked him to date my mother. The closest she ever got to asking him out was shooting him a text when she was fed up with us:

Kids 4 Sale. BOGO. Throw in a cute dog. Free.

He responded:

Can't afford the upkeep.

"Got it!" he cried, slapping his hand on the crossword puzzle. "A-N-T-I-L-E-G-O-M-E-N-A. You know what that means, Aris?"

"The disputed books of the Bible?"

"Yes, and that's all of them, in my opinion. Matthew, Mark, Luke, and John—all Antilegomena. The Old Testament? 'And the unicorns shall come down with them, and the bullocks with the bulls.' Isaiah 34:7. Unicorns, Aris?"

"Maybe that was a typo," I suggested.

"Maybe the Bible is full of typos. I'll be an atheist until the edited version comes out."

"Diane says you baked too long in the Pentecostal church when you were young," I said.

"Well, I guess she baked too long in the Baptist church."

"She did. That's how she became an alcoholic and then found her higher power in AA."

"Exchanging one unicorn for another," said Penn. He ground out his cigarette, flicked the butt, and went back inside. Through the glass door, I watched him linger by the open door of Diane's bedroom. She was on the phone now. From her frown, I gathered she was talking to Grandma. Penn gave her a pope wave, and then he was gone.

When I came inside, she was saying crisply, "Mother, calm down. I didn't say we were moving today. I said we had options. Kanuga really isn't a good fit for us. Am I supposed to wait until you die before I live my life?"

I've heard this conversation a million times. I know everybody's lines. Grandma will tell Diane that she's ungrateful. Diane will deny it. Then Grandma will tell Diane that she can't make it on her own, not with two children to support, not without a husband. Offended, Diane will retort that she can take care of her family. Finally, just when you think Diane is about to win the argument for independence, Grandma will pull the Papa card.

"It would kill your father."

Now Diane was telling Grandma that she had narcissistic personality disorder. She was spelling it for her, N-A-R . . .

Sometimes eavesdropping just wears me out.

I had to step away from the family drama to get back to work on my novel; the clock was ticking! I got my laptop and my mad bomber hat and went out to my office. My office is in the backyard, on the roof of the shed. Often when I'm wearing the mad bomber hat, especially with the earmuffs turned up, my ghost dad speaks to me. This evening, I thought he might help me write the setting for my novel. As *Write a Novel in Thirty Days!* points out, "Nothing happens Nowhere." I gazed out over my world, considering the sign at the entrance of our subdivision:

> THE ORCHARD IS A VIBRANT COMMUNITY
> FULL OF FUN PEOPLE WITH MUCH TO OFFER.

That's a stretch. The Orchard is a community of people who want to avoid the bad elements but can't afford a McMansion. Diane calls it "the fruit bowl." She regrets allowing her parents to ship us down to Georgia after Joe died. If she had had more faith in herself, or more money, she says, she would have made a different decision. Papa bought this house at 17 Plum Lane for us to live in, for free, but he owns it. When Diane took the liberty of painting the green shutters purple, Papa painted them green again, to keep up the value of the property. If he invests in a major change, like redoing the kitchen, he makes her promise to stay here for five more years. She saves boxes in the attic for the day we might move out of Kanuga to someplace where we fit in, but that place is always changing: Taos, New Mexico; the Marshall Islands; Victory, Vermont; Singapore . . .

Write a Novel in Thirty Days! states that your story has to be grounded in the here and now; it doesn't matter where. The author suggests using five senses to create the setting. Only five? Okeydokey, here is my subdivision in Kanuga, Georgia:

THE SETTING

The fruit-bowl smell: Dirty-sock smell from the Bradford pear trees, the stink of the paper mill, and on Saturday mornings, a medley of laundry detergents, which is so strong that I worry about global warming before I've even had breakfast.

The fruit-bowl feel: The dirt in the yard is actually clay; it feels damp and stretchy. It's orange with streaks of yellow and brown and sometimes white. When I was little, I used it to make dishes for my dollhouse. I always scraped out the streaks of white clay, which was probably PCB. Back in the fifties, the Georgia Power plant down the street sold buckets of PCB to the Orchard residents to use as bug killer in their flower gardens. Papa says there is no PCB in our yard. He likes to help people and would hate to think he is killing us.

The fruit-bowl sound: Dogs barking behind fences, the bleep of car fobs, the BLEEP BLEEP BLEEP BLEEP of stuck car alarms, and the honk of vacationing geese.

The fruit-bowl taste: The dirt around here tastes like the tofu corn dogs Diane tries to sneak into our hot dog buns. She says, "You put so much ketchup on it I can't believe you'd notice!" Right, Diane.

The fruit-bowl sights: My least favorite sight in the Orchard is the roadkill at the intersection of Plum Lane and Pear Street. I swear that spot is haunted. There is almost always a dead possum or a dead cat there, especially on Saturday mornings after the teenagers have taken their mothers' SUVs out on the town and come home drunk. Blood, fur, and guts.

My favorite sight is the blue heron that lives by the lake on Muscadine Circle. He is a bluish gray, the color of your shadow on the driveway on a winter afternoon, with a spooky beard that hangs like a broken cobweb around his neck. He stands apart from the silly ducks but never really leaves them. Sometimes I wonder if he's a ghost. If you walk up to him, he'll fly off ahead of you into a cluster of pine trees or over a chain link fence, but when you turn around, he's behind you in a long blue shadow. Diane says he's looking for his mate. IMO, he's never going to find her in that bunch of ducks, but birds aren't exactly brilliant.

There are things you can't see in the neighborhood, like the pedophiles. Diane has located them on an Internet map. She drove us around one day and pointed out which houses to avoid: 4 Muscadine Circle, 28 Apple Lane, 9 Cherry Branch Drive. Diane is paranoid about pedophiles. I don't know what I expected to see—body parts of children hanging from Bradford pear trees? Blood, fur, and guts? The houses looked normal. Diane says that's what's so scary. We never got to see an actual pedophile, but you don't really see people in the Orchard.

I closed my laptop and looked around to see if I had missed anything. Most of the daylight was used up, but there were still a few blue streaks in the gray sky. When a cloud appeared, it turned lavender, and suddenly the whole sky looked like a picture of heaven. I knew I couldn't add that image to my description because it was trite—writers should never be trite. Writers should also never mention unicorns, even though the cloud had taken on the shape of a horse with a horn growing on its forehead. I was embarrassed for the author of the Bible verse with the unicorn in it. Didn't he/she *know* an atheist like Penn would read that and sneer? But maybe Penn was right. Maybe if you couldn't describe something, like God, it didn't exist.

When it finally got dark, I went inside the house. I put Max to bed with a bunch of Legos and his stuffed platypus, Fred, and ran a bubble bath for Diane. Then I climbed into my bed, put my headphones on, and turned out the lights. I was listening to "Greensleeves," a sad, beautiful song. Most people don't know that it's about a prostitute. Diane told me that Joe used to play "Greensleeves" on his sax for his mother, back in Houma. He sang it to me when I was in Diane's womb. Now, if it comes on the radio, she snaps it off. That night I played it four times, but Joe didn't appear. Maybe he was down in the shed, planning a way to turn it into a proper office for me, with electricity and a bay window. Maybe he was still mad that I opened Diane's journal.

Or maybe he suspected that I was going to read all of them.

RISING ACTION

> *Be bloody, bold, and resolute; laugh to scorn*
> *The power of man, for none of woman born*
> *Shall harm Macbeth.*
>
> —William Shakespeare

When life gets hard, Diane likes to remind me that I'm tough. This is the way she was raised. Papa used to slap her on the back, hitting her spine with his heavy gold Masonic ring, and say, "You're a Montgomery; you're tough." Diane tells me something different. She slaps me on the back and reminds me what Mrs. Kierkegaard wrote on my final kindergarten report card: "This girl could get herself out of quicksand."

Mrs. Kierkegaard did not say that Max could get himself out of quicksand. "Max is all heart," Mrs. Kierkegaard said. "I want to marry Max." When Max was in her class, she asked him, in that serious, respectful voice she uses with her kindergartners, to marry her.

He looked way up at her—she's very tall—met her gaze with those big brown eyes, and said, "Yes, ma'am." She was the only one who could decipher his drawings.

"My God!" she exclaimed on parent-teacher conference day. "Would you look at this drawing!" Diane and I, wearing our best casual dresses, sat beside each other on tiny plastic chairs and passed the drawings back and forth.

"This one," said Mrs. Kierkegaard, holding up a manila sheet covered with violent scribbling. "Do you know what this is?"

We shook our heads.

"This is an army of aliens, with curly tails and three arms and four legs. You see, here's one of the tails. They're fighting an army of these birdlike creatures from Earth. They rose up out of the Pacific Ocean, Max told me. He calls it the Specific Ocean. This black thing in the middle is an explosion caused by the friction of these two planets that skidded into each other when the orbit around the sun was reversed." She looked at us, her eyes wide. "This is what Max is *thinking*."

We nodded. "Is that the sun?" Diane asked hopefully, pointing to an orange blob.

"No, that's the pizza the aliens ordered," said Mrs. Kierkegaard, smiling radiantly at us. "None of my other students are doing this kind of work." She waved her arm dismissively at a row of artwork attached to a clothesline. In these drawings, I noted a vase of flowers, a big green tree with a bird in it, and a crooked house with smoke coming out of the chimney, all quite recognizable.

"I mean, my God," she said. "He is *so* talented. *So* wonderful. He's just . . . *Max*." We nodded, but none of us could say exactly how he was going to find his place in the world.

After the flood came the quicksand. Max has no talent for getting out of quicksand—that's my specialty—but we were going to need all of his creative juices to survive Diane's cleaning spree.

On Monday morning, Diane woke up with uncharacteristic enthusiasm at the first ring of her alarm clock. She made the coffee, put on her cleaning overalls and red bandana, and turned on her favorite cleaning music, Bach's *Goldberg Variations*. Diane believes in classical music. Unfortunately, she has the Montgomery musical genes, so she can't actually hear it. When an aria on her playlist gets stuck on repeat, she doesn't realize it.

As Diane sipped her coffee, she texted her department chair

at Kanuga Christian College: Due to a family emergency, she wouldn't be on campus today.

"Mom, don't lose your job!" cried Max. "We'll be poor!"

"I'm a lowly adjunct," she said. "My job is secure because no one else wants it."

"They fired Billy's mom."

"She was *denied tenure*," I said loftily. "Now she is a professor at Harvard."

Briefly, I wondered if Diane could make that transformation—I could live next door to Billy! However, a glance at Diane in her overalls, with the bandana wrapped around her head, dampened that hope. Sometimes Diane looks like a twelve-year-old.

Now she assured Max that she would only miss one day of work to power clean the house. "You all can give me a head start by picking your rooms up before I take you to school," she said briskly. "Get everything off the floor; I'm going to vacuum."

At the word "vacuum," Hiroshima looked up from her tennis ball and glanced nervously at Lucky. The vacuum cleaner was a known enemy.

"Removing physical clutter helps us eliminate the mental clutter that obscures our goals and objectives," Diane was saying in her teacher voice. She paused and then went back to her Mom voice. "I *will* vacuum anything left on the floor."

The dogs headed to the closet.

My room is standard purple. Walls, rug, bedding, curtains, furniture, clothes on the floor, backpack, hairbrush, stapler . . . all purple. Once, when Diane gently suggested that my decor was at odds with the earth tones in the rest of the house, I pointed out that my print of *The Garden of Earthly Delights* was flesh colored. Grandma calls this Bosch masterpiece "that orgy poster."

"Are you cleaning up your room?" Diane called from the hall.

"Yes, ma'am!" I replied, pushing a pair of jeans with the underwear still inside them beneath the bed. I crammed some homework into my sock drawer. Finally, I straightened the muffs on my mad bomber hat and set it carefully on the shelf next to Zimmerman, who was overseeing my work with a satisfied expression on his threadbare face.

I was looking around to see if I had missed anything when my gaze fell on the dollhouse in the corner. It's a three-story Victorian in a run-down neighborhood, and despite the fresh coat of purple paint, it had a sad look about it. Piles of broken furniture were heaped on the porch, and a car with a missing wheel sat on blocks in the front yard. One of the six badly dressed Devereux children was hanging halfway out the attic window.

Inside, I found dirty doll dishes scattered around the kitchen and a half-empty glass of lemonade leaving a wet ring on the polished Steinway. Grandma bought the piano for me one Christmas. She said it was the most expensive piece of dollhouse furniture she had seen in her life, but she bought it anyway. When you hit the keys, it plays music that you can download from iTunes. The memory only holds two songs. On the current playlist, we had "Here We Come," by the Monkees, and "Greensleeves." I played the Monkees because I didn't think Mrs. Devereux could handle a sad song right now. She was slumped over in the bathtub, fully dressed, because Mr. Devereux, who has a drinking problem, was MIA again, and there was no peace to be found in that house with the children and their mess. I straightened up the nursery for her and put the baby to bed. Then I went back to my world to get dressed.

I put on my Lab white shirt (one minute) and my Lab plaid jumper (two minutes) and tied my Converse (two minutes). With the outfit out of the way, I stretched out on my bed to work on a sketch of Billy. I had been working on it all week, hoping to have it done in time for Valentine's Day. His nose turned out remarkably well. He has a straight, perfect nose, but I was having trouble getting the braces on his teeth. No matter how delicately I etched the silver pencil across his teeth, he looked like he was wearing a train track on his face. Given my frustration at the moment, I probably didn't sound as docile and attentive as Diane would have liked when she knocked on my door.

"What!" I yelled.

"Don't use that tone of voice with me, young lady," she snapped.[6] "I'll be back here in fifteen minutes for a room inspection."

The longer I worked on Billy's teeth, the worse they got. He began to look downright ugly. What if he really was? I mean, not *ugly*, but not gorgeous? The more I tried to conjure his image in my mind, the more it slipped away from me. Were his knees actually knobby? Didn't he have big, splayed feet with weird little pointed nails on his pinkie toes? Looking at his photos didn't help because I had looked at them so much I couldn't see them anymore: Billy and me in the backseat of the car, sharing a pair of earbuds as we listened to my favorite Beatles song, "Hey Jude." Billy on the basketball court, caught midair as he went for a lay-in (or is it lay-up?). He was the first eighth-grade boy to get visible muscles in his arms.

I texted him.

F2F? :)[7]

While I was waiting for his reply, I scrolled through our recent texts. When he first moved away, we talked a lot about missing each other and wrote "I love you." Later, we wrote "MYALY," "miss you and love you." Then it was just "LY." Eventually, that was shortened to "459," the keyboard numbers for "ILY," "I love you."

Diane had started her diatribe in Max's room: "Why do you have three wet towels on the floor? Max, something is growing in

---

6 Historical reference: Diane grew up watching black-and-white fifties reruns featuring physically perfect, well-dressed white middle-class people who talked like this. Intermittent canned laughter cued the audience to perceive the shows as humorous, but the social stereotyping and implied moral code were rigid enough to bring on the cultural revolution of the sixties. Call someone a young lady often enough, and she will end up at an orgy dropping acid. I'm just saying.

7 Do you want to FaceTime me?

this dirty dish; it's *moving*! IF I STEP ON ONE MORE LEGO!" I glanced at my phone; Billy still hadn't responded—maybe he was already at school. I texted Kate.

Me:
Is Billy hot, IYO?[8]

Kate:
??? u should know.

Me:
just thinking.

Kate:
weird.

Kate:
NJJS[9]

Me:
trying to draw him.

Kate:
No object is so beautiful that, under certain conditions, it
will not look ugly.--Oscar Wilde

Me:
Thanks. My drawing sucks?

Kate:
Oops. Not flaming you. See him f2f?

8 In your opinion.
9 Not judging, just saying.

Billy still hadn't replied to my request to FaceTime, so I texted:

> Helloooooooooooooooooooooooooooooooooooooooooo
> ooooooooooooooooooooooooooooooooooooooooo

He didn't respond.

Me (to Kate):
He's playing dead.

Kate:
Invite him to visit you in Kanuga.

Suddenly, my bedroom door swung open. Bach's aria, on its fifth or sixth run, filled the air.

"Sweet Jesus," Diane said. She began to rotate in half circles, pointing at piles of clean and dirty clothing, dishes, drawings and bits of poetry, lab reports, doll accessories, sundries, and collectibles. Then she took a deep breath. "Clean it up. Now."

"Okay," I said pleasantly, and sent a quick text.

Me:
Where would he sleep? House is teeny tiny.

Kate:
Couch?

Me:
Dog hair.

"I mean *now*," said Diane.

Looking back, it's clear that I should have made some effort to move my body. That's what Diane wanted. That's what she expected. I should have leapt off the bed and scurried around like a squirrel in the final hour before a blizzard, trying to gather those last acorns before my entire squirrel village starved to death. Instead, I said, "*Okay*, Diane, I'm coming," and scrolled down to see if Kate or Billy had replied.

She lost it.

"Don't use that tone of voice with me!" she screamed. "This room is trashed! Don't you ever put anything away?"

"I'm sorry," I said, but it was too late. Suddenly, Diane was everywhere at once in my room. She descended on my piles, which, however unsightly they may be, are the archives of my personal life—living diaries, so to speak. As I watched in horror, she rooted into the depths of these mounds, dividing my possessions into two new piles: "keep" and "toss." "I never!" she spewed, picking up an Appalachian dialect as she morphed into Grandma. "I never in my life!"

"I'm picking it up," I said. "I'm sorry."

"Lawdee!" she moaned, and then she dived under my bed.

Please God, I prayed, *don't let her find it.* Not *that.* In the following uneasy silence, I shoved a random sock into my nightstand drawer and pushed my hairbrush under the pillow. More silence.

Then, from under the bed—a dry heave. It came out as "Hee, huck, hew, hew," like she was choking on an apple core. I thought, *Oh my God, I've killed my mother.*

"Diane?"

All I heard was "Hew, hew." Finally, she emerged with a dust bunny over each ear, mouth hanging open. In her hand was the training bra with two clementines taped inside the cups. She held it at arm's length because the clementines had gone soft and turned a kind of bluish green with specks of fuzzy white mold.

"Aristotle Thibodeau," she said. "I cannot—CANNOT—do this anymore!"

Max stuck his head around the door. "What is it? What happened?" His cowlick was sticking up at the crown of his head. "My fluff," he calls it. Sometimes it reminds me of the tuft on the head of a baby bird, but when he walked into my room that morning, uninvited, it turned into an antenna roving around my personal space. I wanted to flatten him to the floor.

"Clean up *your* stuff," I hissed. "Or she *will* vacuum up your Legos this time."

"What's that smell?" he asked.

"Get out!" I yelled. "Now! Get out of my room!"

Diane dropped the training bra and fruit into the trash can and pointed at an expensive sweater that had somehow wadded itself into a ball and rolled under my desk. She looked around the room again. I saw it dawning on her that she had paid for all this crap.

"I paid a hundred dollars for this sweater," she said, "and you threw it on the floor? Just *threw* it?"

My phone beeped.

"It's Kate," said Max, who was *still* hanging around. He picked up my phone. "She says that Billy could sleep in your bed if you both wear pajamas."

"What?" said Diane. "You are *not* sleeping with anybody, missy."

"Don't touch my phone!" I screamed at Max. Then I turned to Diane and said calmly, "I didn't *throw* it."

She looked from the phone to me, and then at the sweater on the floor. "I can't take this," she said. "There's too much stuff, too much spending, too much going on—!"

"I might have dropped this beautiful sweater," I said quietly. "Accidentally."

"Well, pick it up!" she shrieked.

"Okay, Diane. Okay, okay, okay. I'm picking it up. I'm sorry."

"Stop calling me Diane. I am your mother. I am a single mother. I will have to work all day to clean up the mess from the flood and the rest of this house. Then I have to grade papers and do a load of laundry and help Max with his homework and get him in the shower and feed the dogs, and you are lying there, *texting wayward nonsense*, with this mess all around you!"

"Kate and I were joking," I said. "I should have been helping.

I'm sorry. I'm helping now." I folded the sweater. Through the tiny window, I saw Mrs. Devereux hunched over in the bathtub; I felt her pain.

"I'm sending both of you to a private school," Diane continued. "I pay for braces, birthday parties, and summer camp. I teach five classes of freshman comp at a Bible college, barely making minimum wage—getting no health insurance, no life insurance, and no retirement—to buy you this overpriced crap, which you wad up and toss like garbage!"

"I appreciate *everything*," I said. "I know I don't always seem like I appreciate the Lab, but I do. I'm going to work hard today, as hard as I can. Please don't cry. Please?"

But she was crying. The tears ran out the corners of her eyes, across the smile crinkles, down her cheeks and neck, onto the straps of her overalls.

Max hugged her and said, "Mom, please don't cry. Please!"

He held her tightly, as if she might disappear. I stretched my arms out to embrace both of them, and we let her talk it out. She was old and tired and ugly, she told us, and a terrible mother. The house, the mess, she didn't know what to do. We lose things because we don't put them away, and that makes us late for everything. It makes her late for work, but she hates her job anyway. The students treat the English Department like the customer service department at Walmart, and why is English so hard for them? They don't speak any other language.

"I am overwhelmed with"—she looked around—"with us."

"I know," I said, patting her back. "I know, Merm."

You might think, wow, what a loser mom. You might expect her to go AWOL on us, like Anders Anderson's mom did. I imagined Mrs. Anderson looking at Anders one day and saying to herself, *Well, it seemed like a good idea at the time, but I'm free to make a different choice today*. Now she's at a ranch in Nevada with other mature spiritual seekers.

Diane is different. Diane has grit. Grit, not to be confused with grits (for you Yankees), is a measurable quality of endurance. A couple of years ago, Diane had everyone take a grit test on the Internet, and we all scored in the top tenth percentile.

"You must have one good student at KCC," I said, handing Diane a clean sock. "Isn't there one student who wants to learn how to write an essay?"

Diane shook her head. "Not in freshman comp."

"What about the boy who loves his mother?"

"You mean Charles Hutchins?" asked Diane. "In 1102?" She frowned. "I have told you not to read my students' work. That's probably illegal."

"My favorite essay was 'Mrs. Octavia Hutchins,'" I said. "The one about his mother." I smiled to show my appreciation of all mothers.

She nodded. "I like Charles," she said, and wiped her eyes with the sock.

It was raining on the way to school. As the water streamed down my window in the car, I felt a sense of foreboding. Even though we don't make it to church often, I've hit the pew often enough to know what happens after the flood. Everybody goes to the ark two by two. What if you have a family of three? I'm thinking somebody gets wet.

We had to walk across campus to the library that morning, and guess who didn't have a raincoat? When I sat down at my table, a puddle of water formed around me. Beside me, Anders Anderson said, "The bathroom is over there," and did his snort-laugh. As stupid as it sounds, I almost cried.

Kate came to my rescue. "I know that boys don't mature as fast as girls," she said, "but really, Anders, you should see a professional about this. I've known you since kindergarten, and you are *not* developing."

"I grew four inches last year," said Anders. To prove it, he stretched his gangly legs out under the table and began to kick our ankles.

"My point," said Kate. She turned to me. "I know you *think* you don't like Jane Austen," she said, handing me a tome with a froufrou cover, "but you really should read *Emma*."

"I've tried Jane," I said. "After a few chapters, I feel like I've been at the Kanuga Country Club with Papa and Grandma, fake smiling *for hours*."

"I've never been to a country club," mused Kate. "I don't know how I'd feel in that setting."

"Max loves it. He could spend all day in a golf cart, eating curly fries with Republicans. Diane says he just wants security."

"The search for security—for a physical place in the world—is one of the major themes of Austen's novels," admitted Kate. She rested her chin in the palm of her hand as she considered this. Then she said, "Of course, she is exploring the idea of security in the context of friendships and relationships. I know the writing is old-fashioned—which I love and you don't—but some of her advice applies to our world."

"For example?"

"Well, you know how you were saying you can't remember what Billy looks like—I mean, not *exactly*?"

"Oh. My. God," said Anders, butting his head between us. "You can't even remember what he looks like?"

"Shut up, Anders," we said at the same time.

"A tandem shut-up? Okay, that's *not* offensive?" he said sarcastically, and left the table.

"In Jane's world," Kate resumed calmly, "when the heroine begins to forget about a gentleman caller, he comes to the manor to visit. He stays for weeks."

"We don't even have McManors in the Orchard," I said. Then I glanced around to make sure no one was listening, and lowered my voice. "BTW, Diane freaked when you texted about sleeping with Billy."

"She read it?"

"The little person grabbed my phone and made an announcement."

"Ergh," said Kate, who co-parents a little sister. "I didn't say you should have sex with Billy—I hope that was clear."

Kate is very conservative about the human body. She wears her skirts below her knees and buttons her shirts to the collar. In her world, sex outside of marriage is taboo, even for old people like our mothers.

"It's okay," I said. "Diane was preoccupied with the mess in my room. She won't even remember. I thought the pajama idea was good."

"Of course, it depends on the kind of pajamas," said Kate, chewing on the tip of her pencil.

"I was thinking about something in purple and gold. Those are the colors of his favorite team—I can't remember the name. It's either basketball or football," I said, but Kate's mind had drifted back to pre–Victorian England.

"There are cottages in Austen's novels," she said. "If the heroine is cut out of the will, she lives in a cottage until she lands a husband with a manor. However, these houses have at least four bedrooms, not counting the servants' quarters. . . . In any case, you should give Jane another try. The setting is different, but relationships are the same."

To appease her, I flipped *Emma* open and read a random passage.

Dear Harriet, I give myself joy of this. It would have grieved me to lose your acquaintance, which must have been the consequence of your marrying Mr. Martin. While you were in the smallest degree wavering, I said nothing about it, because I would not influence; but it would have been the loss of a friend to me. I could not have visited Mrs. Robert Martin, of Abbey-Mill Farm. Now I am secure of you for ever.

"I give myself joy of this?" That's not even a translation.

I glanced at Ms. Chu, at her desk checking out books, and thought about asking for her advice on Billy. Then I remembered that her only marriage lasted three days and decided against it.

Anders shuffled back to our table with his book of Christian fiction. He dropped noisily into a chair.

"Hello, ladies. Did you miss me?"

When we ignored him, he emitted a long series of farts arranged to the tune of "My Country 'Tis of Thee."

He's not without talent, but we stared at him in disgust.

"Ah, that felt good," he said, grinning lecherously at our boobs.

"Developmentally disabled," muttered Kate. "He can't help it."

"Hello, Anders," I said sternly. "My face is up here."

"You are just *so* intellectual, *so* artsy, *so . . . developed*," he said. "How will I ever catch up?"

Until a year or so ago, I had never realized that the whole world revolves around sex. Then one day it hit me: toothpaste commercials I had seen on friends' TVs, the random bumping of Diane's bed against the wall when she was in dating mode, the lyrics to every single song on the radio that wasn't a hymn—and even some of those! Sex, sex, sex. Now I understood why Diane made me wear my red sweater whenever we went to an airport. "So I can find you if you get lost," she had explained. I never get lost. She meant, *So you won't get abducted into the sex-slave trade.* It was an anti–human trafficking sweater.

"Why didn't you tell me that sex is such a big deal?" I asked her then. "It's everywhere! It's everything to everybody!"

She smiled sheepishly and shrugged. "I sort of liked your point of view," she said.

Well, here we are, and there's no going back. Second period at the Lab: Algebra with Coach Bobby.

I settled into my desk, opened my laptop, and sent Billy a Facebook message.

I miss you. I long for your lingering gaze, your lips, your warm touch. Do you want to visit me? PS: What kind of pajamas should I wear?

While I waited for a response, I watched Coach Bobby attack the whiteboard with a marker. His arm swept up and down, always drawing the numbers too large so that he ran out of room and had to erase the first part of the equation to fit in the rest of it. He was actually not bad looking from the back. I'm just saying.

Rule #14 in *Write a Novel in Thirty Days!* states, Do not indulge in superfluous characters. I totally agree; there are enough superfluous characters in the world already. However, I'm sneaking Coach Bobby into my novel because we're short on male characters. Don't look now, but it's a *man.* On the volleyball court, Coach Bobby is in his element. "Move your feet, Thibodeau!" he yells, with his chest all puffed out and his fist in the air. When the ball lands at my feet, he screams, "That was yours, Thibodeau! THAT BALL HAD YOUR NAME ON IT!" When he sits down in the classroom, his knees hit the desk, so he has to pull the chair out and straddle it. Most of the time, he paces around the room. Even with the collar of his shirt unbuttoned, his tie strangles him. He holds a book like a ball he is about to throw.

Anders, who had maneuvered to the desk beside mine, leaned over my shoulder and said, "Billy is online. I wonder why he hasn't replied to your message."

"Aris," boomed Coach Bobby. "Why don't you tell us the order of operations for number seven?"

I jerked my head up in surprise. Anders snickered.

"I haven't quite finished seven," I said softly, meeting Coach Bobby's gaze with a limpid stare.

"Well," he said, shuffling his feet. "Well, okay, who has finished number seven?"

I checked Billy's page for new photos even though I had them all memorized in a slideshow that ran on repeat in my head: red-cheeked Billy making a snowman with his little sister, tight-pants

Billy surrounded by cheering fans as he catches a baseball, slope-shredder Billy in a new North Face jacket, high-society Billy in a coat and tie, receiving honors in history, math, English, Spanish, and science. Billy playing the cello. Billy with his arm around Aris long, long ago in Kanuga, Georgia.

Coach Bobby, with a sweat stain under each armpit, was demonstrating the order of operations for number eight now, putting me at serious risk for a nap, so I decided to break another rule in *Write a Novel in Thirty Days!* Rule #27: Avoid flashbacks. They are usually a sign that the writer is avoiding conflict.

FLASHBACK!!!!!

Aris Thibodeau leaned back into her seat, lifted her water bottle, and looked deeply into its clear color. She took a sip and thought about Billy and their ~~secret, steamy~~ clandestine meeting in the sacristy at St. Michael's on that stormy night last July. Billy wore the scarlet acolyte robe of the chalice bearer, which made his blue eyes even more blue. With both hands, he fumbled at the top button of her robe. His breath, smelling faintly of Eucharist wine, felt warm as he brushed his lips against hers.

After supper he took the cup of wine; and when he had given thanks, he gave it to them, and said, "Drink this, all of you."

"Here, let me help you," Aris whispered to Billy, because he was getting nowhere fast with the button. At any moment, Father James might open the door and discover them. ~~She had the thing off in ten seconds.~~

"This is my Blood of the new Covenant—"

Aris and Billy laughed nervously as the crimson robe pooled around her feet. When she unfastened the top two buttons of her blouse, he pulled her tight against him and pressed his mouth against hers. With ~~tender skill,~~ finesse born of longing, he moved his braces away from her lips as he flicked his tongue over hers. When his hand slid over her breast, she undid another button, allowing his fingers to slip inside her bra. ~~His finger rested on her bare nipple, which~~ Her bare nipple stiffened at his touch.

"Whenever you drink it—"

Tentatively, he stroked her hip with his free hand. "Yes?" he asked breathlessly. She felt beautiful and powerful.

"No," she said, but she didn't push him away. Again, they kissed. Again, his hand glided across her narrow hip.

"Please?" he asked, in his sweet, gruff voice. She paused, considering.

Christ has died.

"Just for a minute," he said. Aris touched his hair and looked deeply into his eyes, smiling. He smiled back. Were those footsteps coming down the hall?

Christ is risen.

They listened, but no one came into the vestibule.

"I think I could love you," she whispered. When he held her close, she felt his hard, hot body pulsing with desire.

"You think?" he said. He held her even tighter, pressing his muscles into her soft curves as she sighed with pleasure. She felt just like Neferneferuaten-Nefertiti, Lady of All Women, Mistress of Upper and Lower Egypt in 1345 BC.[10]

He ran his finger over the outline of her hipbone. "Pretty please?"

She shook her head, just as Queen Nefertiti would have done, because that is the secret to power.

END FLASHBACK

At the whiteboard, Coach Bobby had loosened his tie and rolled up his shirtsleeves. He was slamming out the order of operations

---

10 I made a B in World History, but it wasn't wasted on me.

for another number. Most of the class was on the Internet or fast asleep, but Anders had rested his sleepy gaze on me.

At last, Billy's reply to my message flashed across my laptop screen.

Sry I would but it's basketball season. Pajamas?

Oh. My. God. He rejected me? He did. Slam, bam, no, thank you, ma'am. My face grew hot all the way to the tips of my ears, and my flashback withered. I read it again, in case I had misunderstood.

"That looks like a 'no' to me," said Anders, snooping again.

It's one thing to be rejected, and quite another for this rejection to be witnessed by the one you are rejecting. If I were a violent person, I would have slapped Anders into next week. Instead, I smiled at him, evilly. Then, with a permanent marker, I wrote "God Is" across the white rubber toe of my left Converse. While he watched me nervously, I wrote "God Isn't" across the toe of the other shoe.

Poor reader, I've left you at the Lab too long! I went into zombie mode after I was scorned by Billy. Really? A spend-the-night with Aristotle Thibodeau is tossed aside for mute observation of a televised spectator sport? For the rest of the day, my ego dragged on the ground behind me like one of Max's jackets.

Penn was supposed to pick Max and me up after school— Diane had sent a message to the office that she was "indisposed." Penn was late; he is never late unless his truck is giving him a hard time.

"Where's your nanny?" asked Anders, who has to wait forever for his ride. He watched my feet as I walked toward him, "God Is. God Isn't. God Is. . . ." It was driving him crazy.

"He's in jail," I said. "For murder."

Then I saw Penn's green truck idling in the car line. The placard ARISTOTLE AND MAX THIBODEAU swung from his rearview mirror, so the teachers would know he wasn't stealing us. Penn's truck can't idle for long without going kaput, so I grabbed Max by his backpack and ran. We almost got there in time. . . . The engine sputtered, made a knocking sound, and then went dead.

Penn hopped out, dug around in the backseat, and came up empty-handed. Then, while everyone in the car line watched, he leaned against the hood, rolled a cigarette, and smoked it as he considered the situation. All my friends at the Lab know that our nanny is an atheist and an anarchist; the cigarette that looked like a joint was a nice touch. Somebody's blond mom with a recent boob job waved her fingers at him, but he must not have seen her.

"I need to borrow a pen from one of y'all," he said.

Max still uses pencils, but I found a pen in my bag.

"Thank you kindly," he said. He unscrewed the top of the pen, removed the spring, and handed it back to me. In five minutes, we were all back in the truck. "Fasten your seat belts," he said as we drove out of the car line. None of the seat belts in the truck actually work, but Penn has rigged two up especially for us, using belts from one of his fat uncles. He never smokes in the car when we're with him. Instead, he chews tobacco and spits into an empty Dr Pepper bottle that he wraps in masking tape because that's what they made him do in the navy.

I've asked Diane if she could make Penn stop smoking if she married him. "What you walk down the aisle with is what you get," she says. So it's not like she's never thought about it.

"Well, Lab rats," Penn said as we cruised down the road. "What did y'all do today? Y'all break any government codes or figure out the situation in the Middle East?"

"Nope," I said.

"Anybody write a sonnet that would break my heart?"

"Nope," Max said.

"Well, then, your mama's wasting her money."

"They served us old milk again at lunch," Max said. "I think it said 1973 on it."

"Sounds like a government plot," said Penn.

Max began to worry. "Why would they want to kill the children? That's mean." He was sitting in the middle and squirmed around in his seat belt, looking first at Penn, then at me, with a big furrow between his eyebrows.

"Chill, brother," said Penn as he turned the truck into the Orchard. "The government ain't killing anybody. That's not their style. They want to control us. To do that, they have to keep us alive. It's like marriage."

"Life is so cruel," said Max.

"You've had a hard day," said Penn. "Open that glove compartment and see if you can find a Dum Dum in there. Get one for your sister too. If you see a blueberry one, don't eat it. That flavor sucks. You can just leave it for me."

While Max dug around for the screwdriver that opens the glove compartment, I tried to think of a noninvasive way to open the subject of Penn's failed marriage. I had been able to glean a few facts from Diane, but Penn was closemouthed about his personal life. Here's what we had on him:

- For seven years, he was married to a Japanese woman he met while in the navy and stationed in Okinawa.

- When they moved back to the US, Penn got a job building submarines. She was a housewife.

- One day Penn came home, and she said, "I lost my job."

- Their house had been repossessed.

- Penn thought this was a clever way to put it.

"So," I said, unwrapping my Dum Dum. "What do you think about marriage?"

"Are you asking me?" said Max.

"Of course not." I stretched out as far as Penn's uncle's belt would allow me so I could lean around Max and catch Penn's eye. "I'm asking Penn."

"Oh, look, we're almost home," said Penn.

"I meant in a general way," I said.

"Good. I thought you were going to ask me something personal. In which case, you know my response."

"Not your bizness," said Max. "That's what you always say."

"So smart," said Penn as he pulled into our driveway. "Both of you. Makes me proud."

As we were piling out of the truck, Diane came to the front door. She was still wearing her cleaning overalls and red bandana, and she had a big, satisfied grin on her face, which I took as a bad sign.

"Everybody have a good day?" she asked. From the beatific shine in her eyes, one might assume that she was high from the cleaning fluids. It's true—from the porch I could smell the ammonia—but her joy came from the heart. Diane loves to clean. She doesn't do it often, but when she does, it's a spiritual experience, and she takes it too far. In a standardized test analogy, it would look like this:

    1. cleaning : Diane :: faith : _____

      A. life
      B. prayer
      C. snake handling
      D. train

The answer, of course, is C.

"Please wipe your feet on the mat before you go inside," she said cheerfully. The aria death march was still playing.

"What's that smell?" asked Max, wrinkling his nose.

Diane explained the process of *simplifying* to Max, who was too young to remember our last purge. I'd seen it all before. What begins with a few strokes of the broom ends up in a purification ritual that would shock Dr. Victoria Dhang. Diane actually belongs to an online Simple Living forum, where people count their possessions, bragging about who owns fewer spoons.

"Penn," I said in my calm-but-determined intervention voice. "Diane has been on a cleaning binge. We need your help."

He shook his head. "Y'all are on your own with this one. Watch closely as I demonstrate one of my best moves—the skedaddle." Then he was gone.

"Did you get rid of my stuff?" called Max as he sprinted toward his room. "My Legos? My Dum Dum wrapper collection?" From his room, he cried, "Mom! You did!"

"I kept your platypus!" she yelled. "And a lot of the Legos."

I allowed Max, dear child, the luxury of anger. The yowls of rage coming from his clean room were oddly comforting to me, driving me deeper into the requisite emotional freeze of Family Fixer. I can do postapocalypse. But then I opened a cabinet to find the beans—the beans!—arranged by type in a perfect pyramid. This was worse than I thought.

Before entering my room to assess my personal damage, I took a deep numbing breath of ammonia, bleach, and Murphy's Oil Soap. The effect was brief but intense. Blood rushed to my head; my muscles relaxed. Hello, amyl nitrite! For a moment, I felt the clarity of God.

When I opened my eyes, I found a room decorated in Early Orphan: white curtains, white sheets, white bedspread. Diane hadn't had time to paint my purple walls (thank you, Jesus and Buddha), but she had replaced the *Garden of Earthly Delights* poster with a print of Van Gogh's stark bedroom. "Simple," Diane would call it. Yes, his bed was made.

My bulletin board had been cleared, and a blank to-do list was tacked to the center. On my desk, I found five sharpened pencils, three pens (two black and one blue), and one highlighter. Piles of my sketches and stories, dating back to preschool, had been culled. What Diane deemed worthy of posterity was put in a white scrapbook with my name printed on the cover in painfully neat letters.

Frantically, I searched for my books. Normally, I keep my favorites (*Raising a Happy Child in an Unhappy World*, Anne Frank's diary, *Write a Novel in Thirty Days!*) within easy reach in my bed. When I'm not reading them, they make comforting lumps under the covers around me. Finally, I found them on a dust-free shelf, squeezed between new bookends.

Something was missing in my room—something big—but I couldn't put my finger on it.

The dolls had taken a hard hit. A bustling metropolis of half-naked Barbies with one or two breeder males was reduced to a row of six well-groomed females with one Ken in an ill-fitting tuxedo. The American Girl dolls were arranged on a shelf wearing the clothes from their countries of origin. Kit Kittredge, an American doll from Grandma's era, the Great Depression, was wearing the funeral dress Grandma had sewn, with a black taffeta bow that matched the one I wore to Joe's funeral.

Through the wall, Max continued to yell. "A year's worth of Dum Dum wrappers! Gone, just like that! Poof." When Diane knocked lightly on my door, I didn't answer. She was beginning to perceive that there were consequences to her behavior, and Max and I needed to drive this lesson home.

Diane kept knocking, lightly but firmly. "Aris? Honey? Please open the door."

The Devereux clan had moved out, taking their broken car and their house with them. I sat in the corner where the dollhouse used to stand and sucked in all the loneliness of the place.

"I know you're in there," said Diane. "Please open the door."

I let her stand in the hallway, wondering if I still loved her, for as long as I could. Where was team Diane-and-Aris now? Who had her back now? Surely she wasn't expecting to find an intelligent, insightful, delightful sidekick in this white room reeking of disinfectant. No, sorry, Diane. Aris is gone. An orphan lives here now. As usual, I held out for about a minute.

"Aris isn't here," I said when I opened the door. "She's been raptured."

Diane smiled nervously in my doorway. "Well," she said, surveying her work. "What do you think?"

"It's very white," I said flatly.

"Think of it as a clean piece of paper," said Diane.

"White is the Chinese color of death."

That hurt her feelings. For a moment, she looked like a little kid, with her face so open. I felt guilty, then powerful, then guilty about feeling powerful. It was a good time for me to have my first nervous breakdown, but before I could even begin, Max took the stage.

"I hate you!" he yelled from his room as something hard hit the wall. "I hate everybody! I hate myself!" There was a repeated banging on the wall—his head?—followed by the wail of a hundred dying cats. "I am hurt!" he groaned. "I am dying! Somebody please, please help me." One Mississippi. Two Mississippi. Then he started the cycle all over again. "I hate you! I am hurt. I am dying. Somebody please, please . . ."

Diane and I both glanced uneasily out the window. When Max had a meltdown, you could hear it from the street. It was a wonder no one had called 911. I left Diane to deal with him and firmly shut my door. Stretched out on my bed, I had one of my imaginary talks with Dr. Dhang.

What are you feeling, Aris?

I dunno.

Maybe she would show me the list of feelings she printed out for Max, with faces beside each one, and ask me to select a few.

In Max's room, Diane was saying, "Stop that noise. Honey, listen to me. Okay, stop that. I mean it. Sweetheart. Hush! Max,

I'm losing patience here. Please, please stop. Try to calm down. Did you take your medicine today?"

Calmly, I cracked open *Songs of Innocence and of Experience.*

> *O Rose thou art sick.*
> *The invisible worm,*
> *That flies in the night*
> *In the howling storm:*
>
> *Has found out thy bed*
> *Of crimson joy:*
> *And his dark secret love*
> *Does thy life destroy.*

At least the poems were short. I was typing a long Facebook message to Billy, updating him on Lab life and detailing the cleaning holocaust, when I noticed a new photograph on his page. I clicked on it and then clicked on two more like it.

A girl. Tiffany. Pretty.

She was tall, almost as tall as Billy in the ice-skating photo. Strawberry-blondish hair, blue eyes, and skinny, of course. She had "liked" every post on his page. WTF?

Breathing in, I calmed my body, breathing out, I smiled . . . Then I texted him.

Wasup w/Tiffany?

Typing her name hurt. Oh God, it hurt. I waited. One Mississippi, two Mississippi, three Mississippi . . .

No response. At 273 Mississippi, I realized that an invisible worm named Tiffany had just flown in the night and crawled into my crimson rose.

Maybe she's a friend, I told myself as I reached up to my shelf for the mad bomber hat. *Or a cousin.* He had family up there, right? I wouldn't jump to conclusions. My hand patted the bare flat surface of the shelf beside Zimmerman. Then I stood on the bed and looked.

The mad bomber hat was gone.

"Diane!" I shrieked.

In the living room, Max was sniffling in a corner with his Legos while Diane, on her hands and knees, cleaned out a bookshelf. I planted myself between them, hands on my hips.

"Where is my mad bomber hat?"

"What?"

"The hat with coyote fur," I said slowly. "Daddy's hat."

"That? Oh, honey, I'm sorry."

"You threw it out?"

"I didn't throw it out. I packed up a lot of old clothes that we never wear and gave them—"

"You got rid of the only thing that connects me to my father?" I was crying. Between sobs, I said, "You could have put the bomber hat in the attic. You didn't have to throw it away!"

"Aris, we need to let go of some things. Joe is gone. I know it's horrible, but he would want us to move on."

"Do you want me to hate you?" I said. "Okay, that's nice and simple. I hate you."

"I'm sorry," she said, rising to her feet. "I wanted to create a new start for us, a clean platform." She tried to hug me, but I wouldn't let her. "I put your dollhouse in the attic. I kept Zimmerman in your room. I would never let go of Zimmerman."

Pathetic, Diane. I looked at my feet. "God Is. God Isn't." A dollhouse, especially one inhabited by a low-rent, dysfunctional family like the Devereux bunch, is one thing, but without my father's hat, I was lost. Flopping onto the couch, I stared at the ceiling. It's a big ceiling because our living room, dining room, and kitchen are basically one room. Open concept—who needs walls when you don't have boundaries? Penn had patched the hole Diane made when she fell through the attic last Christmas, but you could

still see an outline over the kitchen table. Our family was almost—
but not quite—falling apart. With my brain addled from grief and
Clorox fumes, an evil thought began to worm its way into the crimson corridors of my subconscious.[11] Now the main character, Aris,
had a second motive: revenge.

11 Crimson prose!

Write a Novel in Thirty Days! warns that two flashbacks in one chapter might kill sales; however, this is my first novel, and I don't see any way around it.

FLASHBACK!!!!!!!!!!!!!!!!!!!!!!!!!!!

It happened on a Wednesday. Diane and I agree that Wednesdays are yellow. My Tuesdays are blue and hers are green, but we both color Sundays black because we feel religiously oppressed. Anyway, on this yellow Wednesday before Christmas break, Diane had to teach, so Penn picked Max and me up from the Lab.

The Christmas tree he had cut for us that morning was tied down in the bed of the truck. It was a truly yellow Wednesday, with the sun streaming through the windows. Penn was wearing thick boots and an army jacket with Batman stenciled on the back; he smelled like wood.

Diane was in the attic when we got home, looking for the Christmas tree stand. We dragged the tree into the living room and started chopping off the lower branches with Max's tomahawk. We could hear Diane's footsteps as she stomped around over our heads. I kept smelling my hands—Douglas fir. I was thinking about reindeer on the rooftop or something, when suddenly there was a loud thump overhead, followed by a yelp.

A chunk of plaster landed on the kitchen table, and then Diane's legs dropped down, dangling through the hole in the ceiling. She had a run in her tights, and one of her shoes was unstrapped but still hanging on her foot. Her dress had caught on something and was bunched up around her hips. That's all we could see.

"Hang on!" called Penn. "Is there something you can hold on to up there? A beam?"

Max was crying. I don't know if he had plaster in his eyes or if he was just disturbed to see his mother this way. She looked like one of those cartoon ladies that pop out of cakes, but upside down. I tried not to laugh.

"Don't you laugh when your mother is hanging out of the ceiling," said Penn, and then of course we were both laughing.

"It's not funny!" Max said, glaring at us. He's a very conventional little boy, and something of a gentleman. "Mom!" he called out. "Are you okay?"

"I'm fine, honey."

"The table is right here, Diane," said Penn. "Right under your feet."

When he reached for her legs to guide her down, his face turned bright red, all the way to the tips of his ears. As I've mentioned, Penn doesn't touch people. The red patches got brighter and brighter as she slid down into his arms. Somehow the dress stayed up in the hole while she shimmied down. Adult Content Alert: She was wearing nothing under the panty hose.

At that point, Max, who was having an oedipal moment or just feeling especially hyperactive, hurled himself into the kitchen table, knocking it out from under Diane's feet.

Penn caught her. From between Diane's knees, he said, "Aris, get me a chair! You can let go, Diane. I've got you."

"I'm hanging on," she said. "I can hang on."

With tears streaming down his face, Max picked up the phone. "I'm dialing 411," he announced.

"Why is he calling Information?" Penn asked as he lowered Diane to the floor.

"Max, honey, don't call anybody," said Diane. "Stop crying, baby. What's wrong with him, Aris?"

"What's *not* wrong with Max?"

"Mom, tell her not to say that!"

"Oh, here we go," said Diane, brushing her dress off as she led Max by the arm to the sink. "Thank you, Penn. I don't know what we would do without you."

After that, no one was allowed to go in the attic.

The next day, when Diane was at work and Penn was in the back-yard building something, I climbed onto the wagon in the garage and pulled the string that brings the attic stairs out of the ceiling.

"We aren't allowed to go up there," Max said.

"No one will find out," I said. "Take the ladder and pull."

"It will fall on me!"

Max's company can be more trouble than it's worth, but I had to bring him with me. For one thing, the attic is a Jungian archetype of higher consciousness. It's the MIND. Since Diane rules our roost, our attic is her mind. In AA meetings, you always hear that the mind of an alcoholic is a dangerous neighborhood, and you should never go there alone. On a more practical note, maybe, just *maybe*, Diane had dropped the mad bomber hat in the attic when she put the dollhouse away. Also, if I left Max behind, he would blab.

"Move it, Max," I said. "We are going up." He was apparently paralyzed with indecision, so I grabbed the ladder, snapped it into place, and started climbing.

As I disappeared through the dark hole, he called out, "What if there's a ghost up there?"

Silently, I felt around for the light string.

"Aris? Are you still up there? Are you dead?"

"Well, look at that!" I cried as the light snapped on.

"What? What is it?"

I waited a moment. I could hear him putting one foot on the first rung of the ladder, taking it off, putting the other foot on, and stepping back down as he weighed the threat of danger against the possibility of delight.

"Oh my," I said. "I never imagined *that* would be here!"

The ladder creaked under his weight. "Is it something of mine?"

"My goodness," I said.

His head poked through the hole. "Is my tomahawk up here?"

We found his old Thomas the Tank Engine train set, all sealed up in Bubble Wrap. Diane had kept the "nice" toys, things bought from catalogs that we might pass on to our own children, but the stuff dear to his heart—the broken cassette tape he'd found in the gutter, the carefully preserved bones of a squirrel, the lemon-juice-powered robot made of curlers that never quite worked, and the tomahawk, which Diane had always said was too dangerous for a child of Max's temperament—were all gone.

My dollhouse was Bubble-Wrapped too. Mrs. Devereux, her lovers, Leonard and Cynthia (hidden in the dollhouse attic for years!), and their odd assortment of children were packed in boxes, lying side by side in corpse poses, as if they had been gassed. Apparently, Mr. Devereux was still off on his drinking spree. Through the wavy bubbles of my cherished bay window, I could see the loaves of bread I had made from the PCB-streaked clay in the backyard, still cooling on the kitchen table. We were in a holocaust.

"Do you think my rock collection is up here?" Poor Max was on his knees, digging through a box of tissue-wrapped Christmas tree ornaments. His tongue stuck out the corner of his mouth as he concentrated on his search. "It's got to be in here somewhere." He ripped the tissue off a blown-glass reindeer and tossed it aside. "I just know it."

How could I tell him that our mother wouldn't save his rocks? She wouldn't even throw them back in the yard. I knew from experience that rock collections went in the trash. I mean, really, how can you throw the earth away, Diane? I kicked a few lampshades over, looking for my mad bomber hat, but my heart wasn't in it. I didn't want to think about my dead father or crazy mother, or everything a person could lose.

"Let's play Anne Frank," I said. "I'm Anne."

When I started stacking boxes to make a bookcase for the annex, Max looked up from his pile of Christmas ornaments. A piece of Bubble Wrap sat on top of his head like a cap. There was a white spot of toothpaste on his shirt, in the same spot it lands every morning when he brushes his teeth. I couldn't bear the thought of the German soldiers stomping up the ladder in their heavy black boots and taking him.

"I don't want to scare you," I said, not sure yet which character he was going to be, "but the SS is outside. They're putting the Jews in the back of a truck and driving them off to a concentration camp."

"Are we Jews?" he whispered back, his eyes big.

"Yes, we are." I decided to write him into the story as Anne's little brother because I really couldn't see him as Papa, Peter van Daan, or that nasty old dentist. "You're Anne's little brother, Hans. It's World War II, and we are a family of Jews hiding in an attic from the Gestapo."

"I want to be a soldier."

"The Jews aren't soldiers. They're victims."

That didn't sit well with him. Diane is always telling us to reframe our personal narratives so that we are the heroes and not the victims. Dr. Dhang gave her a worksheet.

"I don't want to play," said Max, stomping his foot dangerously close to a patch of cotton-candy-colored insulation. "I want to go back in the house and teach Lucky how to sit. Mom got some dog treats."

I could tell he was starting to miss Diane, but then he remembered that she had thrown out his rock collection. I saw the tantrum coming on like a storm, the collision of warm air and cold air, the faint swirl of that ole black twister rising in his little-person soul.

"My rock collection is gone!" he yelled. "Gone forever! She threw it away!"

Brothers! I was crawling to the imaginary window to see if the little Dutch girl had found a blackened hand with her father's ring on it, when I saw Diane's journals. There they were, still wrapped up in that plastic bag, all seven of them. I took one out and opened it.

GROCERY

Soy milk

Fake meat (2)

Spinach

Eggplant

Dog toothpaste

~~Marshmallows ok~~ maybe?

Coffee (FIND COUPON!!!!)

Nicotine gum (~~2 mg~~ 4 mg)

TO DO—URGENT!!!!

1. Grade student papers. Power sandwich: Positive statement—the negative punch—positive statement.

2. Brush Lucky's and Hiroshima's teeth.

3. Find out what smells in the car.

4. Pay bills. Postdate.

5. Do something with the eggplant or throw it out.

6. Call school photographer and ask for a do-over—
   WHY DID YOU PART MAX'S HAIR IN THE
   MIDDLE, YOU IDIOT!!!!

7. Reschedule missed orthodontist appointments—
   two.

8. Get oil changed. TELL THEM TO SCREW THE
   CAP ON TIGHTER. Ask Penn to see if any oil is
   left in the engine.

Max looked over my shoulder. "Is that Mom's journal? You're not supposed to read that, Aris. You'll get in trouble."

His breath was warm on my neck, but I knew he wasn't reading the words. So far, Max has only read two books in his life: *Little Bird, Biddle Bird*, a baby book that I remember Diane reading to me through the bars of my chicken crate, and one of Joe's books, a thick hardback titled *Vietnam—The True Story*. Max alternates reading these two books, repeatedly marking the titles and authors on the reading chart he has to fill out for the Lab every week. So far, none of the teachers have succeeded in expanding his reading list.

Each time he finishes reading *Little Bird, Biddle Bird*, he cries. It's not his emo[12] wail, or the howl of physical pain, which Penn calls "Jake Brake on Ice," or even his baby boohoo. He cries silently for *Little Bird, Biddle Bird*, hiding his face behind his arm, trying to make his sniffle sound like the symptom of a common cold. "I'm crying tears of joy," he explained once.

He has a completely different experience with *Vietnam—The True Story*.

12 Short for "emotional."

When he comes to the last page, he leans back, crosses one leg over the other exactly the way Joe used to do, and says, "You know, we shouldn't have fought that war." Diane thinks this is amazing because he never saw Joe cross his legs like that, never saw Joe at all. I'm like, *Duh, Joe is still here.*

"What does the diary say?" Max asked.

"She's overwhelmed. As usual."

"Is it my fault?"

"Don't try to make this about you."

"It's always my fault. There should have just been one kid. Just you. I'm too much trouble."

"Repeat after me, Max. I am not the belly button of the universe."

He gave me a baffled, hurt look and then bellowed, "I'm emo!" Then he began stabbing an umbrella into the pink insulation.

"Stop it! If you knock that through the ceiling, Penn will know we were up here."

"I don't care! Mom doesn't love us anymore! She hates us! That's why she got rid of our toys. Just THREW them out. I wish she had died instead of my dad." Then the tears came. His button nose turned pink. He squinched his eyes as he squeaked out, "Huh-huh, huh-huh, huh-huh-huh," at an ear-splitting volume.

"I'm warning you," I said, stretching out on my divan with the journal. "The Gestapo will hear you." While he (conveniently) turned himself into a statue, barely breathing, I flipped through the diary until I came to an interesting page. Diane, apparently instructed by a self-help book to make a list of positive statements about herself, had written: *Two men have told me that I'm the best lay they ever had.*

I don't want to shock anybody, but I come from a long line of Calvinist preachers. To be perfectly honest—and given my background, how could I be anything else?—I'm not exactly sure what a Calvinist is, but I know it's hard-core. Papa's grandfather and *his* grandfather were Calvinist preachers. Grandma's side of the family is a little shadier, but she says nobody drank in front of people. They both agree, whenever Diane snags a man from Match.com, that I am at an impressionable age and shouldn't see bad examples. In other words (ahem, Diane), why buy the cow when you can get the milk for free?

I'm actually fine with Diane having sex. Most of my friends say they cannot imagine their parents having sex. It really grosses them out, but Diane, well—it's not too hard to imagine. And don't think I don't know when she sneaks around the corner of the house with Penn to smoke a cigarette. I know every single time. I've put my foot down. Wheedled for three days straight until she swore she'd never do it again. Right now there's a sticky-note affirmation attached to her box of nicotine gum that says, "I am a contented nonsmoker."

I flipped through the journals. She wrote a lot of lists. We are all OCD in my family, but in different ways. With Diane, it's lists. If the house caught on fire, she'd sit down and make a list of what to do.

DREAMS I SHARE WITH ARIS

1. We are calling Joe on the phone and get the wrong number.

2. We are in my parents' house and discover a doorway leading to a luxurious mansion they know about but never use.

3. A pedophile kidnaps Max, and we chase him.

4. We are late for school so many times that Aris is suspended. In my dream, I'm mad because I can't afford to pay someone to stay home with her. In her dream, since I can't afford child care, she takes herself to England. In England, she becomes the queen.

Suddenly, BANG! Something hit the attic floor from below. Max and I looked at each other, and then I grabbed him.

BANG! BAM! BAM! BAM!

"It's the Gestapo!" screamed Max. "They're shooting at us!" He held me around the waist, crying, "Help me! Someone help me, please!"

"Shh," I whispered. "Listen."

For a moment, there was no sound but our breathing. Then heavy boot steps tromped up the wooden ladder. I could feel Max's heart pounding into my chest, hitting against my own heart.

Suddenly, the faded green bill of Penn's cap appeared at the top of the ladder. He held a broom in one hand.

"What are y'all doing up here?"

"We're playing Anne Frank," I said.

"She made me," said Max.

"Yeah, that's what I thought. Come down for a minute and tell me what you think of this playhouse I'm putting up."[13]

Is "the nick of time" a cliché? Diane says that if you need to ask, it probably is. Anyway, Penn got us out of the attic in the nick of time. As soon as he snapped the attic ladder into the ceiling, the garage door opened. Diane had come home early from work. and the car's headlights illuminated the dark corner of the garage where the three of us stood with our hands in our pockets like deer caught in the headlights. That is definitely a cliché. You can see how this works. You let one innocuous cliché slip under the fence, and here come its friends and relatives like a herd of elephants.

Diane opened the window of the car and called out, "Hey— what are y'all doing in the garage?"

---

13 Astute readers will wonder why Penn is building a playhouse. What is his MOTIVATION? A) He's bored. B) He feels sorry for these fatherless children. C) He wants to get into Diane's pants. D) He's a practical man who sees the need for more space in the house.

I don't know the answer yet, but it's coming . . .

Without missing a beat, Penn said that we were looking for some lumber to build a playhouse. I had butterflies in my stomach, but I smiled like the cat who has swallowed the canary and waited with bated breath for Max to blow our cover to kingdom come.

"We're building a playhouse!" Max exclaimed. "How come nobody told me?"

"I believe I was asked to do an intervention," said Penn. "For a cleaning binge?" He put finger quotes around "cleaning binge" before he looked at me. "Old stuff goes out, new stuff comes in." Max and I rushed at him with our arms out, but he stepped back to avoid the attempted hug. "It was your mother's idea."

Diane smiled and pushed her bangs out of her eyes. It was time for a trim, but our new budget stretched the time between salon visits. Diane calls the salon "the beauty parlor" and would rather go to the dentist. She doesn't like being touched by strangers and making small talk because she sucks at it. After a silence that has sent the hair stylist into desperation for any conversation at all, she'll mention that her husband died three months before Max was born. The stylist will go clip, snip, clip, snip while expressing her shock and horror, but before she can whip out the blow-dryer, Diane will ask why we cover dead bodies with sheets. The human is dead. What else can happen? So what if a fly lands on a nose?

"I don't think I'd like flies all over me," the stylist might say, in a voice not meant to encourage further speculation, but Diane can't stop.

Why are bodies put in the basements of hospitals and not on the top floors? Why are funeral homes single-story structures with rooms below the ground? In the big mirror, she will meet the baffled gaze of the stylist. Before the merciful blast of the hair dryer, she will ask, "What are we trying to hide?"

Mostly, I do Diane's hair.

Now, as she got out of the car with a bulging bag slung across her chest, a coffee cup tucked under her arm, a notebook in one hand, and keys in the other, I noted that her bun had worked its way out of the bobby pins. Or she'd pulled them out. At least once a week I have to explain that the style is hair that *looks* messy, not hair that actually *is* messy. She doesn't see the difference.

Penn already had the door to the kitchen open for her, his hand outstretched to take a bag.

"I'm just home for a few minutes," Diane said as she closed the car door with her hip. "I gave my students an in-class reading assignment."

We followed her into the kitchen. The manic postflood cleanup had trimmed a couple of inches off her waist, and in the purge she'd found an outfit in the back of her closet that didn't scream, *I AM AN ANDROGYNOUS MIDDLE-AGED TEACHER. PLEASE IGNORE ME.* She wore black tights and a short black skirt with black boots and a cream-colored sweater. Did I see Penn cast an appreciative glance?

I made a mental note to write down a list of ways I could get him to ask Diane out on a date. Of course, *she* could ask *him* out, but despite the fact that she actually taught a course in feminist literature called Not Chick Lit, she is old-fashioned.

Diane dumped her stuff on the table, blew her bangs out of her eyes, and looked around the kitchen to see if we had messed it up. We hadn't, so she smiled.

"We've cleaned up, Penn," she said. "What do you think?"

"It looks nice," he said evenly. Penn has good home training.

"Nice and neat like a graveyard," I suggested.

"She got rid of my Dum Dum wrapper collection *and* my rock collection *and* Aris's mad bomber hat," said Max. He grimaced at Diane and added, "She has been skipping school."

"I'd have to take a week off from work to think about that statement of faith they're making the faculty sign at KCC," said Penn. "I read about that in the paper." He turned to Diane. "Are they going to make you say you're a Baptist before you can teach?"

"Well . . . ," said Diane. "I haven't seen the form yet—maybe just a Christian?"

"That is bullshit," said Penn.

"It's just a piece of paper," she said. "It's a job. I'm not selling my soul."

"You sort of are," I said, then quickly added, "But you need a job."

"Can you still live without a soul—if you sell it?" asked Max. He put his arms around Diane. "Don't die."

"Let's look at the proposed site for the playhouse," said Penn, who avoids discussions of souls.

As we followed him outside, Max suggested that Penn live in the playhouse. "I could bring you breakfast," he said. I suggested building an office for me on the second floor—perhaps in the tower—while Max insisted on a drawbridge. "I've got an idea," he said, trying and failing to snap his fingers. "We can put some small alligators—very small—in the moat!"

"How much do you think this will cost?" Diane asked Penn. "I can't afford to buy a lot of lumber."

"Nobody buys lumber for playhouses," said Penn. "These are built with the wood that falls off the truck. However, I could turn the shed into a playhouse. That would be easy."

"My father would have a fit," said Diane. "He would say, 'Where will you put the lawn mower?'"

"In the garage," said Penn.

"He would say, 'You can't put a lawn mower in the garage. That's a fire hazard!'"

"It's your call," said Penn. He tapped his measuring tape. "I'm just here to build."

We took turns holding the measuring tape while Penn stretched it across the shed walls. Diane leaned over his shoulder as he scribbled indecipherable numbers on the back of an envelope. After a while, Max was beginning to get nervous. "Mom," he said, "shouldn't you go back to work? How long can your students read by themselves?"

"Depends on the assignment," said Penn. He lit a cigarette,

turning his shoulder so the smoke wouldn't blow our way. "Who's that French fellow who wrote down every little thing that crossed his mind while he was in a cork-lined room?"

"Marcel Proust," said Diane.

"Have your students get started on volume one of that shit. Didn't he write six volumes?"

"*A la recherche du temps perdu,*" said Diane. "*Remembrance of Things Past.* I read some of it in college. He could have used an editor. You might be interested in his ideas about time and space. Some people say that the books are written in the fourth dimension."

"Mom, don't start talking," said Max. Taking her wrist in his hands, he looked at her watch. "You need to go back to school. Your students might tell on you."

"Yes, sweetheart, I'm on my way." As we headed back toward the house, she said, "When he was a child, Marcel was afraid to go to bed because he lost his orientation of time and space when he slept. You know how you wake up and don't know where you are or what time it is? His parents got him a projector, the magic lantern. It flashed scenes from stories on the walls of his bedroom. The magic lantern increased his confusion and fear, but it led to his conviction of nonlinear time, nontangential space. Sometimes a sight or a smell can jettison you into a different reality where you inhabit different places at the same time. It was published in 1913."

"That's around the time Einstein developed the theory of relativity," said Penn. "So he's exploring the idea of non-Euclidean geometry?"

Diane shrugged.

"She doesn't do math," I told Penn.

"He was criticized for his writing; it's all digression, but that was his point. He said everything was happening at the same time."

"That's like our house," said Max. He was walking in a circle, trying to snap his fingers. "We're in the fourth dimension."

"Speaking of dimensions," said Penn, pulling out his scrap of calculations, "I plan to keep the exterior walls of the shed and build up to add a room for Aris's office. Cheaper to build up."

"This is starting to sound expensive—" Diane began, but Penn cocked his head and looked at her just a second too long, and she actually blushed. He leaned against the porch railing with one leg propped up against the wall of the house, rolling a cigarette on his thigh.

"Strictly community service for me," he said. "Repayment for my sins against society."

"What sins?" asked Max.

"I'll tell you later," said Penn. "It might take a while."

Awkward silence.

"Oh shit," said Diane. "I forgot about those papers I have to grade. I meant to do that during the class break." She unlocked her phone and then scrolled through her to-do list app. "There's too much going on."

"Let me grade them," I said. "Please! I know how to—"

"I can't snap!" wailed Max. "I was going to snap to 'Laffy Taffy' in the talent show. I don't have a talent!"

"Excuse you," I said. "You have a talent for interrupting people."

Max threw a modified (out of respect for Penn) temper tantrum, screwing up his face as he stomped his feet and flailed his arms in silence.

"You could dance at the talent show," said Diane. "You can make a costume for it."

Max stopped jumping and huffed, "You threw all my costume stuff away when you cleaned up. You got rid of everything so we could be simple, and now you're going to get fired. My life is over. It was so short!"

"I'm not going to get fired," said Diane, watching Penn amble across the yard with his tape measure, "but I could use some help. After you finish your homework, I have a small job for you and Aris."

"You're going to let me grade papers?" I asked hopefully as we followed her into the house. But no, she had sold some of our books to people on the Internet. We were to put these books, tagged with color-coded sticky notes, into pre-addressed mailers.

"It will be fun," she said brightly, and I felt a headache coming on. "I have to get back to class." She glanced at her watch and mumbled to herself, "They'll leave when the bell rings."

"I'll grade your papers," I said. "Ten dollars a page."

Diane hesitated. "You shouldn't even be reading my students' work. . . . Anyway, I need you to work on the mailers. We have customers waiting for those books."

I picked up a book with Mary Anne Timmerman's name printed across a pink sticky note. *Chop Wood, Carry Water.* Inside the cover, an inscription read, *To Diane with Love from Joe.* The light bulb in the lamp beside me sizzled and went out.

"I just put a new light bulb in that lamp," said Diane. "What is wrong with this house?"

"I'll change it," said Penn, who had just walked in with the stub of pencil over one ear. "You didn't get rid of the spare light bulbs, I hope."

We go through a twelve-pack of light bulbs every month, because, duh, our house is haunted. "Diane is going to let me grade some papers for her," I said boldly. "Five dollars a page. Maybe I can buy a new hat."

"Desperate times call for child labor," said Penn.

"Okay," said Diane, with a big sigh. "Two dollars a page, but I have to double-check your work." As she zipped around the kitchen, looking for something to throw on the table before she returned to her evening class, she said, "Put Charles's paper on top of the stack. I want to leave comments."

Max was in the rocking chair, going about sixty miles per hour. Joe and Diane built that chair in Alaska, before I was born. Once or twice a year, Penn glues the runners back on, because Max rocks them off. Penn was telling him that there would be no mollycoddling the next time he broke them, when Diane got a phone call.

"No, I haven't signed it yet," she was saying. "I'm thinking about it." She held the phone between her shoulder and ear, scowling. "I don't see it as an issue of cooperation," she said. "It wasn't in my contract." After she hung up, she looked out the window and said, "They are serious about this statement of faith. They want to *talk* to me about it."

I started to feel sorry for her, but then I thought about my mad bomber hat. *You shouldn't have done that,* I said silently to her back. *You shouldn't have tried to erase my dad. A playhouse, even with an office for me on the second floor, won't change what you did.* I knew if she turned around and I saw her face, I would cry.

"Just say okay," said Max.

"Do you realize how nonconformist it is for you to be a conformist in this family?" I asked him.

"Society honors its live conformists and dead troublemakers," said Penn. "So everybody gets a reward."

Diane took a deep breath, straightened her shoulders, and faced us with a brave smile.

"I'm a troublemaker myself," said Penn.

"Me too," she said.

"Give me your hand."

"What?"

"Come *here*," he said. "Give me your hand." He took her small hand in his large one and spread her fingers out as he studied her palm. I was like, *Oh my God, Penn is touching another human being. He is touching my mother.*

"What are you doing, Penn?"

"I was looking for a stigmata," he said. "I thought maybe you could just show them that instead of signing the statement."

I forget that Diane is actually a small person until I see her standing beside a man. She didn't look old anymore, just flustered. Even her hair looked flustered. There were big red spots on her cheeks. Sometimes she looks nothing like a teacher.

"I've got this," said Penn. "I'll pour the feed." He held the door open for her. "We'll see you when you get back."

Having papers to grade was an excellent excuse for leaving Penn responsible for both the kitchen and the child. I went into my room with the stack of bombastic, pleonastic, palaverous, magniloquent, grandiloquent, tedious,[14] big-talking, and really boring expositions for the persuasive essay assignment. I was persuaded of nothing until I read Charles's essay—thank God, he had ignored the topic. I read eagerly.

Charles Hutchins
English 1102

> A+++ :)))))) I don't even have to throw the rubric out on this one, Charles.

Should People Be Sentenced to Life in Prison?

Hays State Prison in Trion, Georgia, is a close-security prison in the Georgia Department of Corrections system that houses 1,100 inmates classified as "some of the state's most challenging offenders." One of them is my father, Marvin Hutchins.

> OH MY GOD! That's terrible. I had no idea you were going to say that.

Who is Marvin Hutchins and what did he do to deserve this? He is a 6′2″ black male weighing approximately 200 pounds. On August 13, 1995, Marvin Hutchins stabbed his girlfriend, Lorraine Demeeter, to death. He was under the influence of meth-

> He had a girlfriend when he was married to your mom?

amphetamines at this time, and alcohol. He was a violent man, and I don't know why. My mother says he hurt all the time and couldn't find relief until he hurt something else. It was a kind of relief for him, to watch others feel pain. I remember once when I was a kid I watched him beat our dog with a broom handle. I couldn't scream or tell him to stop because then he would beat me. So I took off my sock and stuffed it in my mouth. You may ask why couldn't I leave. I couldn't leave Betsy, my dog. I couldn't help her either. I was so afraid he would kill her, but she lived,

> He was so mean in that other essay you wrote. I really did want him to go to prison. I'm sorry he's your dad. I'm sorry if that sounded wrong. I don't know what to say, Charles!

> You should never, never hit a dog. Not even with a newspaper.

14 Okay, I used a thesaurus.

with just a broken jaw. After my father beat her, he sat at the kitchen table with his head in his arms and cried and cried. My mother doesn't want anything else to do with him, but she prays for him.

Can God help Marvin Hutchins? Some people would say no. In the Holy Bible, Job tells us, "But the eyes of the wicked shall fail, and they shall not escape, and their hope *shall be as* the giving up of the ghost." Job 11:20. According to Wikipedia, it costs the taxpayers thirty dollars a day to keep a person in a close-security prison.

> That's where that phrase comes from, giving up the ghost. Cool.

Do you think it's worth the money? Do you think he should be executed? I guess that's a topic for another paper. Hays State Prison will be my father's home for the rest of his life. When he isn't in lock-down, he works at various jobs they put him to. Once he was a library assistant, but he can't read very well, so he lost that job. He has the opportunity to completed his GED, but he doesn't. In his letters he says he goes to the prison church service, but he is in lock-down sometimes for acts of aggression. When they take him into the recreation yard, he has to be in kennel.

> "completed" looks like a typo to me.

> Sorry to be picky, but you skipped a little bitty word before "kennel."

Is there any hope for Marvin Hutchins?

> I don't know!

My father has been in prison for most of my life. I have visited him three times. He will never see me graduate from college, never meet my wife or children. He is alive, but also dead. The last time I saw him, he said, "Boy, you done grown on me. You're a man now."

> Profound.

I said, "Yes, sir, I am." Then we looked at each other through the little window, and it was like looking into a mirror because we look alike. That is the worst feeling I have ever had in my life. I can't even describe it. That could be me, on the other side of the bulletproof glass, in a cage for life. At that time, I lost all hope.

> This is so beautiful. Your writing just gets better and better. At first I thought you weren't any good, but now—fame is just around the corner for you, Charles.

Then something happened to me. I remembered the verses James 5:19–20, where Jesus tells us, "Brethren, if any of you err from the truth and one convert him, let him know that he who converteth the sinner from the error of his way will save a soul from death, and shall hide a multitude of sins."

I had my calling then. I cannot save Marvin Hutchins, but I can bring salvation to those who seek it. I will never be on the other side of that glass.

> I agree. Prison would suck.

. . .

After Joe died, Diane insisted that we only keep what would fit inside one trunk. One trunk was something we could handle. His saxophone went in first, and then a crooked pot holder I had made for him in preschool. His hiking boots fit, and odds and ends like his wedding ring, his watch, and the worn leather wallet with his expired Alaska driver's license inside the cellophane cover. On top of everything, Diane had spread a gray wool sweater that still had his smell. Whenever I snuck into Diane's closet to open the trunk, I allowed myself four sniffs—I didn't want to use it up.

When Diane had to identify Joe in the morgue, she recognized him by his clothes. "The corpse didn't look like him," she said. "He wasn't in his face. It's your soul that makes you look like you." Of course, you lose your entire soul when you die, but do you lose *some* soul when you murder someone? I was thinking about Charles Hutchins looking at his dad through the prison window. He said they looked alike. When Charles Hutchins looked at Marvin Hutchins, did he see himself with a broken soul—half-dead? What it would be like to tell people, *My dad got life*? Wasn't that a funny way to say it? His dad got life; my dad got death.

Heavy, heavy, heavy. Now I had a pile of rocks on my heart. *Way to get yourself depressed, Aris.* No one can do homework in that state of morbidity, so I skipped my English assignment and turned to a delightful writing exercise in *Write a Novel in Thirty Days!*

Exercise #7: Sex sells! Here's a surefire way to create a sex scene. Make a list of one hundred food and kitchen items, using nouns and verbs. Write a short sex scene. Now rewrite it, substituting your libidinous words with your kitchen words.

Ah, sex. It's not without its complications. When I was twelve, which seems like ages ago, I appalled one of Diane's friends by revealing certain things about my relationship with Billy, who was living in Kanuga at the time. I was having lunch with Diane and her friend at the Busy Bee Cafe, which is one of my favorite dining spots because the menu lists macaroni and cheese as a vegetable. Fortunately, Diane and I had found a babysitter for Max, and we were both wearing hats. Hers was floppy, with a string under the chin, and had probably been dropped in the river on too many kayaking trips, but it looked good on her. Diane has a cute face when she's relaxed. My hat was more elegant, a broad-brimmed straw hat with a lacy weave, encircled with a purple grosgrain band.

We were discussing men, of course. I happened to mention that Billy and I had considered counseling. We weren't having serious problems, but relationships are hard, and sometimes men just don't know how to communicate. Diane's friend, whose name escapes me at the moment, let her mouth drop open. I could actually see the corn bread she had been chewing.

"He's moving to Boston," I explained to her, "so we have to deal with the long-distance thing. We haven't really figured it out yet."

"It's too far to drive," said Diane.

"There's always time travel," I said. "According to Albert Einstein, if you could travel faster than the speed of light, you could theoretically travel backward in time, $d = rt$." I pushed my hat farther back on my head because it tended to slip over my eyes. "Although breaking the speed of light with any mass is currently considered impossible. I weigh 102 pounds."

"Well, my goodness," said the woman, and took a long gulp of her iced tea.

"Dating other people isn't an issue," I assured her. "We're monogamous."

The woman turned to Diane, her eyes wide. "She's *dating*?"

"It's not like they spend weekends at Barnsley Gardens," Diane said. "They sit next to each other at lunch."

I was a little miffed—it wasn't like Diane went to Barnsley Gardens with her dates (when she had one).

"How cute is that!" said the friend, but I could tell that she had her doubts.

Both ladies could have relaxed. Aside from a couple of forays into the sacristy at St. Michael's, my sexual experience is limited. In fact, after I had made my list of kitchen items, I had to steal a scene from Ian McEwan to finish Exercise #7.

Standing in front of the bookshelf in the living room, I leafed through Diane's copy of *Atonement* while Penn helped Max with his math homework.

"No, man, you tell me," said Penn. "What is seven times seven?"

"I dunno. Have you seen my Pokémon deck? Somebody moved it."

"Okay, let's talk about the Forty-Niners. Did you see the *Forty-Niners* play the other night?"

When Penn finished filling in the blanks on the math worksheet, he looked up and asked me if I was doing my homework.

"Just doing some research," I said. *Atonement* looked like a good book; I was thankful to Diane for excluding it from the sale pile. I took it to my room, closed and locked my door, and wrote Exercise #7.

> *They were beyond the present, outside time, with no memories and no future. There was nothing but an obliterating pot of coffee, thrilling and swelling, and the sound of squash on squash and pomegranate juice on squash as their Gimme Lean soy dogs slid across each other in this restless, sensuous wrestling.*

Done. After I ran a spell-check, I shot the document off to Mrs. Waller for the descriptive writing assignment that had been due last week.

Before we went to bed, Penn brought us outside to see what he had done on the playhouse. Since he had ignored my request for one small, simple tower, I hesitated to ask for the English garden with a maze and a fountain.

"Approve?" he asked.

All I saw was a shed with a square cut out for a window. I tried not to look disappointed. Penn snapped his measuring tape open, mumbling numbers to himself as he took more measurements.

"Can you make it a bay window?" I asked. "With a velvet window seat?"

"I'll study up on it."

"Or a French window that opens out to the garden?"

"How 'bout I put a pane of glass in it and we call it a day?" With a flick of his wrist, he opened the measuring tape again, impressing us with the precison of the swing. He measured some things in sixteenths and asked us to convert them to fourths, and then thirds.

"I don't do math," I reminded him.

"Right, I forgot," he said. "How about a lesson in cosmogenesis? Since space is our way of measuring distance between objects, can there be an element, force, or dimension known as space?"

"Big Bang theory," I said.

"You didn't raise your hand." He turned to Max, who had apparently given up on snapping to rap songs and was blowing air through puckered lips. "Whatever caused this epic explosion occurred in empty space, where expanse and distance are infinite. Are you with me?"

Max blew a weak raspberry from his lips, and I began to whistle "Go Tell It on the Mountain," in key.

Penn nodded, as if we were both whistling agreement, and delivered his summary. "If this cosmology is true, then our universe exists without cause or explanation. In that case, where is God?"

Max looked around. He looked up at the sky, at the playhouse, at us. Finally, he said, "In my heart." Then he made a horrible farting sound with his mouth.

"Shaping young minds is such a satisfying occupation," said Penn.

"Penn," I said, smiling and stepping closer to him, which is what Diane says I do when I'm being manipulative. "If you made a bay window with a window seat, that's one less chair you'd have to build."

"I didn't hear about furniture making in this deal. Y'all can put your beanbags on the floor."

"Mom threw the beanbags away!" yelled Max.

"We have nothing," I said, and I wrung my hands. Penn leaned back against the wall to roll a cigarette.

"Am I being manipulative?" I asked.

"Now that you mention it," he said, and licked the edge of his rolling paper. "Manipulative *and* petulant."

"It's most unattractive of me, isn't it?"

"Butt-ugly," said Max, but we ignored him.

"No, it's just your dark side," said Penn. "Your *shadow* side."

I confess to a secret thrill at the thought of having a shadow side. As the smell of his cigarette mingled with the fresh scent of wood shavings, I imagined people saying, *She seemed like such a nice girl. . . .*

"You have a message from Kate," said Max, who seems to be attached to my phone by some electrical wave, while I never hear the tone. I pulled it out of my pocket.

I briefed Billy on strawberry-blond arrival to his social media pod. Result: Swears she's a cousin. My fact-checking on three sites proved inconclusive, so I friended her on one social media site for further investigation. Uncovered one "Like" of the meme Your husband is cheating on us.

I forced myself to *not* look at her pic again, seeking a family resemblance.

"What's wrong?" asked Max.

"Life, little one, just life." I turned to Penn. "What do you think about the nature of evil?"

"I try not to." He exhaled over his shoulder. "What do you think about it?"

"Well, I read this poem by William Blake."

"Wait a minute. Is that the one about a leopard?"

"It's called 'The Tyger.' I'll read it to you." I got my library book from my room and brought it outside. In the falling winter light of our backyard, over the sound of Max's plaintive efforts to whistle, I read:

> *Tyger Tyger, burning bright,*
> *In the forests of the night;*
> *What immortal hand or eye,*
> *Could frame thy fearful symmetry?*
>
> *In what distant deeps or skies.*
> *Burnt the fire of thine eyes?*
> *On what wings dare he aspire?*
> *What the hand, dare seize the fire?*

Max got quiet and moved closer to me. Deep purple streaks crossed the lavender sky, making it darker and darker. A few minutes later, the night was black without a single star except for the orange glow of Penn's cigarette.

I felt my shadow side growing larger. It had yet to manifest into Evil Aris, but the stirrings were present: Fingerlings of doubt had crept into my relationship with Billy Starr, that god of adolescence, and I was flat mad at Diane. If I failed to bring a new daddy on board by getting Penn and Diane together, I might lose hope in myself—and that is the making of a monster.

Gosh, I almost forgot I was writing. When I'm not visualizing the comments of Mrs. Waller, my English teacher (*"You're rambling, Aris. What's the point here? Where's your outline?"*),[15] I can relax. Writing a novel feels almost like talking. You're not talking to yourself, exactly, but when I'm talking to myself, I'm not talking to myself anyway. I'm talking to someone who may or may not be real, someone who really likes me. If I'm hating on someone— for example, someone who went through all my personal stuff and threw valuable things away without permission—then I'm talking *about* that person to the person who really likes me. Most of the time, I never even move my mouth.

Diane, to our horror, talks to herself at Kroger. She doesn't try to hide it. "Three ninety-eight!" she exclaims. "For a jar of yellow mustard?" Too harried to get her reading glasses out of her purse, she grabs her nearest child. "Read that label and tell me if it has high-fructose corn syrup in it." She talks fast at Kroger because she wants to hurry up and get out of there—the people

15 Imagine this in red ink.

in the aisle probably think she's saying something else instead of "fructose." Which has happened. But she just goes on talking to herself. "I don't need that. Wait a minute, do we have ketchup? Meat loaf . . . what goes in meat loaf? Let's make it with oatmeal, for more fiber."

I have stood in the bread aisle and listened to her plan an entire menu, out loud, over by the pickles. She's not embarrassed at all. She argues that people are always talking on hands-free cellphones, so they probably think she's wearing a Bluetooth device on her ear, under her hair. When I don't buy that excuse, she tells me that the pain I endure as her child is building my character. More or less, I agree with her, but Max suffers.

Max talks to himself too. In the shower he conducts Pokémon warfare (with sound effects), and sometimes on the toilet he will thank God for his family and food and shelter and put in a request for a Mustang. On the Wednesday after Diane got rid of our stuff, he stormed into his room and slammed the door so hard that the crooked sign attached with masking tape slipped to the floor.

PRIVAT. DO NOT INTER!!!!!!

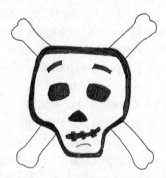

In the safety of his locked room, he yelled, "I hate her!" Legos clattered against the wall. He paused, as if listening for repercussions, and then continued, "She's mean." Mimicking Diane's voice, he said, "'You're the child, and I'm the parent, and you're being disrespectful.'" Another pause. Then, in a calm voice, he confided to the person who really likes him, who may or may not be real, "She's not really even my mother. She's just the maid." For a few minutes, he grumbled unintelligibly. Finally, he said in a loud, firm voice, "You're fired."

This Wednesday was not as yellow as it should have been; it was more of a dark gold until Penn arrived.

"Yo!" he yelled in the doorway. "Anybody home?"

The hallway filled with the light scent of his cigarette smoke and brilliant rays of yellow light. Diane had skipped work again. I was trying not to track her 5.5 absences and 2 tardies, but grading her papers puts me in teacher mode. Perhaps she was edging toward a new career as a trophy wife? As she greeted Penn, standing in that awkward space where southerners usually hug, Penn looked her up and down. I went to my room so they could have some privacy, in case they wanted to start a romance. According to my outline of the novel, if a romance was going to blossom, they needed to get on it.

While I was letting that happen, I crawled under my bed to do some research. Kate had suggested the under-the-bed office as a temporary measure, until my executive suite on top of the new playhouse was ready for occupancy. Since Kate shares a bedroom with her sister, she has innovative ideas about creating personal space.

It was a tight fit, but since Diane had cleaned all my junk out, I was able to squeeze under the bed with enough room to lift the cover of my laptop. Resting on my elbows, I managed to type. A headlamp gave me plenty of light, and the dust ruffle provided privacy.

The small space of wall behind the bed frame held the motivational sticky notes that the author of *Write a Novel in Thirty Days!* suggests for a writer's bulletin board in an exercise called "Remember the Why." You might think it's easy to remember why you are writing your novel, but it's not. Diane says it's like remembering why you married your spouse.

Sticky note #1: I am writing this novel to circumvent the bother and expense of therapy.

Sticky note #2: I am writing this novel to make money so Diane can retire, Max can go to camp, and I can chill.

Sticky note #3: I am writing this novel in case things don't work out with Diane and Penn—maybe somebody else will notice her.

Beneath the "bulletin board" sat the stack of journals I was using for research. What! Cat out of the bag. Yesterday, when I was alone in the house for twenty minutes, I snuck back into the attic and swiped Diane's journals. I knew it was wrong, but my shadow side overtook my common sense and respect for the personal property of others. Anyway, the best fiction is based on research.

I tried to stop reading them. I'd tell myself, *Just one more page, and then I'll put them back.* Then I'd read another one, and another. I was an egg-sucking dog looking down the barrel of a shotgun. Sometimes the Ghost of Dad would appear, flicking a light switch, playing a song on my phone, but what could he do? I learned more and more about him.

A LIST OF THINGS THAT
REMIND ME OF JOE

Jazz

Aaron Neville

French, especially Cajun French

The smell of garlic, onions, and green peppers on the stove

The red flag flapping at the end of a pine on a logging
truck

Snow cones

Car wrecks

Handsome men with broken noses

The mad bomber hat

Aris and Max

How thoughtful of her to mention the offspring. Thanks for the
shout-out, Diane. I couldn't forgive her for getting rid of the hat.
I tried. My enlightened self said, *These memories bring her pain.
She wants to let go of the pain.* My shadow self said, *That was a
stupid way to do it. You should have had all your stupid moments
before turning thirty.*

She wrote a poem about the red flag on the logging trucks, "Death
in Northwest Georgia."

> *It killed him.*
> *Made me stronger.*
> *Strong as a semi barreling logs up the pass.*
> *The wind whistles right through me;*
> *My red flag flaps.*
> *Rain, mud, endless pines.*
> *We're making paper, clearing a view.*
> *How else can a dead man and a strong woman*
> *Keep the family together?*

Joe was never weak. He used to hold his arm straight out, like
a tree branch, and I'd swing on it, do a little flip. I wasn't allowed
to see his corpse. They called it "the body," as if it now belonged
to everybody. I saw a lump covered with a sheet on the side of the

road, briefly lit by a flashlight reflecting off the snow. After that, Diane told me, the body went to a refrigerated room, even though we were in Alaska. Later, it traveled in a temperature-controlled container to Kanuga, Georgia. There, it was burned.

Grandma and Papa said this was a waste of money. If they had *known* Diane wanted to cremate the body, it would have been much cheaper to transport ashes. Diane said she *told* them, but they wouldn't listen. Montgomerys don't like cremation. People want to see the body, they insist, unless it's—well—disfigured. Joe *was* disfigured, a little bit, but Wallace Smithson, down at the Smithson Brothers Funeral Home, could have done something. Used makeup and whatnot. Formaldehyde. Hair spray. Wallace did a good job, the grandparents said. They had seen his work.

Diane said they should have just had the funeral in Valdez.

No, no, no! said Grandma and Papa. They didn't know *anybody* up there. That godforsaken place! Anyway, they were paying for it. Papa said he didn't *mind* paying for it. "We are happy to help," said Grandma, "but everyone in Kanuga wants to see you and your family at the funeral. It's the least you could do."

Joe's family was Catholic, but Papa said that having a priest at the funeral might offend the Baptists. "We could have a priest *and* the Baptist minister perform the service," suggested Papa. "Would Joe be okay with that compromise?" He suggested they take turns conducting the service.

Diane blinked at him. She was ginormous, carrying Max. She couldn't even touch her feet; Papa had to cut her toenails for her. When we went out, with me holding her hand tight so she wouldn't disappear like Joe, men rushed to hold the door open wide for us. Then they edged away, as if she might birth a baby in front of them. Her eyes were empty, just holes in her head. "Joe couldn't care less," she said. "He wouldn't even come to this funeral if we didn't carry him in a pot."

She picked out the cheapest urn, $495.00, but it was the one I liked best, black marble, with a swirl of gray that made me think of a spirit. At the funeral, there was no pastor, no priest. Instead, a Creek medicine man Diane had found on the Internet burned braids of sweetgrass and prayed for Joe's transition into the spirit world. "The spirit is the hand inside the glove," said the Creek, who called himself John Red Fox, "and the glove is gone." John Red Fox had red hair. Grandma said that Diane always gets her way, but she admitted that it was an interesting service. All of Kanuga turned out for it.

When Papa brought the urn to our house, filled with Joe's ashes, he rang the doorbell. He wouldn't carry it inside. "You need to do this," he said, handing it to Diane. "It's not that heavy." So she carried Joe over the threshold, the way Joe had carried her when they got married.

Papa and Grandma couldn't convince her to bury the urn. "We aren't *staying* in Kanuga," Diane said. "I don't want to leave him here." They went yadda yadda yadda, but she said, "Nope. We don't belong here. We're moving."

That was eight years ago. The urn still sits in the same place on our mantel, another thing to be dusted. Sometimes I gaze into the swirl of gray spirit, wondering, *Where's the hand?*

I thought it would be a good idea for Diane and Penn to share their love histories with each other. I knew from experience with Billy that you have to do this carefully. Revealing some information about your romantic past is tantalizing; too much is fuel for future fights.

That afternoon the three of us were taking our coffee break on the back porch while Max practiced an act on the trampoline for the talent show. We had explained that he could not put a trampoline on the small stage at Lavender Mountain Laboratory School, but he refused to listen.

"Dude!" called Penn. "That somersault ain't gonna turn into a flip. You've got to jump high!"

"I'm scared," Max wailed.

"Do it anyway. You'll feel better about yourself."

"Dude, you can do this," Max told himself as he started jumping again. "Dude, this is *so* easy."

He jumped high, bent his head forward, lifted his knees, then chickened out and did a somersault. When he got off the trampoline and came to the porch, he explained, "There was a caterpillar on the trampoline, and my foot slipped on it."

"Must have been a cold caterpillar," said Penn, "out here in February. Was it wearing a fuzzy little sweater?"

"Maybe it was ice," said Max.

"Ice," said Penn, smiling at Diane. "You've got to admire the dogged persistence in his denial of reality. That's a talent."

"It is a little chilly," said Diane. She was wearing a low-cut long-sleeved T-shirt, so thin that you could clearly see the outline of her bra. Definitely in find-a-friend mode. When she crossed her arms over her chest and shivered, Penn had the perfect opportunity to put his arm around her, but he missed it.

I sent Billy a selfie of myself drinking coffee, but he didn't respond. This was becoming a pattern. I'd send him a gazillion texts in one day and get nothing back. The next day, I'd text:

Was it something I said? Where r u?
Did ur fingers freeze?

I'm not a stalker or anything, but he was posting basketball scores on Facebook, so obviously the boy was still kicking. Eventually, I'd break down and send him a long email explaining my feelings. Since Billy *never* remembers to check his email, that's basically like putting a letter in a bottle and throwing it out to sea. Finally, I'd message him on Facebook. Somehow that always feels lame to me. It's like, I know you're on here interacting with all of your other friends, so you have to acknowledge my existence. Then he'd message back that he lost his cellphone again, and oh yeah, he forgot to check his email.

"Billy isn't answering you," said Max as he leaned over my shoulder.

"Thank you for that news alert."

"Aris," said Diane. She was measuring creamer into her coffee with a teaspoon, and cheating.

"I'm busy," I said, staring at my screen.

"I know it's old-school, but men *like* to chase women."

"Right," I said.

"It might be genetic," she said. "The way dogs chase cats. You never see cats chase dogs." She measured a third teaspoon of creamer into the coffee, stirred it, stared at it, and then splashed more into the cup without the bothersome spoon. "You want to make him wonder," she said.

"There are boy cats," Max pointed out.

"Thanks for the advice," I said. "I'll go act on it now." I stood up, ready to hunt down some personal space, but suddenly I saw my opportunity and sat back down.

"Did Joe chase you?" I asked Diane.

She smiled. Max and I love the story of how she met our dad, and Diane loves to tell it. "I was living in Provincetown, Massachusetts . . ."

"And she met the other straight person," suggested Penn. "I've heard of that place. Don't they have the Gay Policeman's Ball there?"

"I didn't see him at first. Maybe I did—he was so handsome—but yeah, Penn is right. You just assume that everyone in P-town is gay. He told me later that he followed me home, five blocks in the rain. "I was wearing green wellies and carrying this huge broken umbrella I found in my landlord's house. He said he wanted to know if I was a crazy person."

"Conclusion?" asked Penn.

"It was a legitimate concern," said Diane. "There are several borderlines in P-town. My landlord had a God complex. He had long white hair, a long white beard, and wore long white robes. He kept my deposit."

"Three months later . . . ," I prompted.

"That was in January? In March, I was sitting in an AA meeting when I looked across the circle and saw Joe. He was so handsome with that dark wavy hair, a scruffy beard, big, dark eyes. Definitely some Cajun there."

I glanced nervously at Penn: bald. He didn't look jealous, though, just interested.

"I looked at Joe and thought, if I were going to marry someone, it would be that guy. I knew. There was something about him, the way he carried himself. He listened with his entire body, taking everything in, but he was also poised to move. He was fast. Oh, that grin! He had a great sense of humor. Once, after we were married, Grandma and Papa came to Alaska to visit us. We were standing on a glacier, and Grandma looked around and said, 'This doesn't even look real.'

"Your father looked her in the eye and said, 'It's not.'"

"You knew at first sight that you were going to marry him," I said, and sighed.

"No," she said. "I was actually engaged to some poor sod, still wearing his ring, but I was about to cut loose. I wasn't planning to marry anybody; I was done with men. When I saw Joe across the room—it was as if I knew him. We went to a coffee shop, a tiny, crowded place where your knees touched the knees of other customers as you hunched over your coveted little table. We drank coffee with cream and sugar. We ate pie. We talked. We smoked. We talked and talked and talked. Somehow, we had known each other before, loved each other before."

"The next day, you moved in with him," I concluded.

"We waited a week," she said primly. "My landlord, God, evicted me, and I had nowhere else to go. Joe lived in an attic over his uncle's Greek restaurant. There were beautiful windows in that attic. The day before I moved in, Joe tied a rope to his waist and scaled the building to wash the windows. The light always changes in P-town—that's why artists go there. When the sun was bright, it sparkled through those windows, and on gray days, you could almost see the clouds roll across the floor. We left the windows open all the time. The air smelled of sea salt and basil and garlic. I can see him in that apartment in his faded khaki shorts, shirtless and tanned. Sometimes he climbed onto the roof and played 'On the Sunny Side of the Street' on his old King sax."

She tried to hum the tune, but poor Diane can't even hum. To our surprise, Penn sang a snippet, in perfect key:

> *Grab your coat and grab your hat, baby*
> *Leave your worries on the doorstep*

He gave us an embarrassed grin. "My mother liked that song," he said. "Sang it to me in the cradle."

"So, Penn," I said, WITH STUDIED CASUALNESS. "How about you? Have you ever fallen in love at first sight?"

I had caught him off guard. For one second, I thought he was going to talk. He scratched his head, looking pensively into the distance. He opened his mouth. Then, suddenly, he stood up.

"Max," he said, "fetch me that broom. It's time for you to watch me sweep out some wood shavings."

Later, as he swept, I heard him softly singing the rest of the song to himself.

In response to the KCC form requesting a signed statement from faculty agreeing to refrain from consuming alcoholic beverages in public, to set "the example of clean Christian living," Diane scribbled, "I'm allergic to alcohol. When I drink it, I break out in jail."

"Mom, don't say that!" Max wailed when he saw the paper on the kitchen table. His ears looked large and pink, the way they do when he has a fresh haircut. "Just say, 'Okay.' If they fire you, we won't have any money!"

You might think that a young child with such concern for the family coffer (am I rocking these vocab words or what?) had great financial ambitions for himself, but whenever people ask Max what he wants to be when he grows up, he says, "A hobo." He's not kidding. He has his spot picked out in Central Plaza, next to an outdoor electrical socket where he can plug in his Game Boy. It's right in front of Domino's Pizza, so when money gets tight, as it tends to do when you're a hobo, he can deliver pizzas and eat the leftovers.

Normally, we eat at Domino's with Grandma and Papa on

Friday evenings, but they were in the mountains with a group of friends who called themselves the EZers. These septuagenarians shared the philosophy that the hard part of life was over for them. When they got together, they lazed around, laughing at the work they refused to do. So this Friday, Diane would have to pick up the check. Since Diane had been smarting off to KCC about their new rules, Max and I were worried, but neither one of us could muster the maturity to say we didn't want to go out for pizza. We love pizza!

Raising a Happy Child in an Unhappy World advises parents that children should never have to worry about money. It makes us feel insecure. Diane hasn't gotten to that chapter yet because every time she picks up the book, she starts all over again with the prologue—she loves beginnings. She's also a fan of affirmations. The sticky note on the visor over the steering wheel reads, "I am sailing on the river of wealth." When I started to worry about the price of dinner, I reminded myself that first-time authors often become millionaires. Several cases are cited in *Write a Novel in Thirty Days!*

As we strolled past Max's hobo camp in Central Plaza, I adjusted Diane's green poncho so it would hang straight. Penn hadn't come out to dinner with us because, of course, he doesn't eat, but it's important for a single woman to look her best at all times. I had my heart set on Penn, but a little competition never hurts.

Unfortunately, there was no competition at the Kanuga Domino's that evening.

I sent Billy a selfie.

"Nope, no reply," said Max, peering at my screen.

"Quit leaning on me, Max. Diane, please make him sit in his chair."

"Sit," Diane said. She handed him her phone with instructions not to download the gun app. He had recently found an iPhone app that turns a cellphone into a gun. Every time he got his hands on a phone, he was armed. If I hadn't been busy watching my own cellphone for a text from Billy, I would have lectured him on the power of nonviolence. Last year, I memorized Martin Luther King Jr.'s "I Have a Dream" speech.

I have a strong memory, which is both a blessing and a curse. It's wonderful because I never have to study. Everything that enters my brain stays there. The downside is that I can't forget anything. Memories flutter around my brain with the damned persistence of moths on a lamp. Sometimes entire pages of Diane's journals flash back to me, unbidden. For example, I might look at a pizza menu and see this:

THINGS JOE TAUGHT ME

How to roll a burrito.

How to roll a baby into a blanket like a burrito.

How to stop hypothermia.

How to make puttanesca, which means "whore sauce" in Italian, because when women cheat on their husbands they don't have time for cooking.

It's okay to dig a huge hole in your backyard.

The difference between jets and unidentified flying objects.

Federal taxes are illegal.

Keep a machete in the car.

How to die before you get old.

I was trying to forget this list when a man tapped on the window and smiled at us through the glass.

"It's Charles!" cried Diane, waving for him to come inside.

A slim young black man stood by our table. He was wearing

creased khakis, a starched white dress shirt (I notice these things because Diane and I don't have time to iron), and a red power tie. I couldn't see his shoes, but he wore a felt hat like the one Papa wears when it's cold, sort of a twenties gangster hat. A red feather stuck out of the hatband at a jaunty angle.

If you have ever met one of your favorite writers IN PERSON, you will understand how hard it was not to jump up and give Charles a big ole bear hug. We had been through so much together: cringing when Daddy gave Mama that mean look and said, "You the smart one . . . ," suffering the humiliation of wearing clown shoes when other kids had new Nikes. When we pulled up in front of Mama's house in a BMW that left our clothes smelling of new car . . . our hearts were one. How we braced ourselves to see Marvin Hutchins's face behind that Plexiglas window in Hays State Prison—

"Children," said Diane, motioning for Charles to sit down, "I'd like you to meet my student, Charles Hutchins. Charles, these are my children, Aris and Max."

"Hi," I said brightly. My ears were hot with excitement, and I didn't know where to look.

"Hello, Aris," he said. "I've heard a lot about you."

I stared at the red-and-white-check tablecloth, thinking, *Believe me, I have heard a lot about* you.

He sat down, working his long legs into the tight space under the table, and smiled broadly. The hat looked pretty strange, with the feather. Papa's feather was a discreet fluff of robin, but Charles's feather was out there, coming right at you. It may have once belonged to some tropical bird.

The waitress brought our Cokes. At first, I thought this was a mistake. Diane says that soft drinks jack up a restaurant bill. Cheap eateries like Domino's don't even make money from their food; it all comes from the soft drinks, which are legal poison. Apparently, Diane had lost her mind and ordered them. She looked a little surprised herself.

"No refills, please," she told the waitress, but she didn't send them back. She asked Charles to eat with us, but he said he couldn't, blah blah blah, and I zoned out. I was watching a baker behind the window to the kitchen knead dough. He wore plastic gloves all the way up his thick forearms, and his muscles popped each time he slammed the ball of dough on the counter and stretched it out again.

"You're coming from the police station?" Diane was asking Charles. "Why?"

Immediately, I forgot about pizza dough and gave Charles my full attention.

He had removed his hat, holding it lightly in his lap. He looked down for a moment while he fingered the brim. He had long, tapered fingers and wore a gold class ring. Other than Penn and Papa, and the occasional Mr. *Friend*, we rarely get close to men, so it was something of a novelty to have one at the table.

"Well, Dr. Montgomery-Thibodeau . . ."

"I don't have a PhD."

"Yes, ma'am. I always forget." He flashed a smile. "*Ms.* Montgomery-Thibodeau." Then he was serious again. "I don't know how to say this, but . . . I got arrested over the weekend for speeding. The police searched my car, and then they took me to jail."

He paused to give each of us a long look, and I could absolutely see him as a preacher. Preachers know that certain silences have a way of waking people up. Even Episcopalian rectors do it (okay, *rector* doesn't sound disturbing), but they don't have the flare that Baptists have for making people squirm.

Max's mouth had dropped open. "You went to jail?" He practically yelled this across the restaurant. Heads turned. Diane and I hushed him at the same time, but Charles wasn't mad.

Charles sat up a little straighter. "Yes, I did, young man. I never thought that would happen to me." He shook his head. "It was . . . I don't know how to say it. It was a low point, Ms. Montgomery-

Thibodeau. A real low point in my life. They didn't find anything in my car," he said softly, "but they took me down to the station anyway. They told me I could call someone." He looked back down at the hat in his lap. "I hated making that call to my mother. She borrowed money from my cousin to pay the five-hundred-dollar fine. The worst part is, I have to spend spring break in jail. The whole week!"

"How fast were you going?" asked Diane. Without looking away from Charles, she reached her hand across the table and slid her phone away from Max. He had started downloading the gun app.

"Eight miles over the speed limit. I don't usually speed, but—"

"That's ridiculous!" said Diane. "They can't search your car without a warrant. They can't just throw you in jail for speeding. Were you drinking?"

"No, ma'am. And this was my first speeding ticket. I had my papers."

Diane went into mom mode. "Driver's license?"

"Yes, ma'am."

"Insurance?"

"Yes, ma'am."

"Car title?"

"Yes, ma'am."

She was probably about to ask him if he'd brushed his teeth, if he was *sure,* now, when the waitress swooped down on us and tried to take his order. He said no, thank you; he had to go see his fiancée. I imagined Billy saying *my fiancée* like Charles did, and looking so proud.

"They can't do that to you," said Diane. "Do you have a lawyer?"

"Yes, ma'am, I think so. My mother talked to someone. He said we could write an appeal."

"I'll help you," said Diane, and I saw the grit coming up in her right there as we moved our glasses to make room for the pizza the waitress was setting on the table. The smell of cheese bubbling on puffy, freshly baked dough and the sight of pepperoni curling at the edges sent stabbing pangs of hunger to my belly. My mouth watered. Diane didn't even notice the pizza; she was looking at Charles with a dangerous gleam in her eye. "Repeat after me," she said. "I am not going to jail."

"I wish I could believe that."

"Repeat," said Diane in her teacher voice.

"I am not going to jail," said Charles. He smiled, handsome and proud.

The waitress asked if there was anything else she could get us. "Just the check, please," I said. She smiled, like I was trying to be cute, and waited for Diane to see her. Diane, however, was blind. "Even Georgia is aware of racial profiling," she was telling Charles. "Let's write an appeal that will bring this case to the national news."

"Thank you," said Charles. When he stood up to leave, he touched his hand to his heart, brushing the red tie with the tips of his long fingers.

"Why is Charles going to jail?" asked Max after he left. He had the phone again.

"Don't talk with your mouth full," said Diane. With a napkin, she wiped some tomato sauce from his chin. Then she dipped a forkful of salad into the small container of dressing on the side. Thoughtfully, she chewed her food. Then she said, "Charles drives a BMW. Charles is black."

"Surprise!" I said.

"You're supposed to say African American," said Max, with his mouth full. You could often see the entire process of mastication in his mouth. It was interesting, but gross.

The waitress came by with a pitcher of Coke but caught herself before she poured refills. Then Max pointed Diane's phone at the ceiling, and the sounds of gunfire filled the restaurant.

· · ·

That night, before I went to sleep, I crawled under my bed and opened Diane's last journal. The binding had come loose and pages were slipping out. On the inside of the back cover, Diane had written an inventory in her smallest handwriting.

INVENTORY

Money in checking account: $47.12. Savings: $2.07. Debt: $0. Gas in car: ½ tank. Milk: ¼ carton. Coffee: 1 bag. Annie's Mac and Cheese: 7 boxes. Nicotine gum: 4 pieces, 4 mg. Monogrammed Christmas hand towels given as wedding gifts: 12. Books: 612. Books of Mormon: 3. Lego pieces: 174,112. American Girl dolls: 5. American Girl doll shoes: 23 pair. Love notes from children: 12. Apology notes from children: 19. Number of students: 66. Passing students: 56. Students who expect to pass: 65. Intellectually curious students: 1. Friends: 2. Acquaintances: 168. Ex-boyfriends: 17. Ex-fiancés: 3. Ex-husbands: 0. Number of times fell in love at first sight: 1. Number of times in love: 1. Urns on mantel: 1 dead person, 1 dead pet. Pets: 2. Number of times forgiven: 1,938. Number of times forgave others: 1,512. Number of times hit by parents: 511. Number of times hit my children: 2. Times father has given me the shirt off his back: 1. Number of years member of a country club: 22. Number of times sold blood for money: 5. Number of miles jogged: 213,000. Number of cigarettes smoked: 2,992,999. Number of kisses blown: 5. Miracles witnessed: 3. Miracles expected: 2,183,173. Number of prayers: 1,319,873,918,000. Number of secrets—

Oh, Diane. What was I going to do with her? What if my novel wasn't any good? A firm believer in beginner's luck, I hadn't seriously considered that possibility until now. Kate said I was a great writer, as long as I used spell-check. True, my English grade was growing shabby, but that's only because I hadn't turned some things in yet. Diane said I could do anything I put my mind to—she wouldn't have given me *Write a Novel in Thirty Days!* if she didn't think I was up to the task. However, after reading these journals, I realized that our family situation was worse than I had thought. If things didn't work out with Penn—and even if they did, since, as Grandma was quick to point out, Penn didn't actually have a job.

Looking at the sticky notes posted on the bulletin board of my under-the-bed office, I reflected on my writing goals.

1. Avoiding therapy.

2. Marrying Diane off.

3. Making money.

Bottom line—the fate of the Montgomery-Thibodeau family rested on my literary success. Even though I wasn't finished with the manuscript, I needed a second opinion. The author of *Write a Novel in Thirty Days!* suggests that the first critic of your work should be someone who has read a lot of books, someone who likes you, but not too much. I thought for a moment, took three deep breaths, and emailed my work in progress to Ms. Chu.

Write a Novel in Thirty Days! says that you should never leave a character alone in a room too long. People don't do anything when they're alone, the author argues, so the story comes to a standstill. When there's no interaction, there's no action.

How I wish that were true.

On Monday night, Diane had arranged to meet Charles at her office to help him with his next essay assignment. Penn came over to watch us and cracked open a taco kit. "There must have been some Mexican jumping beans in that box," he said after dinner, when Max had circled the table for the fourth time, hopping on one foot. Penn suggested a field trip to the Salvation Army, and Max started talking a mile a minute about finding his rock collection there.

"I hope somebody else hasn't already bought it," he said. "That would just suck."

" 'Never say of anything that I have lost it,' " said Penn. " 'Say that I have given it back.' That's Epictetus, or however you say his name. Cool dude."

"If I see someone trying to buy my rock collection, I'll just hit him over the head," said Max. "Pow." He picked up the saltshaker and hit a few imaginary rivals over the head before he got a better idea. "Penn, can I download my gun app on your phone?"

"I hope you know that our correctional institutions are crammed with eight-year-old boys shooting gun apps in thrift stores," Penn said. "Hurry up before the store closes."

Max thought for a moment, shifting his weight on his feet.

Finally, he reached his compromise. "I'll just say politely, 'Excuse me, sir, I believe that's my rock collection.'" He looked up at Penn. "Will that be good?"

"Sweet," said Penn. "You coming, sister?"

"No, thanks." I made my voice sound casual, a little bored. I stretched, yawned, and looked at the ceiling. "I think I'll stick around here and finish mailing out those books for Diane."

Penn's eyes were silvery beneath the brim of his cap. Sometimes looking into his eyes is like looking through a one-way mirror. You can't tell what he's thinking, but you get the feeling that he's reading your brain. "Time to do some good works, or is this penance?"

"I need the cash," I said, and smiled at him.

"Well, all righty, then. Max, load up that gun app, and let's hit the road."

When they left, the house felt suddenly empty. Except for one lamp casting a yellow glow over Diane's stack of manila envelopes, the living room was dark. I watched my shadow on the wall. Every time the furnace kicked on, the lamp blinked and the shadow moved.

Random memory: Once, after Joe died, I was following Diane through a parking lot in Georgia. We had just moved from Alaska, and the sunlight hurt my eyes, so I kept my face down as we walked. Diane was pregnant with Max. As I followed her, I kept my feet on the edge of the shadow of the lady with the big belly.

"Merm," I said, "I'm following your shadow." Suddenly, the woman turned around. It wasn't Diane.

Remembering this made me miss Diane so much I couldn't stand it. Was this the fourth dimension, when then is now and here is there? I was 4 years old and 12.5 years old and 20 years old all at the same time. My entire life was squished into one big Proustian blob.

What if Diane was dead right now? What if she had a car wreck on the way to KCC? Or maybe, driving over there, she had a change of heart, the way Anders's mother did. I imagined Mrs. Anderson on a humid afternoon, exiting the dry-cleaning drive-through. For some reason—maybe she was hardly aware of making a decision—she kept on driving, all the way to Nevada, with Mr. Anderson's starched shirts swinging in the backseat window. Anders told me that she said, "I miss you," on the phone, but he never said it back. There is nothing worse than missing people.

I went to Diane's bed and pressed my face into her pillow to smell her sleep smell. The room was dark and cold, so silent I could hear the tick, tick, tick of the cheap clock on her bedside table. It was 6:16. Penn said they would be back at eighteen thirty Romeo time. As I watched the minute hand s-l-o-w-l-y make its way around the circle, I made a decision.

Having a definite goal, with a sharp deadline, cheered me up. Lucky and Hiroshima followed me into my bedroom and stood with their heads cocked, tails wagging uncertainly, as I scooped Diane's journals out from under my bed. They followed me back to the living room, where I dumped the notebooks in a big pile beside Diane's neat stack of books to be sold.

Each book had a different color sticky note announcing its new owner. *Cooking Vegan for Kids* now belonged to Dr. Patricia Gormez, of Spokane, Washington. That was fine with me. In addition to the cookbook, Dr. Patricia was getting a journal handwritten by Diane Montgomery-Thibodeau, the one with the coffee stain on the cover. This notebook contained Diane's list "Times I Have Seen Double," which a doctor might find interesting.

TIMES I HAVE SEEN DOUBLE

1. This morning driving the kids to school. I guess
   I was tired from speed grading last night. The
   logging truck in front of me split into two logging
   trucks. Immediately, my mind tried to make sense
   of it, to put them in separate lanes. Then my mind
   said, nope, you're seeing double, and the two
   images snapped back into one truck in one lane.

2. My last drink, eighteen years ago.

3. Last Saturday at Kroger. A man held a screaming
   girl over the open trunk of a mottled and dented
   Buick while two women watched with tight faces.

After I sealed the Gormez package and placed it in the "finished" pile, it was easier to slide the next journal into an envelope. This is the case with criminal activity. Does a dog feel a measure of guilt the first time he sucks an egg? At any point, does he quiet his conscience by reasoning that his actions, albeit not championed by the popular majority, are for the greater good? I looked at Lucky, who was stretched out on the floor with her paws placed neatly in front of her, watching me intently. Her look said plainly, *No, dogs do not have a shadow side.*

For Miranda Delmar, P.O. Box 921, NY, NY, who wanted a "like new" copy of *Gone with the Wind*, I chose a journal written right after Joe's death.

STUPID THINGS PEOPLE DO WHEN YOUR HUSBAND DIES

1. Suggest it was your fault.

2. Bring an out-of-state ex-wife to the funeral in your
   hometown.

3. Ask if he was saved.

4. Try to engage both a Baptist preacher and a
   Catholic priest to conduct the funeral.

5. Enlist a Sunday school class in bringing the family
   casseroles. Insist that the widow write a detailed
   thank-you note to each contributor. "We'll buy the
   stamps," my mother said. "I know you don't have
   any money."

Stanley Elke, of Huntsville, Alabama, was next on the list. He
had ordered a book in Greek that Diane has been carting around
for twenty years with the intention of teaching herself Greek—
Alabama will surprise you sometimes. Stanley's journal was
recent. It had the list "How to Die," taken from a conversation my
grandparents had one Thursday night at Applebee's.

HOW TO DIE

1. Write an obituary for yourself and one for your
   wife in case you die first, and she doesn't know
   how to do her own.
   ("Your father is writing his memoirs," my
   mother says when we sit down at the table.
   "Ha-ha," he says, clearing his throat as the young
   waiter comes by with our water. "It's not that long.")

2. Write the funeral program.
   ("He was going to have a soloist at the funeral
   sing 'My Old Kentucky Home.' But there is a line
   in there about naked babies on the cabin floor.")

3. Plan the graveside event.
   ("We've paid for the plot and picked out the
   headstones, so you don't have to fool with that.")

4. Teach your children how to die.

(Oh no, they are telling me in those familiar
voices, you hold the broom like this and sweep in
one long motion. No, not like that! You point the
blade away from yourself so you don't cut your
finger off, but when you set the table, you point
the blade toward your own plate so the person
beside you isn't offended. Keep pedaling and you
won't fall over. Get up and get moving—keep your
dauber up! Don't keep your foot on the brake;
don't lay on it—slow down! You support the
baby's head with your hand like this. Don't let
the children play in the attic; they'll fall through
the floor, and you don't know what's up there.
Tell the teacher you have a concern, but don't
make her mad, now. You've got to use a little
psychology sometimes. Don't marry the first man
you meet—you marry the family. Pay every bill on
time. Open every piece of mail; there might be a
check. Don't throw that away; you can use it again.
You need a lot more kindlin' than that for a fire.
Don't leave the dryer on when you go out—you'll
burn the house down. Don't stay up all night. Look
under the bed before you leave the hotel. You have
the visitation and the funeral in one day. Don't drag
it out. They can't sing "My Old Kentucky Home,"
but they can play the instrumental after they've
lowered the coffin into the ground—while everyone
is walking away.)

As I scooped the remaining journals into envelopes, stuffing
loose pages back into the binders, I imagined myself as one of
the book buyers. I would open the manila envelope and think,
Oh, what's this? Someone's diary? I'd touch the frayed edge of

the notebook, flip open the ruffled pages, check the address on the label. Then I would read it.

A part of me wanted to keep the last journal. It contained a list of my dolls and a story about Diane's own doll, Sheba-Lisa. That was a story of Diane's shadow side. It should at least go to a good psychiatrist, but there was no one left on the list except Shalimar O'Doole, of 1020 Benton Avenue, Pittsburgh, PA, 15016. Shalimar sounded more like a palm reader, but of course you never know.

I wasn't even sure if Diane was finished with the story of Sheba-Lisa. What if she went to the attic looking for it?

"We have to be practical," I told Lucky. She cocked her head, then went to the window to check the driveway; dogs were always practical. Still, I hesitated. A creepy feeling started in my stomach and worked its way down to my toes. I was doing something bad, very bad. Had Diane felt like this when she got rid of my mad bomber hat?

The dogs began to bark, *Penn is here! Penn is here!* and I heard wheels on the driveway. Eighteen thirty hours, on the dot. I dropped Shalimar's sealed envelope on the pile of packages to be mailed. It was done.

Tomorrow, all over the United States of America, little pieces of Diane—and me and Max, and Joe and Penn—would appear in people's mailboxes. People would open us up. They would know us. It wouldn't be the fake knowing of Internet dating or the pinched-smile knowing of the country club. This wasn't the good-ole-boy clap on the shoulder or the old-lady finger press. It wouldn't be the knowing of church, where we were all dressed up and arranged in rows like Easter eggs in a carton, or the way we knew one another at the Lab, with our eyes so worn-out from seeing one another all the time that everyone becomes a blur. It wouldn't even be like family knowing, where you make the person up and try to fill them in. No, this would be knowing from the inside out, from stranger to stranger, like meeting characters in a book, but better.

"You're on the ball this morning," Diane said the next day. She was watching me tiredly over the rim of her coffee cup as I loaded the stuffed manila envelopes into the car. I had weighed them on the food scale and stuck the stamps on before breakfast. When we pulled up beside the big blue mailbox on the corner, I rolled my window down and slipped each package into the slot, waiting for the satisfying plop as it hit bottom before I dropped the next one. Diane drummed her fingers on the steering wheel, afraid we'd be late for school again. I was worried sick that she'd look over her shoulder and say, *Those envelopes look a little thick*, but she'd stayed up all night double-checking the papers I had graded and was half-asleep.

"Close the window!" yelled Max. "I'm freezing! There's snow on the ground!"

"That's frost," said Diane. "Where's your jacket?"

Max thought it might be in his locker. He wasn't sure. Southerners can't keep up with their coats; I don't know what we'd do if we actually needed them. Freeze, probably.

The deer grazing in the meadow beside the Lab seemed comfortable in the cold weather, perhaps more frisky than usual, but the ducks had gone into a huddle at the edge of the pond.[16] On the way to the library, I stomped on a frozen mud puddle. The ice broke easily into shards that floated around my shoes: "God Is. God Isn't." The "n't" was wearing off my right foot; soon both shoes would say, "God Is." *How do you feel about that?* Dr. Dhang might ask me. *I dunno, I dunno, I dunno.*

"Aris, let's wipe our feet before entering the classroom, shall we?" suggested Mrs. Waller as I walked into English.

"Yes, ma'am," I said, and went back outside to wipe my feet on the mat.

"Shall we?" whispered Anders as I slid into the empty desk beside him, which was, unfortunately, the only available desk near Kate.

"There is no future tense in the English language," said Kate. "That's why she says 'shall,' which—"

"Kate," said Mrs. Waller. "Are you talking?"

"Yes, ma'am," said Kate. "I mean, no, ma'am." She blushed. "I've stopped talking now."

I opened the book on my desk to use as a cover for my phone while I checked my email. No word yet from Ms. Chu on my manuscript. It had already been more than three days! I hoped she wasn't sick or dead. What if she hated it and didn't know how to tell me?

Mrs. Waller announced that she would be returning our papers, but first she wanted to go over a few points. While she rambled on about critical thinking, "the intelligently self-controlled process of actively and skillfully conceptualizing, applying, analyzing, synthesizing, and/or evaluating information," I thought about Diane's journals. Had the postman picked them up yet? Were they sorted and separated now—one manila envelope headed to New York, another to Alabama? I wished I had kept the one with the doll story.

---

16   You're probably wondering what happened to the swan mentioned in the Lab catalog. He committed suicide when his mate was killed by a snake.

MY DAUGHTER'S DOLLS

Stud Ken, in bathing suit, Puerto Rican

Barbies, two containers, all women of color

Kaya, a Nez Perce Native American

Josefina from New Mexico

Addy, an escaped slave from Philadelphia, circa 1864

Her Royal Highness Gunnhild, Norwegian ("I know you like dark-skinned dolls better," Aris said, "but I've never had a white one.")

DOLLS NOT ON DISPLAY

Sheba, the fifteen-inch vinyl doll of color, circa 1973. This is Sheba's story:

Like the homes of many childless couples, the small brick house where my uncle and aunt lived in rural Kentucky held within it a certain stillness. In the narrow living room where they put the three-foot-tall artificial Christmas tree, decorated with matching gold and silver ornaments, nothing had changed since our last visit. The couch and chairs, covered in coordinating ruffled brown and yellow prints, remained in their places against the walls. On the mantelpiece over the gas fireplace, the blond, blue-eyed shepherd stared adoringly at the blond, blue-eyed shepherdess. Even the rabbit ears, which sat on a doily crocheted by Aunt Peggy to protect the wood-grain surface of the television set, remained pointed at the same angles.

"Well, I'll be damned," said Uncle Earl, pulling his pipe away from my cheek as he leaned over to look inside the box I had unwrapped. "It's a little nigger." Then he laughed the big laugh that made his belly shake against the tight buttons of his shirt. Even though I loved his smoky smell and the rumble of his voice, blood rushed to my face as if I had been slapped.

"I didn't know if you'd like a Negro doll or not," said Aunt Peggy, peering at me through her glittering glasses, "but I saw her on the shelf and thought she was just the cutest thing."

"What do you say?" my mother said.

I sat paralyzed.

"That's okay," said Aunt Peggy, leaning into her chair without pressing her hair against the backrest. She owned the beauty salon she had worked at since before she married Uncle Earl at fifteen, and even though she could get her hair done for free, she never messed it up.

"She's just looking at it," said my father, smiling to everyone.

"I can take it back and get something else," said Aunt Peggy.

"Oh no," my parents protested, as they fingered the fringe of my doll's brightly striped poncho, examining her red bell-bottoms, the chaste white panties underneath, her platform sandals. "Don't take it back! What do you say, Diane?"

"Thank you," I mumbled. To show everyone my appreciation, I picked up the wide-toothed comb that came with Sheba—that was the name on the box—and began to comb her kinky black Afro. Silently, I changed her name to Lisa.

I don't know when I began to beat Sheba-Lisa. It started as spankings, administered in measured whacks on the bottom as a correction for some misdemeanor: She didn't come to her shoebox bed when I called her, or she

spilled her tea. At first I put her with the other dolls—
gentle Beth, a thin rag doll with giant, uneven stitches
across her neck; Penelope, an uptight vinyl girl who
tended to overdress; and beautiful Heather, who looked
like Goldilocks until you unglued her bonnet and realized
that the back of her head was bald.

These were friendly girls, always smiling and ready to
give a hug, but they didn't like Sheba-Lisa. They stopped
talking when she came over, and they never shared their
toys or clothes with her. Penelope stole her poncho, leaving her bare chested, and Beth refused to use her comb. She
said it was dirty. No matter how many baths I gave Sheba-
Lisa, everyone said she was dirty. Sheba-Lisa just stood
there with that Mona Lisa smile on her face. I spanked
them all that day, with their pants down, but I put Sheba-
Lisa in the back of the closet and never took her out again.

I felt so bad about Sheba-Lisa that sometimes at night
I cried thinking of her alone in the dark closet, hated by
everyone. Finally, I just wanted her to go. I hated having
her there in the back of my closet, reminding me of my
meanness. I couldn't give her away; none of my friends
wanted a black doll, and I didn't want them to know that I
had one. I couldn't throw her in the trash can—I knew that
dolls weren't real, everyone knew that, but still.

Then one day, Lashondra Johnston's house burned
down. Lashondra sat in the back of our third-grade classroom, so far back that it was like she wasn't there at all.
Sometimes, she didn't wear shoes or a coat or have a permission slip, and then she would have to walk up to the
front of the room.

"Where are your shoes?" Mrs. Blankenship would
demand.

Lashondra would stare down at her dusty feet as if
she had not, until this moment, realized that she lacked

shoes. Then she would look quickly around the room, covering her mouth.

Everything Lashondra's family owned burned up in the fire. Mrs. Blankenship made us understand this—everything. Not a sock, not a pair of underwear, not a toy was left. We were each supposed to bring an item to give Lashondra. It didn't have to be brand-new, but it should be something nice.

When Lashondra returned to class, I expected her to look fire damaged, to have singed eyelashes or at least a smoky odor, but she was exactly the same. She wore the same thing she always wore, a cast-off ruffled pink Easter dress over a red turtleneck, and boys' tennis shoes without socks. Her hair was uncombed, as usual. When Mrs. Blankenship called her to the front of the room, Lashondra swayed from side to side, the way children do in a choir. She kept her head down.

No one was snickering yet, but you could tell it was about to start as soon as the first child, Missy Carlton, handed Lashondra a brown paper grocery bag of clothing. Lashondra was presented with lace-trimmed socks, still packaged in cellophane, shirts, pants, and shoes—bags of shoes, some of them hardly worn. There must have been twenty pairs of shoes piled around Lashondra as she swayed before us with dazed eyes.

When a faint snicker sounded from the far back corner of the room, she glanced quickly over there, ready to cover her mouth. Then my name was called, and I walked up with Sheba-Lisa.

"Aristotle Thibodeau!" called Mrs. Waller.

"Ma'am?" I responded automatically, but when I looked up, I almost felt dizzy. I had been far away in the Kanuga public school system with Diane thirty-four years ago—Diane torturing herself, then and now. Other than Diane (and possibly myself), who would even remember a doll named Sheba-Lisa? Then I realized what I had done. I had packed one of Diane's ugliest, guiltiest moments into an envelope and mailed it to a stranger.

"Are you with us today, Aris?"

"Yes, ma'am." I smiled hopefully as she handed me my paper. She folds the papers vertically so that neighbors, like Anders, can't see your grade. I elbowed him sharply as he tried to look.

"She'll ask you to read yours," said Kate. "She always likes yours."

"Nope, not this time," I said. I was getting good at offhand remarks that masked deep pain—a sure sign of puberty. There was a big red "I" written across the top of my descriptive writing assignment. "I" stands for "incomplete." It means F, but we don't get Fs at the Lab—we might get discouraged and blow up the faculty restroom or something.

I thought she'd like it. I had envisioned ole Waller's mouth dropping open as she turned the pages. I'd be asked to read some of it at assembly. Maybe an agent or a publisher, or someone who *knew* an agent or a publisher, would be at the assembly, and I'd get a call. "Are you Aristotle Thibodeau, the author?" the agent or publisher would ask while Diane and Max and Penn were at the kitchen table, watching me. Oh, those dear faces! Those ragged destinies!

"Yes," I would say calmly into the phone. "Yes, I am she."

Wrong, X, Incorrect-as-usual, Aris. Mrs. Waller said that I didn't follow the assigned topic, which was "Describe a person, place, or thing."

"This is definitely a Wally Attack," whispered Kate as she read the red-inked comments on my paper.

"I might be an actress instead of a writer," I said. "No one reads novels."

"What's wrong with it?" asked Anders.

"I don't know yet," said Kate. She chewed on the ends of her hair as she read, then took them out of her mouth and examined them for split ends. "It needs either more detail or less."

"That's helpful."

Suddenly, Anders snatched the paper away from us. Holding it out of my reach, he read aloud:

"'. . . as their Gimme Lean soy dogs slid across each other in this restless, sensuous wrestling.'"

Heads turned. Keller Williams was the first to laugh, a great, hoarse guffaw, immediately joined by Bowers Loudermilk and Frank Harris. I won't stereotype these young men by calling them jocks. They were unique in God's eyes, I'm sure.

"Gimme Lean," shouted Frank.

"Gimme restless!" responded Bowers.

Keller, who was not as articulate as his friends, stood in his desk and shouted: "Sex!"

"Boys!" said Mrs. Waller. "That's quite enough. Everyone, please sit down."

However, Mrs. Waller was too late. Samantha "I'm so rich" Livingston had bestowed her blue-eyed attention on the boys. Samantha has her maid deliver a hot lunch from Arby's to school every day. She carries Prada bags and flies to Palm Beach every twelve weeks to have her highlights done by a man who was once jetted to the White House for a hair emergency. I have seen Samantha throw a bag of change, including quarters, straight into the trash can. When she moves, the boys hold their breath. She's not really even pretty, but she forces you to think she is. Some women are born with that power.

"Really, Aris?" said Samantha. She surrounded herself in a force field of breathtaking beauty, and the room went wild.

I don't know what would have happened—probably a spontaneous combustion that left us all in ashes—if Coach Bobby hadn't opened the door. In two strides, he was in the midst of the fray.

"SHUT UP AND SIT DOWN!" his voice boomed.

Instantly, the room went silent. My heart hammered in my

chest. I am not used to the sound of a man shouting. I swear, the windows rattled. Lisette Fishbourne, a girl with thin hair and a nervous disorder, began crying softly into her sleeve.

"I'm sorry," Coach Bobby said hoarsely, walking over and awkwardly trying to pat her back. "I wasn't talking to *you*." He glared at the football team, who sat with their shoulders hunched, red-faced and abashed. "What's going on here?"

Everyone looked at the corner where the trouble had started—at Aris, Kate, and Anders, the three single-parent kids—products of death, divorce, and abandonment.

"Anders," said Coach Bobby. "Can you explain this uproar?"

"Well, sir," said Anders, squeaking on the "sir." He shifted uncomfortably in his seat, looked at his feet, at the door, at the ceiling, and finally back at Coach Bobby, man to man. "What happened is . . . um . . . Aris wrote a really good essay."

SAY WHAT?

Did that just HAPPEN? Anders stood up for me—whatever—and my essay rocks! YES. YES! OH, HELL YES!!!!!! Clichés can't begin to describe how I felt at that moment. I had to excuse myself, dash into the girls' room, and lock the stall door. "God Is, God Isn't, God Is, God Isn't," up and down my feet tapped out a happy dance.

By lunchtime, the sun was out, and any Lab student who had remembered a jacket that morning had discarded it. Several were tossed over the bushes that lined the stone path to the dining hall. Anders walked beside me, trying to step on the shoe that proclaimed "God Isn't." I allowed this because he was a fan. Also, his hair was growing out of the hedgehog cut. I'm not saying he was cute, just saying.

"It's been proven that Christians live longer than non-Christians," he said. "That's because they're happier."

"Don't start."

"I don't even need to say that Jesus Christ is your savior, because you know that. Even if you deny it, you know it in your heart."

My foot slipped on the path, accidentally kicking him in the shin.

"Go away, Anders."

"Why?" he asked, limping to catch up with me. "Why should I go away?"

"Because." I spun around to face him, spitting mad. "My heart is none of your dang business." We were right beside the fishpond, and I almost pushed him in. "Why don't you try this? Replace the words 'Jesus Christ' with 'My Ego.' Go ahead, say it. 'I want to share My Ego with you. I follow My Ego. I believe in My Ego. My Ego is my savior.'" I stared him down and then stomped away.

"Someone is hormonal," he muttered as he followed me, dog-like, into the dining hall. He flopped into the chair beside mine. With a dejected frown, he unpacked the lunch his dad had made for him. Once, Mr. Anderson had mistaken a can of Coors Light for a can of ginger ale. "My dad sort of has his eyes closed in the morning," Anders had mumbled as the entire table laughed. Today he had two Snickers bars and a can of SpaghettiOs—the kind you have to open with a can opener. And no can opener.

While he watched, I unfolded the cloth napkin Diane packs for me and put it in my lap. Then I spread my lunch out, rather invitingly, so that we could negotiate a trade for one of those Snickers bars. He read the sticky note Diane had attached to my plastic bag of carrot sticks: "I am so proud of you. You are majestic, mademoiselle!"

"What's she proud of you for?"

I shrugged. "She just says that." At the sight of her handwriting, a wave of guilt passed through me. Had I really mailed her journals out to strangers that morning? Why had that seemed like a good idea?

"Half a peanut butter and cucumber on whole wheat for a Snickers?" I offered.

He picked up my sandwich and examined it. "Why do you look so guilty?"

"I don't look guilty. It's just a dumb candy bar."

"No, I mean it. It's all over your face. What did you do?"

I looked him straight in the eye. He looked back. I didn't blink. He didn't blink. I didn't blink. He didn't blink. We stayed that way until the bell rang.

As I was leaving the dining hall, Ms. Chu waved and slipped into step beside me.

She smiled, looking at me as if I had a new haircut or something. Softly, she said, "I like your novel."

"Really?"

"Yes, really."

All of a sudden, it was a beautiful afternoon at the Lavender Mountain Laboratory School. In the fishpond, goldfish shimmered under a slant of winter sun. Afternoon shadows cut across the straight pines in the woods behind the chapel. A few deer were grazing on the chapel lawn, watching us with their sweet dark eyes as we walked along the path.

"It's brilliant," Ms. Chu whispered.

I savored that moment—with the goldfish glittering, the deer gazing, Ms. Chu's skirt rustling as she walked beside me on the curving path of polished stones. *Brilliant.*

"It's not too small?" I asked her. "Too ordinary? The Orchard? Chutiksee County? Kanuga, Georgia?"

"Small is good," she said. She told me about William Faulkner's little postage stamp of native soil in northern Mississippi, how he said he would never live long enough to write about it all.

"I thank you kindly," I said; it's a phrase from the hills of Kentucky that Grandma uses only on special occasions.

"Now," Ms. Chu said, "I have a question for you."

"Yes?" I was watching a doe out of the corner of my eye, having faith that she wouldn't run away. I was at one with nature, God, and man.

"When is your protagonist going to face a situation she can't handle, the outcome of which will change her life?"

"Well . . . ," I said, smiling bravely. I had just died.

My body was there, of course, but it was the glove without the hand. She was criticizing my novel! She hated it! She was trying to be nice, but she hated it. I hated it too. I hated myself for writing it. There was nothing to do but defend it.

"I thought I might make it a literary novel," I said. "Slice of life, you know?"

She didn't say anything. The glow of the afternoon had faded away, and the doe was gone. The air had the greasy, sour-milk smell of Lab lunch. The lovely Ms. Chu took on a hard look, braces glinting.

She whispered, "Something terrible must happen."

All afternoon, I expected the police to knock on the door. I know, I know—why would the police care if someone mailed out her mother's journals? This is what guilt does to your mind. When Penn knocked twice on the door and came whistling into the hallway, I felt my heart hit the inside of my chest. Clearly, I was going insane.

"Don't you dare bark at me," Penn told Hiroshima, who was dancing in a circle, yapping her head off. "What are you barking at me for?" Bending down so she could jump into his arms, he said tenderly, "I would never bark at you."

"It's taco night tonight," Diane said as she whizzed by to get her traveling coffee cup. Evening classes require a caffeine jolt, but she was already pretty wired. She is always happier when Penn comes over. "I found a soft-taco kit with whole wheat tortillas," she said proudly. "Can you believe it?"

"Didn't we just have taco night?" asked Max. "How about a

roast beef? Normal families have roast beef with mashed potatoes and gravy."

"The soy crumbles taste just like ground beef," she replied, tousling his hair. She sped past us, scooping up a pile of jackets without breaking her stride, and disappeared into the bathroom.

When she was gone, Penn explained to Max that soy crumbles come from Japanese soy cows, which are just like our beef cows but are green.

"Green cows?"

"It's weird, but you get used to it."

"You're fortunate I'm looking out for your cholesterol," Diane said as she trotted back into the room, looking for her keys.

"Y'all are so fortunate," said Penn, when she was out of ear-shot again. "Y'all are *blessed*."

At the door, Diane bent her knees and hiked the heavy brief-case farther up on her shoulder while holding her coffee cup with a straight arm so it wouldn't spill. Her high heels swung from their straps on her wrist because she can't drive in them. Penn jumped up to get the door for her, and I made a mental note to put a belt on her the next time she wore that baggy dress.

At least she had remembered to walk through a spritz of Amazing Grace. In case you wondered, perfume is layered with head notes, heart notes, and base notes. We were at the head of Amazing Grace now, a lemony "hello." The scent lingered faintly in the air after she was gone, and it made me sad as I listened to her car backing out of the driveway.

"I don't have any homework," said Max. "I'm practicing my talent."

"You're not doing anything," I said.

"I'm emptying my mind. If you get rid of every thought in your brain, you will rise three inches off the ground. I saw a YouTube of it."

"You haven't moved."

"When you doubt me, I get stuck."

"Have you considered time travel?" asked Penn.

"Yeah, I do that all the time, but no one can see it."

"You'll need something called a wormhole. It's a shortcut connecting two different points in space-time. Albert Einstein and his buddy Rosen came up with it."

"I know where one is in the yard," said Max. "I *think* I can find it."

"Let's study your spelling first," said Penn as he stirred soy crumbles in the skillet. "Spell 'excitement' for me."

"E-c-x," Max began.

"E-x-c."

"That's what I said. I promise! You didn't hear me."

"Try again. It's a weird one. Aris, what are you studying?"

"American presidents," I lied.

"Have you gotten to Eugene Debs?"

"Not yet," I said. I tried to distract him by ripping open a bag of organic blue corn chips and then crunching loudly, but Penn wasn't as easy to divert as Diane. I've noticed that about men in general; they don't have as many things on their minds.

"Well, you probably won't get to him," he said, watching me closely.

"That's not a president," said Max, whose odd little brain had memorized all the American presidents when he was seven.

"Eugene Debs was the Socialist Party candidate for president in 1900, 1904, 1908, 1912, and 1920," said Penn. He flipped a tortilla in the skillet with one hand. "You should know that he ran his final campaign from prison. He was arrested on charges of sedition. Sedition is the 'crime' of speaking out against the established order. You probably thought we had a constitutional right to free speech in this country. Well, think again, Lab rats. Eugene Debs was antiestablishment, and for that reason, you won't see much of him in your textbooks."

"He's like the silent 'e' in excitement," said Max, and then he knocked over the salsa with his elbow and called Lucky over to lick it up off the floor.

After dinner, Penn did the dishes while Max and I built a fire in the fireplace. Max brought out his cards, and we all played Liar. We had to explain the game to Penn: After you pass out all the cards, the youngest player places a card in the middle, faceup. You take turns laying down the next card in the sequence, facedown. You can cheat, but if someone guesses that you're cheating, they can say, "Liar." You show your card. If your accuser is right, you have to take the whole pile of cards. If your accuser is wrong, he takes the whole pile. If you cheat and don't get caught, you say, "Peanut butter."

"I'm not saying 'peanut butter,'" said Penn. "I'm saying 'bullshit.'"

Penn is allowed to cuss because he was in the navy. Diane says taking the cuss out of a sailor is like taking the shine out of the sun. He has a terrible, terrible tattoo that he got one night when he was drunk with some other sailors, but he won't let anyone see it, not even Diane. In the summer, when he takes us to the river to jump off rocks, he blackens it with a permanent marker. I'm always trying to imagine it.

"Just give me a hint," I said once.

"It would fit right in with your *Garden of Earthly Delights* poster," he said.

If you've done something really bad, like mailing your mother's journals out to the whole country, I don't recommend playing Liar afterward. Each time I added my card to the pile in the center of our circle, I felt Diane's glance, even though she wasn't there. How long would it take her to find out what I had done?

On his next turn, Max slapped his cards down and let his face freeze.

"Max," I said, "try to act bored when you're lying."

"I was!"

"Liar." I slid my cards over to his pile. "Your turn, Penn," I said languidly, but inside, my guts were churning. I was picturing Stanley Elke getting his journal in the mail. Maybe he was a fat little man with a big nose who surrounded himself with Labradoodles. He'd lean back on his couch, pat a Labradoodle, and open the manila envelope. *What is this? Someone's diary?* He'd check the return address, then open it up.

THINGS I HIDE

1. Tampons.

2. The fact that I failed fourth-grade math and can't calculate a fifteen percent tip in my head.

3. Chocolate.

4. Attraction to a man who may not be attracted to me.

It was Max's turn. He raised his hand. He does that sometimes, forgetting he's not at school. "Yes, dear?" I said.
"Do I say 'peanut butter' if I lied and you didn't catch me?"
"Yes, honey."
"Peanut butter!"

TIMES I'VE CONSIDERED SUICIDE

1. Age 13.

2. College. I used to wake up on the floor with an empty bottle of Four Roses bourbon and a knife, slowly remembering that I planned to cut off the pinkie of my left hand as a reminder never to drink again.

3. After Joe died. Kill the kids and then myself.

A car turned into the driveway. It was too early for Diane to be home, but the dogs were doing their *Merm is back* bark, and they never lie.

"Sounds like your mama is here," said Penn, reaching into his back pocket for the pouch of Bugler. "I'm going to step outside for a minute."

Through the window, I watched her get out of the car, staggering under the weight of her briefcase, her purse, and the cooler that carried her Lean Cuisine, fresh fruit, and Diet Cokes. My heart was going thumpety-thump, thump-thump-thump! As Penn stepped toward her with his arm outstretched, ready to take a load off her shoulders, she shook her head.

"She's crying!" shouted Max, looking out the window with a stricken face. He rushed to the door, but I stayed where I was, staring into the fire. I imagined her cocking her head as she answered an unknown caller on her cellphone. *Yes, this is Diane Montgomery-Thibodeau. You received* what *in your Amazon.com package? My* diary?

"Move out of the way so Mama can get through the door," Diane was saying. "It's okay, Max. Hush, now. Let me get in the house." Penn came in behind her, ready for action but silent in case it was a personal problem.

"Hi, honey," she said, glancing at me with red, swollen eyes, but she didn't break her stride as she walked through the house putting everything away: cooler in the kitchen (trash in the can and dirty fork in the dishwasher), briefcase on the shelf beside her desk in the bedroom, purse on the coffee table where she could easily reach her cellphone and nicotine gum. When the shit hits the fan in our house, we clean up.

"Hi!" I said too brightly. "You're home!"

My heart had basically stopped. We were at the base note of Amazing Grace now, and I didn't like it. It smelled too personal. Her heels went click, clack, click, clack. *Take everything out of the car as soon as you get out*—that was her rule. *Put everything away immediately*. Click. Clack. *Everything has a home*. Click, clack—like pages rolling off Grandma's old typewriter.

"Okay, everybody," said Diane as she started to clear our junk off the kitchen table. "Here's the deal. I lost my job."

. . .

I've never had a real job, other than writing, but I know what it feels like to lose one. It's like the Turkish Twist at the Chutiksee County Fair, a rotor ride that spins you so fast you're still stuck to the wall when the floor drops out beneath you. You keep asking yourself, *Why did I take this ride?*

Watching the family drama in the living room when Diane got canned was more than I could handle, so I went to my room and rolled under the bed. Bad choice. It was EMPTY under there without Diane's journals. A few loose papers that had fallen out of the notebooks reminded me of the sin I had committed. I could hear every word in the living room.

"You got fired!" yelled Max. "We're poor now, aren't we?"

"We can sit down and talk about it in a minute, but I can't think straight with all this clutter," said Diane. She was picking up our cards from Liar, muttering that you can't play *anything* if you're missing even *one* card. Losing one card makes the entire deck useless.

"I'm going to kill KCC," Max sputtered. "Kill that stupid boss for firing you."

"Bang!" went the gun app. "Bang-bang-bang!" I heard the front door open and then Penn's voice.

"Give me that, Max." The shooting stopped. "Diane, sit down for a minute. I'll make you a cup of tea."

"No, I'm fine. Where's my gum?"

"I'm sorry, Mom," said Max. "I'm really sorry. Let's make a treaty."

It got quiet. I could hear the fatwood crackling in the fire. Diane had probably pulled Max into her lap. Maybe she was stroking his hair, and he was nuzzling her neck in that one silky spot that smells like home.

"It's not as bad as it sounds," she said. "They didn't actually fire me. Apparently, the dean's brother-in-law works in the police department. I can't remember his title."

"Asshole, probably," said Penn. "Sorry for interrupting. Go on."

"I don't think he's the one who arrested Charles, but I'm not sure. Anyway, he found out that I was helping Charles write his defense statement."

"The crime of sedition," said Penn. "I knew it."

"They told me I could finish out the semester. I told them good luck finding someone to teach my class tomorrow."

"You quit?" demanded Max. "You're a quitter? You wouldn't even let me quit swimming."

"She resigned," said Penn. "On moral grounds. She was transformed through Christ at Kanuga Christian College, just like the sign says."

"Where's Aris?" asked Diane.

"Probably hiding under her bed," said Max. "Do you want me to get her?"

"No, leave her alone."

I came out from under my bed and flopped on top of the mattress, where I could get more air. I could have used my mad bomber hat; I always think better in my hat. I checked my social media sites, but that was depressing because everyone was flirting. Consumed by guilt, I had forgotten it was almost Valentine's Day. Billy's "cousin," who was popping up in more pictures lately, posted a dumb "Does He Like Me or Like-Like Me?" quiz. Kate was sharing fun facts about the execution of a Christian saint named Valentine. In his latest mug shot, Anders wore a Snoopy T-shirt with a heart on it. Someone replied, "Dude, settle. R u in love or what?"

There was no love for me on the Internet, but lurking made the time pass. An hour after Diane got home, I heard her putting Max to bed. "Sometimes things don't work out the way we plan," she was saying. "You go to sleep now. Let the adults take care of this."

Adults? My ears perked up. Was Penn still in the house?

Then in the living room I heard Penn's voice, gently telling Hiroshima that she could not sit in his lap. "I don't even *like* you," he said. The tags on her collar clinked as she settled across his knees. His big hand would be scratching that warm, silky patch of fur behind her ears, and then moving to what he called the sweet spot, a place on her back just above the tailbone.

He was STAYING!

I listened to Diane's footsteps. Would she sit on the other couch, the way she usually did, or beside him? I considered moving into the hall, where I could get a full download of the conversation, but decided against it. The chance of being discovered was too great— I wasn't going to blow this.

Penn's voice was deep when he asked Diane if she was okay, but her reply was so soft that I couldn't hear it. Silently, I opened my door and leaned against the frame with my ears switched to full antennae mode.

Diane was telling Penn about Charles. "I mean, can you believe it? He wasn't doing anything illegal."

"He got a DWB," Penn said. "Driving while black."

I imagined him tapping the rolled cigarette behind his ear as if to remind himself that it was there.

"We don't put up with that shit in Chutiksee County," he continued. "If you're going to drive in Where Its Legs Were Broken Off, you better have the decency to be white. Where'd he get the BMW?"

"His mother worked three jobs to save money for his college tuition. When he won a full scholarship, she wanted him to use his savings to buy something nice for himself. He's the first person in the family to go to college."

"Is there a father in the picture?"

"Oh God," said Diane. I imagined her putting her face in her hands. Was she crying? Would Penn *touch* her? I couldn't stop myself! I tiptoed down the hall and looked around the doorframe into the darkened living room before ducking my head back again.

"Hi, Aris," said Penn.

They both sat up straight at the sight of me. I couldn't tell if her hand had been on his knee.

"Aris," said Diane. "I thought you had gone to bed."

"Just passing through," I said, and was forced to go into the kitchen. I opened the freezer and found half a bar of dark chocolate stashed behind the frozen peas. Eighty percent cacao beans. Diane says that chocolate gives you the feeling of being in love, and we go for the strong stuff. "Chocolate, anyone?" I offered as I passed back by the couch.

"No, thanks," said Diane.

"I'm going out back for a smoke," said Penn. He looked at Diane. "You coming?"

I went straight down the hall to Max's room, where I could hear their conversation on the porch through the window. Max was fast asleep with his Spider-Man blanket pulled up to his nose, the platypus clenched in one fist. After adjusting his covers, I cracked the window that looks out over the porch.

At first, I couldn't see them. The lighter flicked once, twice. Diane—no smoking! I smelled the first faint whiff of tobacco smoke. Male voice. Female voice. Male. Female. Female. Silence.

"I think I've met Charles," said Penn. "If he's the guy I'm thinking about, he was over here one Sunday with some of your other students. Back when you were allowed to have those orgies with your students. Guy with a power tie and fedora? Nice looking?"

"That's him," said Diane. I tried to envision Charles, in his ironed clothes and red power tie, sitting on a cot in a jail cell with his head down, holding his hat in his long fingers. "He's a sharp dresser. He grew up poor, wearing hand-me-downs, and he's proud of his appearances. Growing up with a father in prison forced him to earn his own respect. He wants people to look at him and see—a man of honor."

"A murder in the family will definitely ding your reputation," said Penn. When Diane didn't say anything, he said, "I'm sorry. That didn't sound right. I'm not trying to make light of this. It is really terrible. Terrible for Charles and his mom, and for you." He sighed. "What can I do for you? I'll do anything I can. Just ask me."

Then Diane said, "Hold me."

No, Diane! Too soon. Not yet.

Silence. More silence.

You scared him.

Shuffle of feet on the boards of the porch. Rustle of jacket.

Was I breathing? I had to hold my palm in front of my nose to make sure air was coming out.

Silence. Muffle. More silence. Then . . . definitely . . . the sound of a kiss.

CLIMAX

> *Scraps of memory: this is not how a climax should be written. A climax should surge towards its Himalayan peak; but I am left with shreds, and must jerk towards my crisis like a puppet with broken strings. This is not what I had planned; but perhaps the story you finish is never the one you begin.*
>
> —Salman Rushdie

I have no idea where to put this section of the novel. Failed climaxes aren't even discussed in *Write a Novel in Thirty Days!* I mean, how awkward does that sound to your reader? *I'm sorry, but we failed to climax. Let's try again.* People say you can hide things in a novel, unlike a short story, where the reader is on top of every word. Maybe it's because I grew up in a small house, but I'm not good at hiding things. Here is where my story falls apart, smack-dab in the middle.

Penn and Diane were still on the back porch the night she was fired from KCC, still kissing, and I was still eavesdropping from Max's bedroom. I had folded my arms on the windowsill and was resting my head on them, but the cold air from the crack in the window kept me awake. If Dr. Dhang had been in the room, asking me how I felt, I would have said, *Deeply relaxed.*

You have a sense of security, she might have suggested. *A feeling everything is going to be okay. Perhaps that you don't need to be in charge anymore?*

Actually, no, Dr. Dhang. My services are still needed. I'm not a pervert or anything, and I know that Diane is perfectly capable of kissing a man by herself. However, there were extenuating circumstances.

1. Diane was now, abruptly, unemployed.

2. She was putting her tongue in the mouth of my PMI, who did not touch other human beings.

3. What about Joe?

I hadn't talked to Joe in a while—or communed, or whatever— but I knew from Diane's previous forays into romance that he could be trouble. I didn't blame him; Kate says that her parents hate each other, but they still get jealous when the other one is dating. Joe loves Diane. "The sound of your footsteps in the house makes my heart all wobbly," he told her once. "Even when you're wearing those obnoxious cowboy boots."

Sure enough, while I was staring into the darkness of the back porch, the lightning bug of Ghost Daddy appeared. "Hi, Dad," I whispered. "I guess you know about the journals."

He had no comment on this. The flicker stretched into a long green streak, and then a red one, and then a swirl of colors, dancing before my eyes and making me dizzy. I wondered if I was bipolar. "Great writing is ordered madness," Diane had written in one notebook.

Silence settled on the back porch—a bad silence. There should have been some other noise, a husky laugh, the sound of unzipping, a murmured "Let's go inside."

Then Penn spoke. "I'm sorry, Diane. I can't do this. I want to—I really do. But I can't."

"Okay," said Diane. "Goodbye."

Was she crying? Should I go out there?

"Wait a minute," he said. "Will you just wait one minute?"

"I don't want to have a conversation about this," said Diane. "This never should have happened."

"Let me explain, okay?"

Silence.

"So," said Diane. "Explain." Huffy, huffy, huffy! I didn't blame her, though.

"I don't know how to say this," he said, "but I'm going to try. I am not good at relationships. I was married for seven years. You have to be an adult to be in a relationship. I'm not an adult, Diane, but at least I know that now. It's taken me this long just to *recognize* the problem."

"Have you thought about having sex with me?" asked Diane. "Just sex?"

Penn laughed. "Yes, I have. Many times. Have you?"

"Maybe."

"I couldn't do that to you," said Penn.

"I'm not looking for a husband," said Diane. Liar, liar, pants on fire.

"We couldn't do that to the kids. If it didn't work out—"

"You're right. They need you. PMIs are hard to come by."

"You know I was married, right? To Ri-Ri?"

"Who is Ri-Ri?"

"My ex-wife, Chihuro. I've told you about her. When we moved to the States, Chihuro wanted an American name. She chose the name Lily, but her accent made her 'l's sound like 'r's. So 'Lily' came out as 'Ri-Ri.' She hated being called Ri-Ri."

"So why did you call her that?"

"Because she would not ask me to stop. She would not ask for anything, just hint. If she had asked me to stop, I would have. If she had asked me for a car, I would have bought her one."

"Did you buy her a car?"

"I bought her a couple of cars. I was making good money. She kept most of it, though. 'I don't need Japanese salaryman,' she would say, and then hold her hand out for the paycheck. I was mainstream back then, chasing the dream: car, wife, house, kids. Then I woke up."

"Was she pretty?" asked Diane.

"Yeah," said Penn. "She was *fine*, very fine."

Poor Diane. He could have just said she was attractive.

He lit another cigarette in the following silence.

"She didn't drink?" asked Diane, finally.

"Not like I did. It was fun at first—you know, that warm, fuzzy feeling—and then having the balls to fight the biggest man in the bar. Not really caring when he stomped you into the warm, fuzzy ground." I heard him walk to the edge of the porch. He was probably leaning against the rail. "I stopped paying the bills. I had a couple of booty calls. Then one day Penn-san was having a seizure at the kitchen table—delirium tremens."

"Oh."

"Yep."

"She called you Penn-san? Isn't that like calling you 'mister'?"

"It was 'Penn-sama' at first. Master. Then 'Penn-san.' Mister. We scaled that down to plain 'Penn.' Somehow, 'Penn' morphed into 'Asshole.' Finally, there was no Penn at all. Suddenly, the woman who had never been able to ask for anything, not even a glass of water at a restaurant—*a glass of water is so nice*—demands a divorce. Okay, she doesn't demand. She *asks*. Plainly."

"You said yes?"

"I didn't try to talk her out of it. If I had . . . who knows?"

"Most people try a separation first," said Diane.

"Like I said, I was not an adult. Around this time, my dad got sick, and I came back to Kanuga to help my mom out. Then my grandmother fell and broke her hip, and the economy crashed . . . One day of mowing the lawn turned into another day of mowing the lawn; sometimes I get a booty call. The rest of the time, I try

to live in the present moment, zigzagging the three poisons: igno-
rance, aversion, and attachment. You can get knee-deep in that
shit—the Buddhists call it *samsara*, which means 'the indefinitely
repeated cycles of birth, misery, and death.'"

When they launched into a long conversation about karma, I
started to yawn. A normal woman would be crying or breaking
something, but Diane and I can squeeze our feelings down into
tight spaces when pride is at stake. From the sound of her teacher
voice, you'd think she had stepped out on the porch that evening
to attend a lecture on the wheel of life. I left those clowns to themselves and went to bed.

On the Tuesday after Valentine's Day, a rumor was going around the Lab that Billy had dumped me because he forgot to send me a gewgaw.

Anders Anderson was all over it. "Long-distance relationships never work," he said, offering me a sticky bag of Cheetos.

"Commercialized love," I said. "Really, Anders?"

In the girl's bathroom, I texted Kate an SOS.

OMG is it over?

She told me to ask Billy himself if it was over. I knew she would say that, but I was hoping she would come up with something better. All the same, when I went home that afternoon, I doused myself with Diane's Amazing Grace and psyched myself up to text Billy Starr III. "Always wear good perfume," Diane told me, "even if you can't afford it. Cheap perfume destroys a woman's character faster than one-night stands and bad credit." I looked in the mirror, fixed my hair, and then went outside and did a few flips on the trampoline to knock some endorphins into play. I didn't want him to think I was *sad*. Finally, I was ready to send the message.

Did u break up with me? #:-)[17]

I had counted to 3,025 Mississippi when Diane called me into her room to check her outfit.

"Job interview?" I asked.

"I have a date," she said. "So what do you think?" She held her arms akimbo and turned slowly in front of me: black skinny jeans and a road-sign-yellow sweater with red heels.

"Make it stop," I said, covering my eyes.

"Is it that bad?"

"Yes, Diane. It is that bad." I flopped onto her bed. "You have a date? Do we have a new Mr. Friend on the horizon?"

"Not a date-date. I'm just meeting someone for a latte." She pulled a dress and a pair of black boots out of the closet. "Did you get any valentines at school today? Hear from Billy?"

"Romantic love is overrated," I said. I pressed my face into her pillow, and for some reason, I wanted to cry. I felt like a little girl, afraid she would leave the house and never come back.

"I hear ya, honey," she said. "I need to go out, though. Things have been so serious around here lately. Time for some mandatory fun."

Diane always says that getting ready for a date is more fun than the event itself. However, both of us sensed the dutifulness of this particular date. She might or might not have seen my face in the window the other night, but Diane had long ago recognized that I was an Indigo child. Reading her mind was the least of my psychic powers. Frankly, I didn't need my superpowers for this case. Anyone with critical thinking skills (apply, analyze, synthesize, and/or evaluate information) could see that Diane had been scorned, in her career and her love life. She had hit rock bottom here in Where Its Legs Were Broken Off, Georgia. What she wanted to do was drop into a granny gown and break open a bag of cookies, watch

17 I added the "smiling with a fur hat" symbol because I miss my mad bomber hat. Also, I didn't want to look like I cared, if the rumor was true.

some sad movies, call an old boyfriend. Maybe she wanted to throw down a bottle of Jack Black and have a car wreck. As I may have mentioned, Diane was no stranger to the blues. After Max was born, three months after Joe's death, she went into a postpartum depression that could have ended it for all of us. I have vague memories of hanging out with her and baby Max in the bathroom for long periods of time, with the door locked, but I failed to realize the significance of these episodes until I read a scary journal entry from that year.

> Now I understand why those women kill their children and then themselves. You can't leave them here alone. I want to be with Joe, dead with Joe, but I can't leave them here. Who would take care of them? My parents? Ha. Ha ha ha ha ha ha ha ha ha ha ha ha ha ha.

Batshit crazy. It makes me wonder why women get pregnant in the first place. What are they thinking? *Oh, baby showers will be fun! I'll eat cake and get those cute little suits with panda ears on the hoods.* Here's the recap of the postpartum journal entries:

After birthing Max, Diane rolled straight down the hall to have her tubes tied. (No offense, Max.) Papa and Grandma invited the members of their Sunday school class to visit her hospital room at this time. Several of them watched her throw up when the nurse gave her a tiny cup of ice. Grandma reminded everyone that Diane's husband had died three months earlier. Then, while Diane made fruitless gestures for them to leave, Grandma told the ladies that Diane had always wanted to be a writer and now she certainly had a lot of material! They said things like, *Oh my goodness*. A couple of them said they liked to write too. Grandma said Diane would be glad to help them, once she felt better.

On the way home from the hospital, Diane begged Papa to stop and get her a Coca-Cola.

He said they had Cokes at home and it was a waste of money to buy one.

She pointed out that she had just had a baby and then an operation, and she really wanted a Coke.

He refused. It's hard to believe that Papa was that mean.

Grandma, meanwhile, outdid herself. She left town. "I can't take this," she said, after Diane had been in her house for two days with her newborn and her four-year-old and her weeping.

"You don't love me," said Diane.

"Well, you don't love me either," said Grandma, and off she went to a cabin in the mountains to get some rest.

Diane made Papa take her back to her house with her children. Once inside, she locked herself in the hall bathroom with me and baby Max. I remember that part, sitting in her lap while she leaned against the toilet with her knees braced against the wall. We had wrapped Max in a towel and put him in the dry bathtub.

"You need to write a thank-you note," Papa was telling her through the locked door, because one of Grandma's church friends had baked us a casserole. "Right away. People have been good to you, and you need to show your appreciation. Do it now, or you'll forget."

"Get out!" Diane screamed behind the bathroom door as the baby started crying. "Get out of my house!"

"I won't stay where I am not welcome," said Papa. His feelings were hurt.

I could tell Diane felt a little guilty. All the same, she put the chain across the front door so he couldn't open it with his key. When someone from AA dropped by to check on her, she talked through the chain. A few days later someone else from AA, a guy named Penn, came over to mow the grass. He didn't even come to the door.

I watched him through the window—the faded brim of his cap hid his face as he bent his head over the lawn mower. I wanted him to look up and see me in the window wearing my princess gown. I had been wearing it for a week, day and night, so it had a rip and a few stains, but it was still so beautiful. While Diane and the baby were sleeping, I had accessorized with her wedding pearls and tried out some lipstick.

Through the glass, I waved at the guy. He didn't look up. Men! I put on my sparkly plastic high heels, climbed on a chair to unfasten the chain on the door, and tottered out to meet him.

He turned the motor off as I wobbled across the uneven grass. "Hi," he said.

"It's nice out here," I said. "It doesn't smell like blood."

"Somebody's bleeding in there?" he asked me, but I had found a dandelion and had to concentrate on my wish. "Hey," he said. "Is somebody hurt?"

I closed my eyes and blew with all my might, scattering seeds over us. "It's just baby blood," I said. As he headed into the house, I had to kick off my heels to catch up with his long strides.

He found everyone alive. Diane allowed him to wash and bleach the sheets stained with afterbirth. When he made the bed, he bounced a quarter on it and gave me the quarter. While Diane slept on clean sheets, he cleaned up the kitchen and fixed tacos for everyone; then he vacuumed and mopped and cleaned the bathrooms.

"You know that's going to come out the other end," he said, watching me give Max his bottle. "I'm just telling y'all now—I don't do diapers."

"Should I call you Dad or Daddy?" I asked.

"Call me PMI," he said. "That stands for positive male influence."

After he left, I wrote the thank-you note for Diane and addressed it to PMI. I put it in the mailbox, where I put my notes to Santa Claus, and sometimes to God. The next day, when he brought the mail in, he held it up.

"Is this for me?" he asked.

"Of course," I said, but I was nervous—I couldn't write anything except the letters of the alphabet. He read it anyway.

That was a flashback, in case you didn't notice. So . . . 8.5 years later, here we are helping Diane get dressed for a Match.com date.

She was out of the road-sign ensemble and into outfit number two, a short gray hooded sweater dress with a full-length front zipper, thumb holes in the cuffs, and tall black boots. "How about this?"

I stared in silence.

"Just say something. I can take it. Give me two words."

"Space suit."

"It's just a coffee date," she said, frowning, as she turned in front of her mirror. "There's not going to be a photographer or anything."

Tiredly, I rolled off the bed. Even though my legs were aching from a recent growth spurt, I marched into her closet and got to work. In the end, we went with black velvet boyfriend pants, a fitted white tee, her jean jacket, the short black boots I coveted, and her wedding pearls. Hair teased in the back and tucked behind her ears in the front, a touch of mascara, red lipstick, and, of course, Amazing Grace.

"Well?" she asked with a hopeful smile, turning in a slow circle in front of me.

Both Diane and Kate's mom like to think they will date a man for six months before introducing him to their children, but this never happens. At 5:30 P.M., Mr. Friend materialized in our kitchen. He wasn't eating with us—you have to know somebody pretty well before you start passing around baked rutabaga fries. When he said something to Diane about going out for Italian after their coffees, she hesitated. "I didn't get a sitter," she said. (Obviously, I'm too old for a babysitter, but I can always use help with Max.)

"Go ahead," I said. "I'll take care of everything."

"Are you sure?" asked Diane. She nibbled on her thumb, the way she does sometimes when she's trying to make a decision. "I can pull out a potpie . . ."

"You should call Penn," said Max. "Why isn't Penn here? He always takes care of us."

The date watched Diane with a big, polite question mark on

his face. Diane looked distraught. "I think he's busy tonight," she said. She was careful not to touch her left ear—she knows that I know she does that when she's lying. Had they talked since the Rejection?

"Penn is never busy," said Max. "I mean, he practically *lives* here." He pointed to the shoe basket by the door. "He even leaves his shoes here."

"Who is Penn?" asked the date.

"Just a friend," said Diane quickly.

"Your kids will be fine," said Jack or Tom or whatever his name was. "This little lady seems quite mature. How old did you say you were?"

Dude was way older than Diane, and he'd never had kids. One of those. When they meet us, they're all like, *Oh, I love kids. Everyone always said I should have kids. Kids keep you young.* Then after a few months of Max's meltdowns, my sarcasm, picking up the dinner tabs for four, and maybe a trip to Florida, they're like, *Gotta go!*

Jack or Tom was okay. He wore khakis, a short-sleeved polo shirt, and old-man shoes. He had some hair left, but not much, and it was cut over his ears. He liked Diane's outfit, which made me proud, and he clapped heartily when Max showed him a dog trick he does with Lucky and Hiroshima. Max called him "sir," like Diane and I had taught him. I was proud of him, but when he admitted that, no, he didn't play any sports, there was a conspicuous hole in the conversation.

I pointed out that we were Bulldog fans, but since apparently it wasn't football season, and none of us had any idea who had won the Super Bowl or the Orange Bowl or whatever, that line of conversation was dropped.

While Diane was setting the table for our nuked faux-beef pot-pie, Max insisted on having the pink napkin. Pink is his favorite color.

"Pink?" said Mr. Friend, and he slapped Max on the shoulder in a rough-and-ready, hale-fellow-well-met, we're-just-guys-horsing-around-in-the-locker-room-slapping-each-other-with-wet-towels way. It didn't go over well.

"Ouch!" said Max, pulling away. He glowered at the man as only Max can do.

"Pink is for girls," said Mr. Friend, smiling too hard. "You're not a girl, are you?"

Max's eyes had turned very dark.

"He's male bonding with you, honey," I said, stepping between the two of them. I smiled brightly at Mr. Friend, who glanced at my chest and then looked quickly away.

"Excuse me," said Max coldly. He snatched the pink napkin off the table, stuffed it in his pocket, and stomped off to his room.

Diane sighed as the door slammed. We were both thinking the same thing: Warning to Suitor: Single mother can't control her son. At that moment, we disliked Mr. Friend, but I hadn't given up on him yet. I bustled around the kitchen after Diane, being the Helpful Daughter, laughing gaily at any witticism either of them shared, praying we could avoid the topics of politics and religion until it was time to send them off on their date.

"What's that perfume you're wearing?" asked Mr. Friend, stepping close to Diane to help her put the sugar up in the high cabinet. "It smells delicious."

He took a deep, appreciative sniff, and she half turned to face him. They looked nice together, standing close like that, blond and dark, small and large, female and male.

When a crash sounded in Max's room, I murmured, "I'll take care of it," and slipped down the hall so they could kiss or whatever.

Max stood in the center of the room, clenching a pair of scissors in his fist as he kicked his bed. Little pieces of pink napkin covered the floor. "Hello, Emo," I said, closing the door softly behind me. "Overreacting, are we?"

I could fill the rest of this page with his outbursts, but it's repetitive, so here's a narrative summary.

1. Max pitched a fit.

2. My attempt to coach him through his feelings using the "I" statements recommended by Dr. Dhang was, as usual, an epic fail.

3. I resorted to a time-tested technique. Reaching under his pillow, I pulled the stuffed platypus out by a webbed foot. "Fred," I said, "would you like to go for a little swim in the toilet? The current is a bit strong, but that makes it exciting."

   "No!" cried Max.

When I went back into the kitchen, I fully expected to find Diane and Mr. Friend groping each other by the sink. *Get a hotel room, why don'tcha,* I would say with a smirk, but they were sitting across from each other at the table. They already hated each other. Diane's mouth was set in a hard line, and Mr. Friend was laughing one of those tinny, fake laughs that mean, *F you.* Evidently, someone had made the mistake of bringing up either politics or religion.

"Jesus was a bastard," Diane said. "The reason he turned to God the Father is that he didn't have a father, and in those days, in Bethlehem or wherever, an illegitimate child was a social pariah." She factored in the educational level of her audience and amended, "A social outcast."

"He was born in Nazareth," said Bob or Ed or whatever his name was. There was that laugh again. "Jesus is the Son of God, and if you don't believe that"—he held his meaty hands out in an expression of futility—"well, then I feel sorry for you."

It was Diane's turn for a mean, fake little laugh. "Carl Jung said, 'Religion is a defense against the experience of God.'"

"Hi there," said Mr. Friend, noticing me.

"You probably wish we had a TV," I said, smiling at him. Somebody had to be nice to the guest. He smiled back. He had very nice teeth, and you don't see that much around Kanuga.

"Y'all must read a lot," he said, looking at the neat bookshelves lining our walls. "I guess the last book I read was in school," he added, with a rather alarming lack of embarrassment.

I happened to know that on his Match profile, Mr. Friend had checked "Some College" under "Education," and "$75,000–$100,000" under "Income." Diane says you can knock two years off the education and $25,000 off the income. She had gone back to her bedroom to get her purse and jacket, so Mr. Friend continued talking to me.

"My ex-wife used to read all the time. She liked Sidney Sheldon. Do you read her books?" I shook my head, but just then the dogs announced Penn's arrival, so I ran to the door. Max was already there.

"Whaddup!" said Penn, grinning at us as we crowded him in the doorway. He took Mr. Friend in with a swift glance, noting Diane's date getup, the whiff of perfume. He hesitated for a moment, as if he were about to leave, but Hiroshima wouldn't let him go. She was walking on her hind legs, balancing her forepaws on his thigh as she tried to keep up with him.

"Hiroshima, you get away from me," he said, scooping her into his arms so she could nuzzle his ear. Hiroshima crushes on Penn. "Quit loving on me," he said, holding her close. "I don't even *like* you."

"Look, Mom, I told you he would come!" cried Max. "Hey, Penn, will you play Pokémon with me?"

"Sure. That is, if it's okay with your mom."

He and Diane looked at each other. Mr. Friend cleared his throat. According to the rules of polite society, it was time for an introduction. However, Penn had a certain look on his face I've only seen a few times before: when we see a cop flash his lights to get through a red light, for instance. Then he would mutter, "You motherfucker."

"Looks like she's getting ready to go somewhere," Penn said now.

Diane's good home training failed her completely. She stood at the door—in her black velvet pants, holding an evening bag just big enough for a lipstick, a driver's license, and a ten-dollar bill—struck dumb. She looked the way she does at a party when she can't remember the name of the person who has spoken to her. She looked like she didn't know any of us.

Mr. Friend stepped forward and tried to introduce himself, but Max interrupted him. "So, Penn, I was looking for a breeded Sentret, low level," he said, beginning to spin around in the foyer between the two men.

"Let's get out of the hallway so you'll have more room for aerodynamic speech," Penn said. "Careful not to knock that picture off the wall."

Mr. Friend saw his opportunity to introduce himself and lurched forward with an outstretched hand. When he explained that he was here to take Diane out to dinner, I held my breath. Would Penn walk out the door? No matter how hard this guy in the polo shirt tried, he would never make PMI. He wouldn't even come close.

Penn shook his hand, but he didn't offer any explanation for his presence in our house. This clearly irritated Mr. Friend, especially when Penn started making a pot of coffee and knew exactly where to find the sugar.

"Penn is our nanny," Diane told her date, when she finally found her voice. Penn acknowledged this role by telling her that she looked very nice this evening. For a moment, Diane blinked at him as if she couldn't quite place him. Mean Diane![18] When she thanked him for the compliment, the temperature in the room

18 Yep, hell hath no fury like a woman scorned.

dropped two degrees. I wanted to scream: *We get it, Diane—you are unattainable, but this is our PMI! What are you doing with our lives?*

"Nanny?" asked Mr. Friend.

"Left my apron and ruffled cap in the truck," said Penn. "Aris, if you'll get me a flathead screwdriver, I'll fix the hinge on this cabinet. It's hanging cattywampus again."

"Why don't you ask Max?" I said. I was afraid to leave Diane without a coach even though I didn't know exactly how to save us.

"Because I am making a conscious decision to sidestep the prescribed sexist roles of our society, which dictate that only boys know the difference between a flathead and a Phillips," Penn said.

"I'll just run to the bathroom before we go out," said Diane.

I glanced at Diane's date, who stood in the corner with a painful smile plastered to his face, and reminded Penn that the South has always been a matriarchal society.

"Yes, ma'am," he said, dipping his head to hide a smile.

"We'll be back by ten," said Diane, striding back into the room. A long strip of toilet paper was attached to the back of her pants, floating behind her like a tail.

My heart did a small flip-flop. Everyone stared and then looked away except for Max, who grabbed one end of the toilet-paper tail and waved it up and down. Joe was responsible, of course. He always does something like this when Diane has a date. Last time it was a broken heel on her shoe; she had to come home early.

"What? What is it?" Diane was saying, looking around the room. In a flash Penn was behind her, slipping his hand into the back of her pants so fast that if you blinked (I didn't), you'd miss it. The toilet paper tail was removed and discarded.

Diane was back in half an hour.

"How did it go?" asked Penn. He was too much of a gentleman to smile when she grimaced, but I detected a spring in his step when he fixed her a cup of coffee. At the risk of sounding literary, may I add that I heard the faint notes of a song in his heart as he sat down at the kitchen table with her?

"I hope I didn't interfere with anything when I came over earlier," he said.

"Oh no. That's okay."

"I should have called—can't find my phone."

"I should have told you."

"Told me what? You don't have to tell me anything."

"There's nothing to tell—"

I decided to give them some alone time. In my room, I checked my phone, but there was no word from my betrothed. Just a text from Anders Anderson.

> just a line . . . 2 keep in touch . . .
> coz u r on my mind so very much . . .
> & even though, I've nothing 2 say . . .
> U'll know . . . I thought of u 2day . . .

I decided to respond.

Me:

:-&[19]

Anders:

will u forward to ur friend kate?

Me:

srsly?[20]

19 Tongue-tied.
20 Seriously?

Anders:

add swak[21]

Me:

Dude she friend zoned u

Anders:

when?

Me:

last week

Anders:

tttt[22]

Me:

iyo[23]

Anders:

jj[24]

Me:

ig2r[25] new Mr. Friend was here. :b[26]

Anders:

ifyp.[27] :'(

21 Sealed with a kiss.
22 These things take time.
23 In your opinion.
24 Just joking.
25 I've got to run.
26 Tongue sticking out.
27 I feel your pain.

I hadn't heard from Billy in over a week. I refused to go on Facebook and stalk him. What if I unfriended him? I imagined him calling me, his beautiful growly-Billy voice asking me to friend him back, to come to Massachusetts and move into the basement with him. I imagined myself pinching my lips like Grandma and saying tartly to the imaginary Billy, "Well, we'll see about that."

A couple days later, Max and I had to go to Grandma and Papa's house because Diane had made a fresh kill on Match.com. She insisted on wearing the black velvet boyfriend pants for the next Mr. Friend. After the last date, I thought we should pack them away as bad-luck clothes, but I let her have her way.

"Now, who is the man again?" Grandma asked Diane as we walked into her house. "Where did you meet him?"

Max and I were silent. We had been taught not to give Grandma any information. This isn't hard, because Grandma never listens.

"Henry!" she hollered before anyone could answer her question. "Henry! They're here! The children are here!" When Papa failed to materialize in two seconds, she said, "I don't know where he is. He goes off and hides."

Their house is huge. It's so big that they had an intercom installed back in the seventies, but Grandma never uses it, because she likes to yell.

"Henry!" she yelled again. Two seconds later, she said, "I give up," and turned to us. "I bought some Cokes and strawberry ice cream. I guess we're having pizza for supper, if that's okay with your mother. I know she's picky."

"All that sugar and processed white flour isn't good for them," said Diane. "Have you read *The China Study*?"

"The what? I'm sorry. This was last-minute. Who is this fellow? You never did tell me where you met him."

"Under a bridge," said Diane.

Grandma didn't think that was funny, but Papa did. He was coming down the stairs with a big grin on his face. "Well, here are my long-lost grandchildren and my long-lost daughter. Coming to see your old Papa!" I hugged him, careful not to disturb the tiny Band-Aid on his bald head. Papa takes blood thinners to prevent a stroke, and this makes him bleed from the slightest nick. When I was small, I usually had a Band-Aid on my bear, Zimmerman, so this is a nice association.

"What time will you be back?" Grandma asked Diane. "Do you want them to spend the night?"

"I'll call you," said Diane.

"I hope this isn't a spend-the-night date," said Grandma. "I know you don't want to hear this, but your father and I think it's important for you to set a good example for Aris. She's getting to be that age."

Diane glared at Grandma.

Grandma glared back.

"You are amazing," Diane said coldly.

"Excuse me," said Max, but we ignored him. I could tell this was going to be a good fight, so I settled into my favorite chair in the den, a mamasan with faux-leopard-skin pillows from the seventies, and dug my spoon into the pink ice cream.

"Why am I amazing?" asked Grandma.

"You have no boundaries," said Diane.

"Well, I hope you have some," said Grandma. "There's no reason to buy the cow if you can get the milk for free." Having won that battle, she turned to Max. "What is it, honey?"

"I forgot," said Max. "Are we getting a cow?"

"Come in here and let me give you a present," she said, taking him by the hand. "I don't know if you'll like it or not." He skipped along beside her, asking for a horse "to keep the cow company."

Papa patted Diane on the back and told her she looked pretty. Then he asked her if she needed any money. "Let me just give you something," he said, taking out his wallet. "You might need to buy some milk. Do you have gas in your car?"

"She has no boundaries," said Diane. "I can't put up with this."

"Well," he said, patting her on the back some more. "Your mother is just that way. We all have to forgive each other sometimes," he said, counting out crisp twenty-dollar bills. "She means well."

He looked at me and made a monkey face. I made one back. Diane pocketed the twenties and left.

I spent most of the evening on Grandma's manual typewriter. I like the way it makes a song of my writing, clackety-clack, clackety-clack, clack, clack, zing! The zing is the return key.

"I see you're still writing your novel," said Grandma. "What's it about?"

"Well," I said, and then I froze up. What was my novel about? I had no idea.

"I'm illuminating reality as I transcend it," I said.

"Aren't you smart." She pushed the typewriter back on the table so it wouldn't fall on the floor—manual typewriters sometimes dance while they sing. "You're not going to tell me what it's about?"

I tried to remember the story statement I had to write for an exercise in *Write a Novel in Thirty Days!*, but all I could think about was how Grandma's face would look when she was reading about herself.

"Is it about me?" she asked. "Am I in it?"

I fake smiled. Luckily, Grandma doesn't wait for people to answer her questions.

"Your mother wanted to be a writer once," she said. "I guess she gave up."

"She's not dead yet," I said, and that made Grandma laugh. Grandma almost never laughs. Once, I tried to read her jokes from a *Far Side* book. Not a single one made her laugh, or even smile. She says she doesn't understand jokes.

I asked her if I could have the typewriter.

"No, I use that," she said, but she gave me a dusty black velvet hat with a rhinestone pin that her mother had worn to church and funerals. Max got a hundred-year-old coffee grinder that you crank by hand. We were instructed to return these items if Diane ever tried to take them to the Salvation Army. Grandma and Papa grew up during the Depression, so they never get rid of anything. Their house is like a time capsule. It pains them to hear Diane talk about Simple Living.

"Now, don't you get rid of these things I gave the children," Grandma said when Diane came back (early) to pick us up. "Just give them back if you don't want them."

"They might be worth a lot of money someday," Papa said, carefully carrying Max's coffee grinder to the car.

"Money, money, money," said Grandma. "That's all you ever think about, Henry. You think the world revolves around money."

I decided not to add to the tension by telling her that the world actually revolves around sex. "We are keeping these things because they have *meaning*," she said. "No one is *ever* going to sell them."

"We have to keep them in the family," Papa agreed.

I wore the hat to make Grandma feel good, but it itched and made me sad because I missed my mad bomber hat. On the ride home, while Max sat in the backseat finding things on the floor to grind in his coffee grinder, it occurred to me that the meaning of an object varies significantly from one person to another, and the question of ownership has historically been a matter of controversy. Furthermore, "keeping it in the family" is really a moot point since all humans are descended from a small group of Homo sapiens in East Africa. It would have been interesting to discuss this with Diane, but she was hunched over the steering wheel, scowling through the windshield. Every time we came to a stop sign, the car bounced with the pressure of the brake.

After a respectful silence, I asked, "Was he married or separated?"

"Yep," she said. It's funny how sometimes we all talk like Penn.

I sighed and checked my empty phone. If Billy did break off our engagement, would I have the strength left to find a man for Diane? I wondered if love could just run out, like money.

When we got home from Grandma's house, we all went to our own rooms. We always do this when we come home. After prolonged exposure to other human beings, Diane and I have to rebuild our psychological infrastructures in solitude. Max, who leans toward extroversion, goes to his room because no one will talk to him.

My room had slowly been returning to its comfortable state of disorder, but I missed the presence of Diane's journals under the bed. Their absence created another big suckhole, like the mad-bomber-hat hole. Things were always disappearing in my life. Frankly, even though I'm too old for dolls, I missed the Devereux family. I missed the living-on-the-brink-of-disaster wonder of their world in all its shabby detail: the three-wheeled car, the sagging porch, the half-naked kids hanging out the windows. Poor, crazy Mrs. Devereux. Mr. Devereux would probably turn up one day, stuffed in an old sock that Diane had missed on a cleaning binge, or wedged into the corner of an air vent, one foot chewed off by a young Hiroshima. He'd ask about his family. What happened to the house? Where on earth did he leave his car?

I found Diane at the kitchen table, drinking a cup of tea called Smooth Move. I made a mental note to hide it in the bottom of the tea basket before Billy came to visit. I chose licorice tea for myself.

"I thought you might like some company," I said as I brought the honey jar to the table.

She smiled sadly at me. "You're my darling."

On the other side of the wall, we could hear Max in his room, grinding something in the coffee grinder. "This is really hard," he was telling Fred or some personage. "But it's worth it. You-just (grind), have-to (grind), keep-try (grind) ing."

"Grandma gave him something good for him," I said.

"Papa is right," said Diane. "She means well. And she loves you guys."

"Does she love you?"

"I don't know," said Diane, "but she's been a good teacher. In the Buddhist sense." She stirred some extra honey in her tea and passed the jar to me. "You and Max should go to bed. Children are supposed to get ten hours of sleep every night."

"I'm not a child."

"Technically, you are a child."

"I don't feel like a child. I feel like your partner."

"Oh, honey. Dr. Dhang says you don't need this kind of emotional responsibility. We need to let you have a real childhood."

"I can handle it. I'll have a late childhood when I'm forty. I have big plans for us, Diane."

"Big plans." She gazed into her teacup. She looked so pretty in the broken light of a chandelier with only one working bulb—it was sad that no one else could see her. "Joe could see me," she told me once. "Until I met him, no one had ever really seen me before. Different people saw different pieces, but they didn't add up to me. When Joe looked at me, his eyes had that light of recognition."

"So," I said. "How was your date tonight?"

"Ha," she said. "Ha, ha, ha."

"Go on," I said.

"I asked him, 'Have you ever been married?' He replied, 'Yes, twice.' I took that to mean he was now single."

"Well, of course," I said.

"Men suck," she said.

"What about Penn? He's already used to us."

"You know, Aris, the three of us *are* a family. When you and Max were little, I felt so conscious about all the four-square families in your storybooks: mom, dad, dog, cat. . . . I thought I needed to find the missing man, but maybe we are whole now, the way we are. We are a single-parent family of three."

"What's one more?"

"Penn is an atheist," she said. "He smokes. He lives with his mother."

"We're open-minded?" I suggested.

She shook her head. "He doesn't love me."

"Oh, Merm. How could anyone not love you?" I reached out and touched her short hair, warm and silky all over, like the fur behind Hiroshima's ear. "You're beautiful. You're strong. You're smart. You're even organized!"

"Old and fat," she said. "Short and poor."

"Careful," I said. "I'm looking at my future. You don't want to discourage me."

"Okay, erase that. The organization, however—it's an act of desperation. I'm a reformed slob. When I wake up in the morning, I feel like I'm coming out of a coma. I don't have any idea what date it is, or even where I am."

I nodded. I knew this from reading her journals. In so many dreams, she was lost, driving through a fog that grew denser with every mile. She forgot to attend entire courses at some cosmic university of life. The hands of clocks spun backward. In most of these dreams, she carried a baby, sometimes two, and she was terrified of losing them.

"You're a survivor," I said. I paused, wondering how to proceed with my argument for Penn. I didn't want to diminish Diane's self-esteem, but we had a PMI at stake here. At last, I resorted to one of her AA slogans, "If you stay in the problem, the solution goes away; if you stay in the solution, the problem goes away."

She smiled at me; everyone likes to be quoted. "Solution," I continued. "If Penn moves in with us, he won't live with his mother anymore. As for atheism? You always said people have a right to their spiritual beliefs."

"Penn isn't having nice, quiet, personal beliefs. He's a rabid atheist."

"At least he smokes outside," I said, but I was losing heart.

"I'm lonely," she said. "I admit it. I'm lonelier in my home-town than I was in Alaska, and that is one empty place."

"We should move back there."

"I want to move, but Alaska is too hard. Beautiful, but hard."

"What was it like in Alaska?" She's told me all the Alaska stories, but I always want to hear them again. I love to hear about my dad.

"Well," she began, "I remember one spring, just after the roads had thawed, your father decided we should have Easter dinner at the Arctic Circle. So we took a big halibut out of the freezer, which was just a box on the porch, and drove up Haul Road. The road was all broken up because of the thaw. After we passed through Fairbanks, we never saw another rig. Just caribou, eagles, and two black bears. Joe had already used the extra five gallons of gasoline we brought with us, so we really needed to find a gas pump.

"Finally, at the Yukon River, we spotted a shed with an ancient gas pump in front of it. As we climbed out of the car, this skinny man came out of the building. He was as weathered as an old fence post, with a grayish beard, wearing four or five shirts. I will never forget the way he smiled.

"He said, 'Call me Ned.' Some people out there had changed their names so no one could find them. It didn't matter. We came inside the shack for coffee, of course, and sat around a homemade table beside the woodstove. Ned was crocheting."

"How old was I?"

"Two or three. I remember that you were saying 'Hot' every time you came near the stove—that's the first word Alaskan babies learn. Ned crocheted a little doll for you while we sat there, drink-ing coffee and talking. His voice was rusty because he hadn't spoken to people in months. When we finished our coffee, we went outside and looked at the heavy, broken chain his dog had snapped on a negative-thirty day. We met the dog, who was mostly wolf. Everything around us was white and still. It was just the four of us, and the wolf-dog, in the world. Before we left, Joe hacked off a hunk of the halibut and gave it to Ned."

She paused and looked back into her teacup. "Do you know what I'm saying?"

"We belonged," I said.

"Exactly." She scratched the foil from a piece of nicotine gum and chewed it reflectively. "Down here, you spend your time sorting through categories: political party, religion, school, family, income . . . there's no simple human connection. Even with family."

I held out my hand, palm facing her. "Human connection," I said. As soon as we touched palms, the last kitchen light bulb died out.

Back at the Lab, I was avoiding Ms. Chu. I kept hearing her words, *something terrible must happen*. As Kate pointed out, Ms. Chu wasn't going to walk up to me and say, "Hi, Aris. Has your protagonist faced a situation she can't handle, the outcome of which will change her life?" But she would *think* it.

However, Ms. Chu has a highly developed sense of social context clues, and she left me to myself during library period. After recommending an Italian play, *Six Characters in Search of an Author*, she busied herself with several rowdy boys in our class who have zero social context clues. Drunk on their own hormonal cocktails, they were turning our cool, quiet library into a dark, noisy tavern. Anders nosed around the edge of the group, looking seedy.

When he sidled up to me and asked if I had heard from Billy lately, I said sternly, "This is a library. I am reading. That's what people do in libraries. Get a book."

Actually, I had not heard a peep from Billy Starr. During science, I found three new pictures of his "cousin" Tiffany on his Facebook page. At home later that afternoon, I discovered that Tiffany had followed him on Twitter and Instagram. When my cellphone rang, I jumped, thinking, *He's calling me!* That was ridiculous, of course—my friends and I haven't "talked on the phone" since third grade.

It was Grandma, who rarely begins with "hello."

"I cannot get your mother to pick up her phone," she announced. "I called her phone twice. Where is she?"

"Taking a bath."

"A bath? I thought she was supposed to be at work."

"Oh, that's right. She's at work. Maybe you shouldn't call her at work?"

"Well, I can't keep up with everyone's schedule. Who is over there with you? Is Penn there?"

"Uh, yeah. I mean, yes, ma'am. He's over here."

"What's he doing over there while she's in the bath?"

"She's at work."

"Well, it's late. I can't imagine why she would be working so late. She'll have to pay Penn a fortune."

My head had begun to spin from telling lies, so I didn't say anything. Grandma eventually answers her own questions.

"I guess she's giving a makeup test," she said. I could hear her shouting over the phone to Papa, "She's not home yet. Giving a makeup test to her students. The children won't tell me when she'll be home."

Finally, she got down to the real reason she had called. She and Papa were coming over for dinner on Saturday night to celebrate her diamond jubilee wedding anniversary. "*My* diamond jubilee," she called it, as if Papa wasn't even a player. She wanted to know if we had that gold tablecloth she had given Diane a while back. She hoped Diane hadn't thrown it away. She wanted us to put that cloth on the table, if it wasn't too much trouble. Gold, she informed me, is the color of the diamond jubilee wedding anniversary. We might all want to wear something gold too, for the pictures.

"Only queens are allowed to call their anniversaries diamond jubilees," I said.

There was a pause in which her feelings got hurt. Then she forgave me because I was under the age of thirteen.

"Well, shoot," she said. "I guess I can call my anniversary anything I want. I've put up with your grandfather for a long time." Then she went into details about how he was losing his hearing and too proud to admit it and wasn't any fun and didn't like to go to movies and picked up after her all the time, just moved her things around so she couldn't find them, blob blob blob.

I put her on speakerphone while I checked my Facebook page. Tiffany and Billy had begun appearing in photos together. Tiffany had "liked" Billy's basketball photo. Billy had "liked" some dumb picture of her. Apparently, she played girls' basketball.

"Aris!" Grandma yelled into the phone. "Aris? I can't hear you. Something is wrong with your phone."

Max walked into the kitchen. "She put you on speakerphone, Grandma!" he shouted, thumping his hand along the counter as he made his way down one side of the galley kitchen and up the other.

There was a pause while Grandma digested this information. Then she said, "Well, I guess I better go. Y'all are busy."

"Aris," said Max after she hung up. "Will you play Pokémon with me?"

"No."

"Why not?"

"I'm busy," I said.

"What's wrong with you?" He stepped closer and stared into my face, but I brushed him away. "Have you been crying?"

"No."

"You look weird."

"Thanks. You too."

He started thumping on the counter again. "We're going to be poor," he said. He opened a cabinet and shut it and opened it and shut it and opened it and shut it. "We are going to be poor and hungry. Don't you care, Aris?"

I stared at a cracked tile in the floor, imagining myself getting smaller and smaller until I could slip inside that crack and disappear forever. Did I care?

"Will you play with me later? At seven fifteen?"

"I have to do my homework."

"You never do your homework."

It was true. I had been letting my homework lie fallow while I finished the novel.

"Will you play with me tomorrow?" He opened the cabinet again and pulled out a bag of ancient marshmallows. Diane quit buying them after Penn told her they were made of petroleum.

"Probably," I said.

"What time? Will you play Pokémon with me at nine o'clock in the morning?"

"Probably." I swiped some marshmallows and walked down the hall, pausing in front of Diane's bathroom door to listen to the soft splashes in the bathtub. In my room, I sat down at the little white desk from Sears that had taken Diane a week to put together and which I never use. According to the calendar she had hung on my bulletin board, I had less than two weeks to finish my novel.

Two weeks! I put on my headlamp, grabbed my laptop, and dived under the bed. A few more dust balls had formed since I cleared out Diane's journals, and one sticky note had fallen off the wall. I gathered the loose papers that had slipped from Diane's notebooks: an old gym schedule, a couple of bills, and then—I don't know how I missed this—a short story, stapled together and folded in half. Under the bed, in the dim, dusty light, I read it.

Greensleeves
By Diane Montgomery-Thibodeau

When Joe's mother died, we flew to Houma for the funeral.

"Will Mr. Lafontaine be there?" I asked.

He shrugged like it didn't matter; then he looked hard at me. "I am asking you not to say anything or do anything," he said. I tried to shrug like him, but he wouldn't have it. Kept looking into me. "I am asking this of you," he said.

Before we were married, he said, "Now I have to put the dead fish on the table." I saw him in the kitchen of the restaurant where he worked, wearing a white apron spattered with blood, leaning into a halibut with a thin knife half as long as my arm. The fish eye stared straight up at the ceiling. Scales glittered along the backs of his brown hands like silver sequins. Then I looked out the trailer window at our blank, white world in Alaska and felt the butterfly kick of the fetus.

Victims generally choose similar victims, I read from a library book. So it would be a seven-year-old boy, a neighbor's son, someone whose dad had recently died, a big brown-eyed kid with five siblings and an overwrought mother, a boy who needed a mentor, perhaps a deacon and the chief of police in the town of Houma, Louisiana. He would give him rides to Little League practice. It would happen again and again and again, in the basement of the man's house. The boy wouldn't tell because if he did, Chief/Deacon Lafontaine would tell his mother that he had been drinking. I tried to imagine the glass a man would pour whiskey in for a seven-year-old. Was it a plastic cup that wouldn't break if he dropped it on the basement floor? This went on for three years.

"Why did he stop?" I asked Joe.

"I don't know," he said, putting his hands in his pockets, his head nearly grazing the water-stained ceiling of the trailer. "He got tired of me? Found someone else?"

"I'm going to kill him," I said.

"Okay. You do that." He pulled on his coat, took the snowshoes off the nails on the wall, and went outside.

I sewed a little black velvet jumper for Aristotle, a funeral dress. I stitched pink ribbon around the hem and saved a piece for a pink bow. She was a beauty, with his big, dark eyes and ruby studs in her ears.

"Maybe you'll see an alligator," I told her.

The velvet dress was too hot for Louisiana, even in February. Aris took it off in the middle of the funeral service after she'd slipped out of my arms and dashed up to the casket, where her grandmother lay in her favorite red dress, eyes closed in a forever sleep. I caught Aris, carried her screaming outside.

"Hot!" she cried, pushing me away with her damp arms as I tried to get the velvet back over her head. So I let her walk with me around the parking lot in her big-girl pants and Mary Janes, looking for alligators. When she began to cry because the sunlight hurt her eyes, I put Mickey Mouse sunglasses on her face. The ribbon held fast on her shiny head.

As we passed by the window of the funeral home, she stopped to listen to the recording of "Greensleeves."

"It's Daddy's song," she said. They had asked Joe to play his saxophone at the service, but he wouldn't. He used to play it for his mother when she called, putting the phone on speaker and strapping the sax across his chest. They spoke French to each other. *"Je t'aime, Maman."*

When people began filing out the door after the service, I looked for Mr. Lafontaine. I thought that somehow I'd recognize him, but I felt confused in the crowd. After so many dark months in Alaska, the sunlight made me dizzy. The Creole drawl sounded more like French than English.

"My wife," Joe would say in introductions. "My daughter."

"Yo wife," they would drawl. "Yo daughtah," with the accent on the end.

"Mon cher," an older woman said to him, pulling him into a hug, and he was eased away from us into a blur of shoulders and backs the colors of shadows.

"I'm tired of the funeral," said Aris. "I want to go home now." She handed me her glasses and pressed her face against my leg to hide from the light. "I'm hot," she said. "I'm thirsty. Merm, my shoe came off."

One afternoon when the ice on the roads had begun to melt into a beer-colored slush, I stomped home from my job at the coffee kiosk to find Joe stretched out on our mattress with the baby. He was wearing what we had worn all winter, in and out of bed, long underwear with sweatpants, a turtleneck, a pullover, and two pairs of wool socks. She lay in his arms, shocking in her pink flesh. Even the diaper was gone.

"Why did you take her clothes off?" I asked him. It was the way I leveled off each word, making them all flat and even, as if I was cutting something out.

He looked at me, looked into me. "She's always so bundled up," he said. "I want to see what she looks like."

The baby focused her eyes on my chest. She was pale and long in the belly and too thin, I thought. At night, I would reach into the sheepskin bag we tucked between us, where she lay soft and warm, and put my finger under the tiny nose to make sure she was breathing. "Do you tell her that you love her?" he had asked me.

"She doesn't know words yet."

"She understands," he said.

Later I would remember getting a new doll, taking its clothes off to look at it, to know it, but the memory came too late.

"It's just weird," I said, and I took the half stride that led into the kitchen. Over the miniature sink, there was a window slightly bigger than my face that looked out over the rusty wall of the next trailer. A few weeks ago, the snow had been higher than the window, but it was melting away. I could see through the ashen light into the other window, but there was no movement there.

"I know what you're thinking," he said from the bed.

I dumped a cup of cold coffee into the sink and then carefully scraped the grounds away from the thimble-sized drain so it wouldn't clog. I prayed. *Please, God. Please help me. Please help us.*

Mr. Lafontaine came upon me suddenly, while I was bent over putting the shoe back on Aris's foot. "Hello," he said. I stood up too fast, trying to blink away the colored spots that danced before my eyes. He looked nothing like I had imagined. *It's not him,* I told myself.

When Joe first told me about Mr. Lafontaine, I called a nun hotline. Having grown up Baptist, I had an image of nuns as sweet ladies with pink cheeks and kind wrinkles around their eyes.

"It happens all the time," said the nun in a Brooklyn accent. There was a long pause on the line, as if she was giving me a chance to tell her something she didn't already know. "Be glad that your husband lived," she said. "A lot of them kill the victims. Keeps them from telling."

I thought about the man handing the little boy a glass of whiskey down in the basement. There must have been a dart board, maybe a foosball table, some posters of football or baseball players. Little League. "I'd be happy to take Joe to practice when I take my boys," he must have said to the mother. There was a Mrs. Lafontaine and two children, a dog, and a cat.

I imagined the sweaty gray Louisiana sun thickening the air around them on the ball field, wet circles widening under Chief Lafontaine's armpits, the smell of deodorant. "Strike one! Choke that bat, boy! Choke up on it."

Later, his big hand clapping him on the back, resting for a moment between the birdlike shoulder blades. "I'm proud of you, son. That was a good effort."

"Mark Lafontaine," he said, pumping my hand as he called me by the name of Joe's ex-wife. He had sandy hair, streaked with gray, and light-colored eyes. He was tall, with a slightly athletic stance, but just an ordinary man, somebody's husband, somebody's father.

"It's so good to see Joe after all these years," he said.

The words sat waiting in my mouth. I had practiced them in front of mirrors, recited them to myself as I fell asleep, repeated them upon awakening. There were many versions: *So you're the man who molested my husband when he was a child. Nice to meet you at last. / Hi. Nice to meet you. Raped any little boys lately? / Mr. Lafontaine! Yes, Joe has talked so much about you. He told me everything.*

Then I would punch him in the face. Then I would draw a Smith & Wesson and pull the trigger. Then I would scream and scream and scream.

The humidity was a steady, suffocating entity, pressing evenly all around me, squeezing the air out of my lungs, making the zipper of my dress hot against my back. He was looking down at Aris.

"And what is your name?"

Suddenly, Joe cut in between us, smiling, saying something about the LSU season.

They talked about football.

As we drove to the graveyard, Aris and I pressed our faces against the windows, searching for movement in the murky swamp on the side of the road. "Ooze," said Aris. "Ooze, ooze, ooze." She beat her hand on the car seat. "Bite you!" Every stick floating in the water looked like an alligator.

"You can't see them," said Joe. "They show up when they want to."

"I saw bubbles," I said, but he wouldn't stop the car.

That night at a restaurant we ordered crawfish with corn on the cob and iced tea. The crawfish came in a plastic bag stuffed inside a bucket. Someone called them mudbugs. Joe took one out, delicately twisted off the head, and sucked the juice out of it. I watched him dig the fat out of the head and then break the tail.

"Daddy's eating roaches," said Aris, watching him intently. He grinned at her, teeth flashing, bringing that light all around him.

My God, I thought, *he's forgiven the bastard.*

I left Diane's story under the bed. I sat down at my white Sears desk, scooting the chair all the way in even though my knees scraped the wood. I felt safe at my tiny desk, in control. Once upon a time I was a little girl who thought growing up meant having birthday parties. I had never read my mother's journals, learning more about my past than I wanted to know. I had never heard of *Chief Lafontaine.*

It was too late; I knew what I knew. For the rest of my life, the image of my seven-year-old father being molested by a man in a basement would live in my head.

Through the wall, I could hear Diane getting out of the bathtub. She would be standing on the mat in the steamy room, smelling of lavender bubble bath, humming tunelessly as she patted herself dry. A few bubbles would remain in her hair. When I was little, we all took baths together. "Just keep his head out of the water," she would say as we passed a slippery Max between us. You wouldn't think cleaning such a small body could be so much work, but it was. "It takes a village to wash a baby," I said, and she grinned under the tall bubble hat I had made on her head.

All of a sudden, I wanted to run to her and tell her everything. I would say, *Merm, I read your journals. I read about the basement.* Maybe she would say, *Oh, Aris, that's just a story. That's fiction.* She would say, *There is no such thing as Mr. Lafontaine.*

But there is such a thing as Mr. Lafontaine. I knew this. Deep down, I had always known. That's why she drove me and Max past the pedophile houses in the Orchard. That's why she dressed me in an anti–human trafficking sweater to go to the airport. When a man sometimes looked at me funny, Diane was instantly by my side emitting danger vibes like an electric eel. News flash: Aris, there is evil in the world. I know, I have always known, but—

I don't think I can do this anymore, I imagined telling Dr. Dhang. *I can't hold on.* I saw myself stretched out on the velvet divan while she adjusted her glasses to peer at me across a long room.

Are you having thoughts of suicide? she would ask me.

It's complicated, I would say. As my Montgomery genes kicked in, I would retreat into the safety of analysis, approaching the issue from a practical standpoint.

The author of *Write a Novel in Thirty Days!* is generally opposed to killing off characters. The chapter on endings warns writers not to chase the characters off the edge of a cliff like bison hunters just to finish the story. Apparently, this is a temptation. The book points out the obvious—as soon as you wipe out a first-person narrator, your story is finished.

Even if I could, logistically, kill myself in my own novel, there is the matter of method. We are probably the only people in Kanuga who do not own a gun. In Georgia, you don't even need a license to have a gun unless you are wearing it. Kanugians keep a pistol in the glove compartment, a rifle hanging in the truck window, and a few AK-47s back at the house. You can buy guns at Walmart, and Max is always pestering Diane to put one in the cart. "No," she always says. "We have a machete."

No, Dr. Dhang, I am not having thoughts of suicide. I have a better plan. The idea came like a firefly, like the spirit of Dad. It grew into a streak, and then, the more I thought about it, into a sky popping with fireworks. I would go to Houma, Louisiana, and confront Mr. Lafontaine.

I imagined holding the blade of the machete to his bobbing Adam's apple, watching his eyes dart fearfully as I said, "I am Aristotle Thibodeau, Joe's daughter." Diane had failed to challenge him, but I would succeed.

I would bring Billy with me, in case I needed a backup. *Billy,* I would say, standing at his doorstep in Boston with snow blowing all around me, *I know that you have been ignoring me and that you are in all likelihood dating your cousin, but I need your help to settle a score.* Of course, Billy would fall in love with me all over again on our heroic mission, but I tried not to dwell on those details: the sunglasses we would wear, how I would sweep his hand aside and knock on Chief Lafontaine's door myself, the way the moon hung over the bayou when we had put that evil man away and Billy held me close. I could fix this.

On Friday, February 20, after everyone in the house was asleep, I removed the machete from the car and hid it under my bed. If there were a police report of what happened on Saturday, February 21, it would look like this:

Incident Report 001001
Kanuga Police Department

At 2300 hours on February 20, Aristotle Thibodeau, of 17 Plum Lane, sent a Facebook message to Billy Starr, of Northampton, Massachusetts.

> I need you. We have something important to do.
> Call me.

There was no response.

2430 hours Ms. Thibodeau sent a second message to Billy.

You say I'm an idealist, but if we aren't going to change the world, who is? I know where we can start. I found out something terrible about my father. We can make the world a safer place. Will you help me?

0116 hours Ms. Thibodeau sent a third message to Billy.

I know you're not asleep. I AM NOT STALKING YOU, but your Facebook status is ONLINE. Hello?

0430 hours

You haven't answered ANY OF MY EMAILS OR TEXTS in forever. I don't mean to sound desperate or anything, but really? Am I, like, nothing to you?

0800 hours There is a knock on Ms. Thibodeau's bedroom door. Her mother, also of 17 Plum Lane, is reported as saying that she is going to run errands and will be back in a few hours. Ms. Thibodeau is informed that Penn MacGuffin, an employee, will be on the premises before 1000 hours to continue construction work on an external building on the property (shed/playhouse).

0840 hours There is another knock on Ms. Thibodeau's bedroom door, which is apparently locked. A brother, Max Thibodeau, age 8, requests entrance. He knocks repeatedly and then slides a note under the door.

you sade you'ld play Pokémon wih me

0850 hours Ms. Thibodeau opens her bedroom door. Max Thibodeau, of 17 Plum Lane, is waiting in the hall, holding a shoebox of Pokémon cards sorted into bundles and wrapped with rubber bands. He says:

"I'm training for the title of Most Talented Ten-and-Under Pokémon Player, and I need your help. I've made you a special fire deck. Fire-type Pokémon can be tricky because they require a lot of energy, and you have to somehow pull that energy out of the discard pile after an attack, but I've given you a Reshiram and an Emboar with Inferno Fandango Ability. Which means that you can play as many Fire Energies as you want with each—"

[His speech is interrupted by a text message to Ms. Thibodeau's cellphone from an unidentified caller.]

Hi this is Tiffany hope ur ok? Billy is worried about u

When Ms. Thibodeau fails to reply, Max gains her attention by shaking the cardboard box and resumes his speech. "With each turn. You can use the Blue Flare Attack. So, basically, a Pokémon with 130 HP can do 120 damage every single turn!"

At this point, Ms. Thibodeau makes a false statement, promising her brother that she will meet him in the shed/playhouse to play Pokémon at 0915 hours. He is instructed to wait for her there.

0905 hours Ms. Thibodeau, wearing jeans, Converse high-tops, and a dark hooded sweatshirt, carrying a machete, exits the residence on foot.

Transcript: It was cold. Although I was wearing a sweatshirt, the string had come out of the hood, so the wind kept blowing it off my head. My ears were freezing. As I walked, I changed the machete from one hand to the other so I could warm the free hand in my pocket.

A few ragged clouds hung in the gray sky, and the air

smelled like damp clothes. All along Plum Lane, the houses were silent. Occasionally, I saw the blue flash of a TV screen through a living room window, or a minivan rounding the corner, but cold affects southerners the way it does lizards, making us still.

Only the dogs were alive, barking frantically behind their fences as I turned the corner onto Peach Street. In the driveway of the house with the green shutters, a boy was riding his bike up and down the driveway. He was about Max's age, wearing a thin hoodie zipped up to his raw, red face, with the cuffs pulled down over his hands. He pedaled furiously to the edge of the street, slammed on his brakes, turned, and pedaled furiously back up the driveway, where he slammed on his brakes and turned again. When he came flying back down, I could see that his eyes were watering from the cold, or maybe he was crying. He was the age of my father when Mr. Lafontaine brought him into his basement. Not Max—I could not think of Max being hurt—but this boy about the same age as Max; he was small. He had to say, "Yes, sir." If he cried, he would be called a baby. He would believe anything. He would be terrified.

0912 hours Ms. Thibodeau reaches the end of Peach Street, which dead-ends into Muscadine Circle, a street that encircles a small lake.

Transcript: If I turned left, I would pass number four, the house of the pedophile on Muscadine Circle, but out of habit, I turned right. In my mind, I could see the Google map of the Orchard on Diane's computer screen, with red pushpins marking the addresses of child molesters. "He might look like an ordinary person," Diane had told us. "Like a teacher or a friend's father. Never let anyone touch you in a private place." It upset her to talk about child molesters. The wads of chewed nicotine gum would pile up in a yellow mound on her desk. If she'd had a husband, he would have put his arm around her.

0915 hours Ms. Thibodeau continues on Muscadine Circle.

Transcript: When Kate saw a picture of Joe, she said, "Oh-mygod, he is hot."

I said, "Don't creep on my dad, okay?" Billy is hot too, but he looks nothing like Joe. He has the all-American-boy look, which Diane says is not my style. How would she know? We could use a normal person in the family. As I plodded around the lake, switching hands in my sweatshirt pocket to keep them warm, I thought about our first date. (The sacristy meetings don't count.) We were at the movie theater, sitting five rows behind Diane, with Max sandwiched between us until Billy sent him out for popcorn with a five-dollar bill. I don't remember the movie. Billy's tongue tasted like Junior Mints and Coca-Cola and the metal of his braces. His mouth seemed separate from him somehow, connected but not. I felt connected to him but not. The whole time we were kissing, I was wondering if he would say he loved me.

The heron won't show up at the lake if you're looking for him, so I kept my head down and watched my feet. "God Is, God Isn't, God Is, Isn't, Is, Isn't." My phone was vibrating against the warm hand in my sweatshirt pocket.

0920 hours Ms. Thibodeau receives a text message from a number she has recently identified in her iPhone address book as "SKANK."

Billy used to talk about you 24-7 but hes over it just saying ywsylsbfn[28]

---

28 You win some, you lose some. Bye for now.

0921 hours Text message from Ms. Thibodeau to SKANK:

wdalyic?????[29]

Transcript: I would have said more, but my fingers were freezing, so I put the machete under my arm and stuck both hands in my pocket. My hood blew off my head again, and when I looked up, I saw the heron.

He appeared bluer than usual, poised against the flat silver water, just a few yards ahead of me. I walked softly, hoping to catch a closer look at the strange web of beard he wore around his neck, but even though he didn't turn his head—he was much too cool for that—he knew where I was at every step. There were three or four ducks in the water, black and gray ones that missed the last flight to Florida, floating with their heads tucked under their wings. The heron seemed to be looking over their backs at something in the bleak limbs of the trees. A blue heron will never look straight at you. When he rose into the air with three soft flaps of his wings, it was as if he had been swept up by an invisible hand. Then he was gone.

0930 hours Ms. Thibodeau exits the Orchard neighborhood via Apple Lane and approaches Highway 11.

Transcript: The heron was ahead of me and behind me and ahead of me again, always appearing mysteriously from nowhere before disappearing with three wing beats into nothing. It seemed like more than one heron, but it never was. Poor lonely bird. This is what I was thinking: *Screw Billy. Hitchhike to Louisiana. Find Mr. Chief Lafontaine and settle the score.*

0935 hours Text message from Billy Starr:

29   Who died and left you in charge?

sry i haven't been in touch lost my phone r u ok?

0936 hours Ms. Thibodeau throws her phone into the street on Apple Lane and continues walking south toward Highway 11.

Transcript: I stood on the curb for a few minutes, looking at the sun. If the sun was rising in the east, which of course it was, then it should be on my left if I was heading south, to Louisiana. I had to cross the highway to catch a ride in the right direction, but there wasn't much traffic, mostly logging trucks.

0938 hours Ms. Thibodeau gestures to passing vehicles (sticks her thumb out).

0942 hours Clement P. Harris, of Waycross, Georgia, an employee of S&P Trucking, stops his vehicle and offers Ms. Thibodeau a ride.

Transcript: It takes trucks a long time to stop. I had to walk almost half a block to the place where the wheels finally stopped turning, and then I wasn't sure if the driver had stopped for me. Maybe he just stopped? This was my first time hitchhiking. I stood on the curb awhile, not sure what to do. The cab was actually pretty high off the ground, and I didn't want to climb up there and hang on the door like a monkey, especially if he hadn't stopped for me. I felt stupid, standing there, and I started to walk away. Suddenly, he leaned across the long seat and opened the passenger door.

"You want a ride?" he asked.

I thought, *No.* Diane says you should always listen to that first answer, the one that comes from your gut. My answer was definitely no, but I was embarrassed to say no after I had stuck my thumb out and followed the truck all the way to the point where it stopped, and then stood there until he had to open the door himself. I climbed up and got in.

He had fuzzy red hair. It came out in wisps under his cap, and in a scraggly beard. His eyebrows were red too. There were red hairs on the knuckles of the hand that gripped the wheel, no ring. He had almost no eyelashes, and his eyes were dilated, the way they are when the optometrist puts drops in them. An air freshener shaped like a cross hung from his rearview mirror.

"Where you headed, young lady?" he asked.

"Louisiana."

"Is that right?" He looked at me, too long, and I stuck my hands in the pocket of my hoodie, pulling it tighter around me. I held the machete between my knees.

"That's a mighty big knife you got there," he said. "That's damn near as big as you are." Then he started to laugh. I laughed too, which is a bad habit of mine, laughing at things that really aren't funny to make the other person feel like his joke was funny. So we were laughing, and he was looking at me so weird that I couldn't make myself into a small enough ball, when a horn honked.

0948 hours Penn MacGuffin arrives on the scene. 1989 green Mazda truck.

Transcript: "What the fuck," said the trucker. Penn had pulled up beside us even though there wasn't exactly a lane over there. His window was rolled down. He honked again.

"Yeah, buddy, what is it?" said the trucker through his window.

"Let her out," said Penn.

The trucker took a swallow of his Mountain Dew, rolled up the window, and hit the gas. We couldn't go very fast because we were going up a hill.

"Louisiana," he said slowly. "What's down there? Your boyfriend?"

"No," I said. "My boyfriend is in Boston. We broke up."

"Ain't that a shame." He lit a cigarette, not even asking me if I minded, but he rolled his window down when I started coughing.

There was Penn again, pulling up alongside us. He was actually driving on the median.

0955 hours The driver of the green truck passes the logging truck, on the median, and pulls across the highway, blocking the flow of traffic in both lanes. He steps out of the vehicle and approaches the logging truck, on the passenger side. He motions for Ms. Thibodeau to dismount the vehicle, but she remains inside the cab.

Transcript: I couldn't move. Penn must be able to see the gun, even though the trucker was holding it behind the Mountain Dew bottle. (Did he buy it at Walmart? Point at it through the glass case with his red-haired finger, drop it in the shopping cart? Attention, Walmart shoppers! Was he thinking, *Someday I might need this. I might need to put a bullet in someone's heart.*)

Now, the trucker had the Mountain Dew bottle in his left hand, the gun in his right. So if a car passed us, the gun was hidden. Penn kept walking toward us, straight into the barrel. When he opened the door on my side of the cab, he shouldered me out of the way. Now there was nothing between Penn and the gun.

"Walk to my truck, Aris," he said. "Get inside. Floorboard."

"Okay," I said, but I walked backward, slowly, with my machete in my hand. I couldn't turn my back on Penn.

"I'll kill you," said the trucker. He dropped the Mountain Dew bottle, revealing the gun, aimed at Penn's chest.

"I understand that," said Penn. "She's twelve."

The trucker was watching me walk backward through his windshield. Did he think I was older? Was he a child molester? Through the glare of the glass, his face looked like the red mask of a face, with nobody behind it. "If you ain't gone in two minutes," he told Penn, "I'll run right over your truck."

1000 hours Ms. Thibodeau and Mr. MacGuffin enter the green Mazda and make a U-turn on Highway 11, heading north.

Transcript: While I was in the floorboard of Penn's truck, my ears were frozen up, prepared for the sound of a gunshot. It didn't come. During the U-turn, it felt like we were going around and around, forever, but Penn is a good driver.

After a while, he said, "Coast is clear." I climbed back into the seat and fastened the seat belt. I tried not to look at him, so he wouldn't look at me, but I couldn't help it. His face was drawn up tight, and there was a strange, sharp smell to him. Thick blue veins stuck out on his hands as he clenched the steering wheel.

When we were back in the Orchard, driving down Apple Lane with the familiar small brick houses, the bikes in the driveways, the garbage cans on the street, Penn slowed the truck down. "That your phone in the middle of the street?" he asked.

I nodded.

"You stay IN THE CAR," he said. Then he got out to pick it up.

When he handed me the phone, I said, "You can smoke if you want."

"Damn right I can," he said, lighting a cigarette, but he rolled the window down. Turning onto Muscadine Circle, he said, "We're gonna loop around the lake and talk for a minute." The heron wasn't at the lake. Even the ducks had gone somewhere. The water was a flat gray disc.

"You okay?" he asked. "Did he touch you?"

"He didn't touch me."

"Were you hitchhiking?"

"Yes."

"That sombitch was on some high-speed chicken feed. Where is the ever-vigilant Chutiksee County Police Department when you need them? They'll catch him, though. The cops may be asleep when an armed driver picks up an underage girl, but they put the sirens on for a missing red flag on an object extending four feet beyond the bed of a vehicle." With one hand on the wheel, he reached into his back pocket and pulled out a tattered red square of cloth.

I wanted to ask him how he got the flag, but my phone started going boing, boing, boing in the pocket of my sweatshirt. That was Max's ring.

"Answer him," said Penn. "Tell him we'll be there in a minute." He picked up his lighter and put it back down. "Never mind. Give me the phone." He took the phone out of my hand. "We'll be there in a minute, Max," he said, and hung up. He shook his head at me. "Aris, where were you going, if you don't mind my asking, with a machete?"

"Houma, Louisiana? Where my dad is from?"

"I guess I don't need to tell you how absolutely fucking dangerous that was." He lit the second cigarette and then dug around under his seat until he found a dirty towel. "One corner of that is clean. I cannot stand to see a girl cry."

"Are you going to tell Diane?"

"No, I don't have to. You will."

"Do I have to?"

"No, but you will." We drove in silence while he blew his smoke out the window.

Then I cleared my throat, took a deep breath, and said, "Penn? I don't know how to say this, but about the weirdness between you and Diane?"

"What weirdness?" he said with a poker face.

"I mean, it didn't work out, right?"

"Can we talk about this some other time?"

"Sure," I said, but I was afraid there might not be another time. If Diane hadn't blown it with Penn, I certainly had. Who wants to be the dad of a girl who gets you caught at the wrong end of a gun?

As soon as we pulled into the driveway, Max dashed out the door. "Where were y'all?" he demanded, wiping his eyes on his sleeve. "Aris left me here alone. I called and called, and she wouldn't answer." He cast a suspicious glance at my hands. "Did you get ice cream without me?"

1020 hours Ms. Thibodeau enters her home at 17 Plum Lane. She is unharmed, but shaken. She reports paranormal activity in the living room: The empty rocking chair her parents made for her when she was a baby is in motion.

Transcript: All I wanted to do was hide in my room, but as I passed through the living room, I stopped. The room was dim, lit only by the weak winter sun, and eerily still except for the empty rocking chair, which was rocking. Was Joe here?

I locked myself in my room. Even though I could hear Penn banging on the playhouse in the backyard, and I knew that Diane would be home soon, nothing felt safe. Billy was finished with me, had been finished with me for a long time, probably ever since he moved to Boston. Diane had lost her job. I had scared away my PMI and probably just missed a gruesome death. I remembered the way the truck driver had looked at me with his empty eyes, and the red hairs on the backs of his hands—

Max's knock on my door sounded like a gunshot; I jumped.

"Go away," I yelled.

"You said you'd play Pokémon with me."

"Later."

"You said that this morning. You promised."

"Stop it!" I screamed. "Just stop it, stop it, stop it, stop it!"

There was a short silence. Then, through the wall that separates our bedrooms, I could hear Max talking to himself. "Stop it," he said, mimicking a girl's voice. "Stop it, stop it, stop it." In his own, calm, male voice, he said, "Stop what? I just invited you to play Pokémon. Is that a crime?" In the voice of someone else, he agreed with himself. "No, that is not a crime. Is she your sister? Really? Dude, I'm sorry."

I leaned my elbows on my dresser and stared into the mirror. There I was, a 12.5-year-old girl with frizzy hair and brown-not-violet eyes—a total stranger. I had stood on the highway with a machete, holding my thumb out. What was I going to do? Slice Mr. Lafontaine's head off with the machete? The blade wasn't even sharp. Was I crazy? I probably was crazy. Penn was right—I had to tell Diane what had happened. When I heard the dogs barking, and her voice as she opened the door, I was ready to tell her. She would listen. Holding my hand, she would say, *You hitchhiked? You were going where? Are you nuts? Dear God, Aris. Honey! He had a gun?* She would grab her phone and make me that appointment with Dr. Dhang.

The plan to spill my guts was foiled when Diane walked into the house with Charles. "Look who I found at Kroger," she said, beaming. They both had their arms full of grocery bags. When Penn came in from the backyard to help, she said, "Penn, this is Charles, my former student."

"Former?" said Charles.

"I'll explain in a minute," said Diane, flipping her bangs away from her eyes. "I hope you don't mind, Charles, but I've told Penn about your court case. He thinks it's awful." Penn and Charles reached around the bags in their arms to shake hands.

"That sucks, man," said Penn. "I'm sorry. I hope you can fight this."

"I invited him to come over here so we can do some final edits on his statement," said Diane.

"I appreciate your help," said Charles. "I've rewritten this thing so many times that I can't even see the words now. Nothing like this has ever happened to me before. I was going over the speed limit, but jail?"

"Once again, injustice prevails in Kanuga," said Penn.

"I don't know if you saw my picture in the paper. That really upset my mom. All my relatives were calling her."

"Isn't that illegal?" asked Diane. "You haven't been convicted."

"A human interest story," said Penn, squeezing the last bag onto the kitchen counter. Diane had apparently blown the grocery budget. We were laying up for a long season of deprivation with bags of frozen like-chicken nuggets, like-pork sausages, and like-beef patties.

Max pawed through the bags, looking for something edible. He opened a bag of raw almonds, took one out, licked it, grimaced, and put it back inside the bag.

"Max!" exclaimed Diane. "Don't do that."

"It was gross," explained Max.

"Now you have to eat every one of those raw, unsalted almonds," said Penn. "Until you find the one you licked. After that, we'll go bang some nails into that playhouse."

"Ms. Montgomery-Thibodeau," said Charles after they left, "I hope I didn't jeopardize your career."

"You can call me Diane now. I am no longer your teacher, and no, you didn't jeopardize my job. I quit, actually."

"That's a shame," said Charles. "It's a loss to KCC. You were a great teacher. I never thought about writing essays as anything more than a chore until I took your class. When you told us, on that first day, that if the writer who finishes the essay is the same person who started it, he has failed—I thought, man, this is going to be a tough A to earn. You changed me."

"You changed yourself, Charles. You took risks." She sighed the way she does before she gives a speech, and I cringed. Even when her orations are good, I cringe. "Your next teacher will find you," she said in a low voice. "Nobody knows when or how it happens. Prepare yourself and wait." Effective pause. When she resumed the speech, I started putting groceries away. As soon as Charles left, I planned to make my confession. However, before I could balance the last can of pinto beans onto the bean pyramid, Diane had him doing a freewrite at the kitchen table.

"I'll set the timer for three minutes," she was saying to poor Charles, "and you write without stopping. You remember this exercise from class. Write whatever comes into your head—anything. Write as fast as you can. Don't use punctuation. Keep your hand moving at all times. If nothing comes to your mind, just repeat the last word you wrote." She walked over to the stove and put her hand on the kitchen timer. "Whatever you do, don't stop. Ready?"

"Ready," said Charles, and his pencil started moving across the paper.

"Diane," I said. "I need to talk to you. I have something important to tell you." She glanced at the timer and then at Charles. "Okay," she said, motioning me away from the table so we would not disturb him.

"Is something wrong, Aris?" Her face was so dear to me at that moment—her mother face, with the sweet, worried eyes, the hopeful smile. *She can take it,* I told myself. *She can do this. She can take care of me. Diane,* I would say, *Merm. I did something stupid. I need your help.*

The kitchen timer went off.

"Ouch," said Charles. He leaned back in his chair, then stretched out his long fingers. He cracked his knuckles. "That was hard."

Penn opened the door. "Charles, I have a book I want to loan you. Or maybe you've read it—*Walls and Bars, Prisons and Prison Life in the 'Land of the Free,'* by Eugene Debs?"

"No, I haven't," said Charles. He smiled. "You carry that around with you?"

"Actually, I do. In my truck. I'm a goner if I ever get stopped. Of course, the cops would need a search warrant. No, wait—they wouldn't. Come on out to the truck with me, and I'll give it to you."

When they were gone, and Diane wasn't looking, I leaned over the kitchen table and began reading the memo pad.

> *Whatever you do don't stop stop stop blue lights flash-*
> *ing stop step out of the car hands up I said hands up*
> *in the air hes clean I dont care open the trunk shut up*
> *hands up hands behind your back back of the line for*
> *visitors yes sir hes my daddy my father who art in no*
> *sir yes sir you broke the law son dont you respect the*
> *law son son you grown on me hard on me life one week*
> *aint nothing boy you're just getting started*

"Aris! Are you reading Charles's freewrite?" Diane snatched the memo pad out of my hands and turned it facedown on the table. "I have taught you not to read other people's writing without their permission."

Where the hell did that come from? We were grading papers together a few days ago. Was I or was I not the co-parent in this family, an equal partner in the management of the Montgomery-Thibodeau enterprise? Did I even *want* this job? It had always been my life's goal to grow up. Every year, I came closer to achieving adult status—but now—I wasn't sure. I felt as if I had been crossing a long, narrow bridge and realized I might not want what was on the other side. I couldn't go forward, and I couldn't turn back. I thought this must be the place where people have nervous breakdowns.

I looked at Diane's outfit: gray leggings, white artist smock, gold bobby pins that disappeared into her blond hair, failing to hold anything back. Nails filed down for working hands. Eyes played down, lips played up to emphasize the desire to communicate. We were at a new beginning, and oh, how she loved beginnings. This was a prologue to a new book. It was all about starting over on bright, clean pages. The possibilities stretched into the horizon. We would never get to chapter one.

Outside, Charles had joined Penn and Max on the renovation site. Bang, bang, bang went the hammers. Suddenly, they stopped. Penn was telling Charles something. Charles was telling him something back. They both shook their heads and laughed. The hammers were making a song now: bangbangbang bangety-bang-bang.

"Diane," I said, "we're not going to make it this time."

"I have some ideas," she said. "I can start a business."

"Doing what?"

"I was thinking about becoming a professional organizer."

"Really?"

"Really."

Her voice was tight with self-control, but I had to push it. "Cleaning out people's closets? Taking their stuff to the Salvation Army?" I lost it. "Diane, what are you going to *do*?"

"Do about what?"

"Your life," I said quietly. "Our lives."

Diane decided to blip out on this conversation. "Well," she said, as if everything were normal, "I'm going to start something for dinner. Remember, Papa and Grandma are coming over tonight for their anniversary. I thought I'd try a soufflé, or maybe—"

"Diane," I said, "you are unemployed."

"Okay," she said, crossing her arms over her chest. "I know that."

"We are stuck," I said. "Don't you see that?"

I had never said this to her before. I had never expressed my lack of faith in our ability to survive. I had been the strong one, the voice of hope, but all that was gone now. I knew how dangerous it was for me to abandon her like this. An alcoholic might remain sober for twenty years, and then bam! One drink leads to the bottle, which leads to the case, and Defax is at the door. I had heard this story a hundred times in AA meetings.

"This may look like an ending," said Diane, "but it is actually a new beginning. Sometimes, you have to close one door before a new one opens."

"Excuse me," I said. "I'm going to have a nervous breakdown."

"What?"

"How inconvenient of me," I said. "I know you don't have time for this. Even if you did have time, you aren't grounded enough to catch a falling star." Immediately, I wished I hadn't said "falling star" in that dramatic voice! She was probably thinking, *Bad poetry*, but the look on her face was pure bafflement.

"Call Kate's mom," I instructed. "Tell her I'm coming over because you're fed up to here, and you have a dinner party with your difficult parents."

"Aris, are you okay?"

"I'm fine. What's the matter with me?"

"You seem a bit fragile."

"It's probably just my hormones having a party," I said in my old reassuring voice, but it sounded false.

With a worried frown, she picked up her phone.

At Kate's front door, Diane said, "Aris seems a little tired and out of sorts. It's probably hormones."

"I know, I *know*," said Kate's mom. "Believe me. I have two tweens over here. Sometimes there's only so much you can take as a single parent."

"Well," said Diane, "I think I might be the problem. I quit my job."

"Oh no! I'm sorry. Or was that a good thing?"

I left them commiserating on the porch and found Kate in her room. Kate and her sister share a room because they all had to move in with her grandmother after the divorce, but there's an invisible line down the middle that we all respect.

"I *think* I'm having a nervous breakdown," I told Kate, "but I'm not sure." We were stretched out on our backs on her twin bed, head to toe, so we would both fit. "I don't actually feel nervous."

"You can be completely calm while having a nervous breakdown," said Kate. "It's a rather mysterious process."

Kate's sister was on the other bed, lining up Barbies for a session of speed dating with the only Ken in town. "Out of my way, bitch," said the second Barbie in line. "It's my turn."

Kate shot her a reproachful glance, but you're allowed to say whatever you want in the privacy of your own room—that was their rule. Kate's half of the ceiling was strung with Christmas tree lights. The lights reminded me of the Ghost Daddy sparks I hadn't seen in several days. What if I never saw him again, not even a spark of him? He hadn't been around much. Was he swept away (mostly) with the mad bomber hat? Or was I changing? I had been a cute little girl without a shadow side when he died. Maybe Mr. Lafontaine was once a cute little boy without a shadow side. Eventually, everyone eats fruit from the tree of knowledge of good and evil. You eat that apple and then you find yourself alone.

"What happens now?" I asked Kate.

"Well," she said, staring up at the ceiling, "that depends. Every culture has its own method of responding to a nervous breakdown. The Oglala Sioux Indians regard the event as an opening of the window into the spirit world, possibly the beginning of a career as a shaman. In the Middle East, where only women lose their minds—yeah, I know, who's writing history here, guys?—a drum ceremony called Zar placates the evil spirit. Koro is a Malaysian malady, brought on by stress, in which a man thinks his penis is shrinking back inside his body. The cure is to have friends and family members hold on to it. Believe it or not, this disease is contagious. Indigenous Canadian tribes dealt with an anxiety disorder called Windigo, in which a person was seized with the uncontrollable desire to eat everyone else, by burning him into a pile of ash. In our culture, Kanugian white middle class, we respond to crack-ups by ignoring them."

"You've been reading again," I said.

"It's never too soon to find your direction in life. I don't know if I want to be a linguistic anthropologist or a cultural anthropologist."

After a few minutes, she said, "I told you my mom has a new 'friend,' right?"

"Do you like him?"

"He totally creeps me out."

"He undresses her with his eyes," said Kate's sister.

"You too," said Kate.

On the other side of the room, two of the Barbies sidled over to the edge of Kate's sister's bed and started to whisper to each other and giggle. When Kate took her shoe off and threw it, the Barbies turned away and went creeping after Ken.

Silently, I began to cry. Kate handed me some toilet paper, and I blew my nose.

"You can talk whenever you're ready," she said, stretching her hands behind her head. Good old Kate. Dr. Dhang charges a hundred dollars an hour to do this.

I licked my salty lips and blubbered, "I am a huge, epic fail."

"I'm listening," said Kate.

"I read all of Diane's journals."

"Ah," said Kate.

"Then I mailed them out to people who had ordered books from her on the Internet."

"That is rather shocking," said Kate. "I'm not judging, just saying."

She glanced at the closed bedroom door. We could hear the tap-tap-tap of her mother's footsteps going up and down the hall as she talked to Mr. Friend on her cellphone. On the other side of the room, the Barbies had swarmed upon Ken in a fit of passion, and now he was missing a leg. Abruptly, they abandoned him, piling into their Jeep and driving off the side of the bed without a second glance at the man they were leaving crippled but smiling.

"Be right back," said Kate. "Nature calls." She went to the bathroom, where the walls were thinner and she could hear her mother's conversation better. While she was gone, my phone started beeping and buzzing like it was having an orgasm or something. When I looked at the screen, I figured the world was coming to an end—Billy had responded to a text I'd sent three weeks ago.

Then he responded to an email I had sent him around that time, outlining my plans for the novel.

He answered another text.

Then another email.

He was even answering texts like, "Watup?" He was opening links in my emails and thanking me for them, one after another.

When Kate returned, I said, "Billy is texting me. A lot."

"The Mayan end of the world isn't until December," she said, and looked over my shoulder.

> Sry for all the pain I caused you.

"What should I reply?"

"Count to five," said Kate. "Or maybe fifteen." She had opened a dresser drawer and taken out an oversized garment she calls her security sweater. It was navy blue and came to her knees. "Then maybe ask him if you can talk. Texting distorts reality, IMO."

"I don't want to talk to him," I said.

I sent him a Botox smiley (|:( ) Then he started blobbing on about how the long-distance thing just wasn't working for him. He hoped we could be friends, blob blob blob. I replied with a whatever, wry smile (:-1 :-7).

Two minutes later, Anders texted:

> Did Billy brk up w/u?

When I got home from Kate's house, I found Max alone at the kitchen table with *Vietnam—The True Story* propped up in front of him. He was reading as he attacked a whole rotisserie chicken that had been set before him. "Mom got it for me when she went back to the store to get some gold candles for the diamond jubilee," he said, clamping down on a chicken leg. "She said I could spoil my dinner."

Something was very wrong. I spotted the gold tablecloth folded neatly on the counter.

"Did she go in the attic?"

"Yumph," he said through the carcass in his mouth. Before I could get anything else out of him, Diane stormed into the kitchen, her face white, hair standing on end.[30] "Aristotle," she said between her teeth, "I'd like to speak to you alone for a moment. In my room."

The walls of Diane's bedroom are painted a color called Relaxing Green, which she chose for the name because it's not a great color. Her furnishings are minimalist: bed, desk, chair, with clothes organized in labeled boxes in the closet. Her incense smells like Penn after he's been chopping wood.

"Aristotle Thibodeau," she said, closing the door behind us. "Where are my journals?"

I made direct eye contact and was careful not to touch my nose, because studies show that liars tend to avert their eyes and touch their noses. "I dunno," I said.

Diane wasn't fooled. "You took them out of the attic," she said, putting her hands on her hips. "Where are they?"

The dogs began to bark. From the living room, Max hollered, "Grandma's here!"

---

30 Hyperbole #2. Sorry, but I have a deadline. Anyway, have you seen Diane's hair?

"Hello in there!" called Grandma, tapping on the window. She was wearing a metallic gold jacket, black pants, and lots of fake diamond jewelry. She carried her enormous pocketbook on one shoulder and held a newspaper article in her hand. After she rang the doorbell twice, she knocked on the door, which wasn't locked, making the dogs go berserk. Papa was still getting out of the car, which takes a while because he has to double-check to make sure everything is turned off. Then he has to get all the things Grandma left in the car and pick up any litter that might have accumulated on the fifteen-minute drive.

"Shit," said Diane, giving me one last frown before she checked herself in the mirror. Her hair wasn't combed, which would upset Grandma. I didn't comb mine either, to show support.

"Yoo-hoo!" Grandma called, opening the door herself. "Anybody home?"

Grandma is always fun at first. There are those sparkly moments when we are all bunched up in the hall while she tries to step over the dogs to get through the doorway with the enormous pocketbook. She talks nonstop, careering through a conversation like a car without brakes, bouncing over anything that gets in her way.

"I finished your quilt, Aris," she said. "Henry is bringing it inside. It took me six months to make that thing. I got so sick of it, I almost quit. I told my Sunday school class I was making a quilt about the story of your life, and they said, 'Well, that must be a little one.' I said, 'Ha! You don't know! That child has so many stories to tell I could have made a king size.'" She patted me on the shoulder. "I hope you like it, because I'm not making another one."

"Thank you, Grandma."

"Henry!" she yelled. "He's such a slowpoke. Move, dog, I can't get in the house. Diane, I brought you a newspaper article. I know you don't like us to bring you articles, but your father thinks you need to read this one. Henry, bring that quilt!"

Papa finally squeezed in the door behind her, grinning. His eyes were shining because he was so happy to see us. He hugged me and Max and then held us at arm's length to get a better look. "My goodness!" he exclaimed. "You are both growing like weeds!" He bent down to pet Lucky and Hiroshima. "How are my grandpups?" He told them they were fine dogs, so good and smart and well behaved. "Arf-arf-arf," he called out while they hopped around his feet.

"Henry!" Grandma yelled, even though he was only a few feet away from her. "Did you get my quilt out of the car? Henry! The story quilt I made for Aris. Do you have your hearing aid on?"

"Arf," Papa said quietly to Hiroshima, and then he looked up with wide blue eyes, as if coming out of a dream, and saw his wife of sixty years.

"Henry, where's that newspaper article?" she demanded.

"You have it," he said.

"No, I don't. Oh, here it is, in my hand. Diane, take this." She walked over to the stove, waving the newspaper, and tried to give it to Diane, who was now wearing oven mitts.

"Put it on the table," said Diane. Her words were clipped, as they usually are with Grandma, but she was looking at me. When Diane is angry, her eyes blaze into a supernatural green glow. In a horror movie, people would scream when she looked at them, but we were used to it.

"Your father and I want you to read the article," Grandma was saying. I know we're in trouble when she includes Papa in her directive; it gives her more clout. "It's about your student, and it mentions your name. That black boy they arrested. They don't know what all he did. It mentions your name, as his teacher. I know you don't get the paper, so you might not know about it. They're saying you tried to help him write something to get him out of trouble. Henry doesn't think you should get involved."

"What black boy?" asked Max.

"Honey," said Grandma. "That black boy in Diane's class. He was speeding in a BMW. An expensive car."

"Oh, you mean Charles," said Max. "He's not a boy. He's a man."

"Don't you start on me too! I can't take much more criticism."

"It doesn't matter what color he is," said Papa. "You don't want to do anything to jeopardize your job. You've got a family to support."

"Henry!" Grandma slammed the newspaper on top of the salad and glared at Papa.

"What?"

"Don't you do that." Papa didn't ask what he had done; he knew she would tell him. "You are just as racist as you can be," Grandma said. "Don't pretend it's all my fault."

"Why don't you go sit down," said Diane. "Dinner isn't ready."

"Aris, please go comb your hair. You look just like your mother." I glanced at Diane to see if she appreciated my messy-hair solidarity, but she was good and mad. When she opened the oven door, smoke poured out.

"You burned something," Grandma announced, as Papa went to look for one of the three fire extinguishers he had installed in our house. Luckily, it was too dark outside for him to see that Penn was turning the shed into a playhouse, which would make him ask about the future home of the lawn mower, and that potential fire hazard.

"There's not a fire," Diane called after him.

"That's not the point," he said when he came back. "There could be a fire, and you don't want to go all over the house looking for a fire extinguisher. You might not have time. Why, if this kitchen caught on fire—"

Diane dropped the blackened soufflé in the sink, removed her oven mitts, and took the newspaper article, "Kanuga Christian College Teacher Helps Student Write Defense for Arrest," from Grandma's outstretched hand. Then she wadded it up and threw it in the trash can. There was a sudden, rare moment of silence in our house.

"Well, I never!" said Grandma.

Diane stood firmly in front of the trash can, arms crossed over her chest.

That day my grandparents had officially endured each other for sixty years, but none of us could stay in the same room together another minute. I spread the new quilt on my bed. There, in Grandma's taut, angry stitches, was the story of my life. I had watched her sew while wearing her big reading glasses, sitting directly under the lamp. She frowned while she worked, and sometimes she drew the thread up and snapped it in two with her teeth. When she got to a hard part, she'd say, "I give up! I can't do this! I am going to throw this thing in the trash!" Then she would keep on working.

The quilt was beautiful. On a black background, a swoosh of green light from the aurora borealis in Alaska celebrated my birth. My stories were told in symbols: an angel for Joe, a heart for Max's birth, a cross for my baptism, and a star for my engagement to Billy Starr III. Diane was a white snowman on a square of black. Inside her snow-belly was a baby snowman, Max. A small snowman, me, stood beside her, and we held hands. Our helpless little hands were made of twigs. "Don't wallow on it," Grandma had warned me. "I wouldn't even put it out unless you have company."

When Diane came in my room, I was standing in front of the quilt like a visitor in a museum.

"I've ordered a pizza," she said, closing the door behind her. "Now, tell me what's going on." Then she sat on my bed, right smack down on the quilt. "Where are my journals?"

"Well, let me think . . . ," I said. I didn't know where to sit. Standing in front of her, I shifted my weight on my feet as she looked anxiously around my room.

"Sit down," she said.

Gingerly, I sat down beside her on the quilt.

"I mailed them to people," I said.

"People? Which *people*?" I can't describe her face, but I know that's my job, as the author, so—imagine a clown who has just stepped in a bucket of dead squirrels. Okay, I know that's gross. But her face was all stretched out and sort of caught between expressions.

"I put them in the mailers," I said, "to the people you were selling books to. When I filled the orders, I put a journal in each one." Quickly, I added, "I sent the books too."

"Okay," she said, staring at me with her mouth open. "You did that." She took a deep breath. "That's what you did. You mailed my most personal possessions to utter strangers."

I nodded, working on my breathing: *Breathing in, I calm my body, breathing out, I smile. Breathing in, I dwell in the present moment—*

"I suppose you read them," she said.

"Yes, ma'am."

"Good God." Leaning forward so that her elbows rested on her knees, she put her head in her hands.

"There's something else," I said.

"No," she said. "There can't be something else, Aris. This is it. This is enough." She took a few more deep breaths. "Okay, what is it?"

I tried to speak, but the words wouldn't come out. I felt myself walking through the cold that morning: Plum Lane, Peach Street, Muscadine Circle, Apple Lane, seeing Diane's child molester pushpins on the map as I switched the blade in my hands to keep one hand warm in the pocket where that damn phone shook and buzzed . . .

"What's going on here, Aris?"

"I dunno," I said. I looked down at our hands. We have pretty hands. She had one age spot on her left thumb, and she still wore Joe's ring. Finally, I confessed.

"I read 'Greensleeves.'"

"The song?"

"Your story. About Dad and Mr. Lafontaine, the child molester."

"Greensleeves," she said slowly. "Joe's story? Oh no!" She rolled over onto the quilt and pressed her face into it, holding her hands over her ears. Her feet (shoes on) were touching the aurora borealis.

"Merm?"

In the hallway, Grandma's voice rang out, "We did *not* order a pizza! You are mistaken."

Suddenly, she was rapping on the door, demanding to know why Diane was holed up in there with me when she needed to come out and make a decision about the pizza.

"I can't handle this," Diane said. She kicked her feet on Grandma's quilted heaven and punched the pillow. When Grandma knocked again, Diane sat up. In a cold, level voice, she said, "Mother. Go away." Grandma went nah nah nah, but Diane was determined. She put her arm around me and whispered, "Until you see an ax come through that door, we are safe."

"We aren't safe, Diane. The world is not a safe place."

"Because of Mr. Lafontaine?"

"Joe *thought* he was safe. Everybody *thought* Mr. Lafontaine was normal."

"I know. Maybe they still do."

"He should die!"

"Aris," said Diane, laying her hands over my tight fists. "Aris, what did you do?"

"I told you. I read your journals and mailed them to people."

"What else?" She stared me dead in the eye.

I had no choice. In the calmest voice I could muster, with as few details as possible, I related the events of my very short hitch-hike. "We only went about two miles," I said. "Penn was on his way over here when he saw me get in the truck, so he followed us. First he cut the red flag off the back, so the guy would get stopped by the police."

"A logging truck?" She looked at me the way I have seen Papa look at her sometimes, and said what he says to her: "Honey, you just don't have good sense."

It was strange, seeing Diane morph into Papa like that. We had entered into a time warp. I was Diane as a little girl. Diane was Papa. Everything was happening over and over, and in some weird way, we were all the same person, splitting and merging back together and splitting again.

"Where were you going?" asked Diane, suddenly herself again.

"I dunno," I said.

"Were you trying to go to Boston to see Billy?"

"At first, but then he broke up with me. He has another girl-friend, I think. Maybe. It's messy, okay?"

"You were going to find Mr. Lafontaine, weren't you? You were going to Houma, Louisiana, to find that man. You wanted to kill him."

"I'm sorry!" I cried, and I began to sob. "The world is evil, and I'm evil."

"Hush," she said, pulling me close.

"I wanted to kill him!"

"Aris—*I* wanted to kill him when I found out. I saw that dark side of myself—relishing the death of another human being."

"Maybe he'll go to hell," I said. "Do you believe in hell?"

She thought for a minute, chewing on her lip. "Hell is hating people," she said finally. Sighing, she stroked my hair. "I wish you didn't know about this."

"Maybe I'll forget about it?"

"Some people would," she said, pressing me tightly against her. We were so close that our hearts began to beat together. "Some people would refuse to see it in the first place. You're like me, though. We don't have thick filters. For a while, I thought I could drink to keep the world away from me—but that doesn't work very well."

"What can I do?" I asked, wiping my nose on my sleeve. "How can I stand it, Merm?"

"I don't really know what to tell you," she said, and her shoulders slumped. Her voice grew faint, and somehow, even though she still had her arm around me, she seemed further away. I saw the familiar confusion in her eyes, a harried, scared look—*I am a single mother I don't know what to do there is too much going on I can't handle this by myself*—

"Tell me *something*," I said. "You're my mother. You have to tell me something."

She blew her bangs out of her eyes. Then she sat up straighter, faced me squarely, and said, "Don't hitchhike." She pressed her hand firmly against my head as if she could speed my mental development along, perhaps shape my future. Softly, she added, "Please stay alive, Aris. I couldn't stand it if you died."

We leaned into each other, breathing together. Our thoughts were spiders scrabbling to build a new web. In the spaces between the thoughts, I tried to pray. *Our Father, who art in heaven*, I began, but I didn't want to think about fathers, and heaven seemed far away. When Diane got sober she was an atheist, so she prayed to a pink elephant. She said it worked. I imagined a medium-sized pink elephant in the corner where my dollhouse used to be and prayed, *Hello.*

Suddenly, I felt a cool current around me, as if I had hit a cold spot while swimming. When I opened my eyes, Joe was leaning against the bedroom door with his arms crossed over his chest, looking down at us with a mixture of exasperation and love. No, he wasn't gone forever.

"Well, *there* you are," said Grandma when Diane and I came back into the kitchen. "I thought this was supposed to be my anniversary party; I didn't know I was going to have to do everything."

Max, whose bangs were pinned back with a clothespin, had already opened the pizza boxes on the table. "Aris, Mom ordered us Cokes!"

"Your father paid for everything," said Grandma. "I thought you were cooking dinner for us, but I guess that didn't work out."

"I'll pay for the pizzas," said Diane.

"No!" cried Grandma and Papa at the same time.

"I don't mind paying for the pizza," said Papa. "I want to pay for it."

When we were all seated at the table, Diane raised her glass of Diet Coke with a trembling arm and said, "A toast. To sixty years of grit."

"Har-har," said Papa, grinning. He kissed Grandma and launched into the old story of their romance. They had a class together in college, and she was the prettiest girl in it. She sat in the front and made As. He sat in the back until he started dating her, and then he made As too. He had dated another girl before Grandma, but she was *too* smart. *That* girl could just look at a book—

"I guess we'll make it another day," Grandma said, and we all clinked our glasses.

Twenty minutes later, the refined carbohydrates had sent Max into a tailspin. He sat in a sea of Legos on the living room floor, still determined to practice building Legos for the talent show. Grandma got the camera out.

"Don't spread them out so much," Papa said. "You're going to lose those tiny little pieces."

"Leave him alone, Henry," said Grandma. "He's creating. Max, what are you going to do for the talent show?"

"I'm doing it," Max said.

"What are you doing, honey?"

"I'm building a starship." He snapped on a Lego the size of my little finger.

"I can't see anything," said Grandma.

"Max," said Diane gently. "Honey—"

"Oh Jesus," I said. "Are we doing this again?"

"All right, that's it!" screamed Max. "That's final!" He jumped up and threw the Legos against the wall. "I don't have a talent! See? I'm stupid. I'm dumb. I am not going to the stupid, dumb talent show." Tears streamed down his face. He kicked the coffee table, then started slapping himself. Diane took a deep breath and did what Dr. Dhang has been telling her to do all along.

"Max, if you hit yourself again, I'm putting you in time-out."

Max socked himself in the stomach.

"Eight minutes," said Diane. She set the timer, one minute for every year of his life, and Max went to time-out in the laundry room, dragging Lucky and Hiroshima with him. After a couple of body slams to the closed laundry room door, he was quiet.

"Diane, I don't think you should lock him up like that," said Grandma. "He might hurt himself."

"He doesn't hit himself without an audience," Diane said wearily.

In the laundry room, Max was saying, "Sit. Now, lie down. Roll over. No, Lucky, not like that. Roll *over*! No treat for you, Hiroshima. Try again."

"Let him out of there, Diane," said Grandma. "I want to say goodbye."

"The timer has to go off," I said.

"Speak!" called Max from the laundry room. There was a sharp bark; then the timer went off, and Max was out on parole. He swaggered into the living room, pockets stuffed with Pup-Peroni treats, Lucky and Hiroshima at his heels.

"Ladies and gentlemen," said Max, striding to the center of the rug. "You will now witness a miracle." Holding out a Pup-Peroni, he issued an imperious command for Hiroshima to sit. "Now, shake," said Max. Hiroshima, looking up at him with bright expectation, raised a paw to Max's outstretched hand.

"Now, that's a talent," said Papa.

"Whose talent?" said Grandma. "His or the dog's?"

"Ignore her," said Diane. "You've got an act, buddy."

"Don't ignore me," said Grandma. For a split second she

228 · *Melanie Sumner*

looked stricken. Then she gathered her giant pocketbook, which is always spilling something out, and stood up. "Henry," she said, "they're tired of us. Let's go. Hurry up."

Papa did what he usually does when Grandma tells him to hurry. He killed time. While she shot him evil looks, he did this, and he did that, and then he took the trash outside. A few minutes later, he returned with the newspaper article he had retrieved from the trash. He smoothed it out and set it on the kitchen table. Then he wrote a check for eight hundred dollars, clipping it to the article so Diane would be sure to read it this time before she threw it out.

The Chutiksee County courthouse sits in the middle of the cotton block in historic downtown Kanuga, a brick pavilion where cotton, slaves, and sometimes bad wives were once put up for auction. All that has changed now, of course. Except for the ten-foot statue of Nathan Bedford Forrest, founder and grand wizard of the Ku Klux Klan, who sits on a horse in front of the courthouse, you would never know that racism once existed in Kanuga.

Inside the thick walls of the courthouse, the cool, moist air smells of crumbling brick. A woman at the front desk, wearing glasses on a chain, was eating potato chips when the heavy doors closed behind us. Diane waited for her to finish chewing before she asked for directions. Meanwhile, Max and I were peering everywhere, looking for criminals.

"That's municipal," the woman said at last, dabbing at the corners of her mouth with a Kleenex. "First door to your right, past security." After we were wanded, a process that Max and I handled more smoothly than Diane, we entered a long room filled with tall, old-fashioned windows. On a raised platform, flanked by an American flag and the Georgia state flag, an upholstered leatherette chair had been reserved for the judge. A railing separated him from We-the-People, who sat in molded plastic chairs. Charles and his mother were already seated.

"Mama, this is my teacher, Ms. Montgomery-Thibodeau," said Charles as he stood up.

Miss Octavia stood up too, a head taller than Diane, a hundred pounds heavier. She wore a skirt and blazer with panty hose and pumps, accessorized with a long strand of pearls and matching earrings. Her glossy black hair was straightened into a pageboy; it didn't move when she bent over to exchange a formal little hug with Diane.

We had decided on a little black dress for Diane, one that should have transitioned from cocktail to courtroom with flats and a blazer. Unfortunately, Diane didn't have a real blazer. In the glare of the courtroom light, I could see now that the jean jacket she called conservative, because it wasn't faded, wasn't our best choice. It covered the spaghetti straps of the cocktail dress but did nothing to hide the cleavage. Instead of panty hose, she wore black tights, and her flats were actually ballet shoes. The whole outfit screamed "HIPSTER."

My ears grew hot as Charles's mother looked her over, but Miss Octavia smiled, showing the gold tooth in the back of her mouth, and said, "Charles and I really appreciate the help you've been giving him on his statement. You have gone above and beyond for my son."

"Charles is a fine young man," said Diane. "He's one of my best students. This charge is completely unfounded."

Miss Octavia smiled warily and took her seat. Sitting by her side, I could see the brown rim of her eyes around her purple contact lenses.

Charles wore a dark suit and a pale yellow tie, no hat. As we learned when Penn entered the room, hats are not allowed in a court of law. The bailiff gestured angrily for Penn to remove his hat. When he did, I tried not to stare at his shiny bald head— definitely a new look.

When everyone had taken their seats, the bailiff said, "All rise. The Municipal Court of Chutiksee County, State of Georgia, is now in session, the Honorable Burr Wiglett, presiding." His Honor, a short white man whose robe trailed on the ground, entered the room and settled into the big chair.

"The court will now come to order," Burr Wiglett said in a weary voice, and tapped his gavel. He had serious bags under his eyes. As his voice droned on through a stack of requests for post-ponements, unlitigated motions, and arraignments, my mind wandered to the last Charles Hutchins essay I had graded for Diane.

Charles Hutchins
English 1102

Descriptive Essay: My Elephant

"I saw the elephant" is an old army expression that means, "I saw combat." Two years ago, at the age of nineteen, when I was called into active duty in the United States Army, I saw my elephant. I never thought I could describe this, but I will try.

War is loud. This is something I didn't think about before I found myself in the Pech Valley in Afghanistan—the ricochet of artillery, the thud of mortar rounds, the head-ringing explosion of rockets, all going over the sirens and static call of Big Voice, the loudspeaker on base: "Exercise, exercise, exercise. IED detected outside the wire. Take cover, take cover."

Outside the wire, the radio was blaring, "Contact, contact, Blue 4, where are you? Mortars, three KIA, seven WIA. Black on fuel, ammo." I flipped the safety off my M4 and ran to the zone, zigzagging down a dusty road lined with cornfields. The stalks were tall and bright green.

Back in Georgia, I had helped my grandmother with her gar-den. Close to harvesttime, she would send me out in the maze to find the cobs with dry corn silk—mother's hair, she called it. The corn wasn't ready until the hair on top was thick and dry, but my Mee-mee always picked a few early ears, with the shiny, silky yellow hair she used to make a tea for her arthritis. When I

So I wrote some comments in the text, but I erased them. After reading this essay, several times, they sounded stupid. It's an A paper, with as many +++++++ as there are stars in the sky.

squeezed those early ears, sometimes a thin, white milk seeped between my fingers, and I thought of her stiff, crooked fingers, the relief of pain.

The green seemed brighter out here, where everything else was the color of dust—moon dust we called it. It feels like flour, like you are covered in flour. It covered our uniforms and weapons, our bedding, our food; we breathed it.

He came through the corn, almost on me before I saw his arm raised. Was it an IED or just a rock? I never think, was his arm raised in surrender? You think that, and you die. I fired. There was a sickening moment when all the noise around me seemed to stop. No sound but his grunt. His brains had blown out the back of his head. But that's not the image that kept going through my mind as I tried to rack out in my bunk that night, or every night afterward. What I saw, and what I can't forget for some reason—my elephant—was corn silk, the shiny yellow stuff dripping with milk, on the ears that weren't ready to be picked.

When Penn touched my shoulder, I jumped. Then I looked at the window, where he inclined his head. Outside, in the parking lot, a group of men wearing orange jumpsuits were filing into a Chutiksee County Prison Work van. I recognized the fuzzy red hair of the guy who had picked me up in his logging truck.

"Red flag violation will get you stopped every time," whispered Penn. "Not a good idea to be high then."

Diane glanced over at us, then looked away before Penn could meet her eye. I sensed some tension, but I couldn't pinpoint exactly where we were in that relationship. Initial attraction—check. First rejection—check. Jealousy revealed—check.

"Charles Hutchins," announced the bailiff.

The judge motioned to a police officer who had been sitting off to the side of the room. At the podium, the two men bent their heads together, conferring in mumbled voices.

"What the fuck?" whispered Penn.

Charles's long fingers picked nervously at the edges of the

statement he held on his lap, printed out on crisp white paper. A second cop was summoned to the podium. More mumbling.

"Guess that's the witness," said Penn. "He's invited to the pow-wow." He leaned forward in his seat, fists clenched. "Maybe the rest of us should just leave. This seems to be a private party." The bailiff gave him the stink eye.

Miss Octavia sat perfectly still in her seat, her hands folded in her lap. Her lipstick was perfect. You could not tell from looking at her face that her husband was serving a life sentence for first-degree murder or that her son was on trial, so to speak, for a speeding ticket that would most likely result in a week of jail time.

When Charles was called to the stand, he towered over the two officers who had arrested him. Judge Burr Wiglett had to crane his neck to look up at him from his seat. When the judge put on a pair of reading glasses and bent his head down to read the paper in front of him, a wattle of chicken skin settled around his jaw. Charles tried to hand him his statement, but the judge waved it away.

With a shaking hand, Charles held on to his statement. He shifted from one foot to the other. When the judge spoke to him, Charles had trouble finding his voice. His Adam's apple bobbed up in his neck, and his eyes had a wild, hunted look as he searched the room for his mother.

"Look at me when I'm talking to you," said the judge. "What's that in your hand?"

Up and down went the Adam's apple. Charles cleared his throat. "I wrote a statement," he said, holding the paper out, but no one stepped forward to take it from his hand.

"Does the defendant have counsel?" asked the judge.

The two officers looked at each other. One of them shrugged. The lawyer had dropped the case because Octavia couldn't afford his fees.

"Sir," said Charles. "Your Honor. I have written a statement in my own defense. If the court would please, if I have permission, I would like to read it."

"How long is it?" asked the judge. Charles fumbled with the document. He dropped it, picked it up, and dropped it again. "Ten pages," he said quietly. "Or eleven?"

"It's only five!" whispered Diane.

"How fast were you going on the evening of February first, in a fifty-five-mile-per-hour zone?" asked the judge.

Charles swallowed. "Around sixty," he said.

"Correction," said the police officer. "Your Honor, the defendant was clocked at sixty-three miles an hour." He showed the judge a document, and the judge nodded.

"Correction sustained." He looked up at Charles, who was shaking from head to foot, smiling erratically. "Young man," he said, "I understand that you are a student at Kanuga Christian College."

"Yes, sir. Yes, Your Honor."

"Now, KCC is a fine institution. My daughter graduated from there, and several of our friends' children as well. As you might expect, I am no stranger to the classroom. I hold several degrees from very fine schools. I believe in education. However, I also believe in the brevity of truth. At the time you were clocked by these officers at a speed of sixty-three miles an hour, were you on your way to a hospital?"

"No, sir."

"No one was in the backseat of the car about to have a baby?" A thin ripple of laughter lifted through the room and was immediately hushed.

"No, sir."

"You weren't fleeing a fire, were you?"

"No, sir."

"No tornado chasing you?"

"No, sir."

"No lion or tiger or bear, I presume." The judge shuffled through a folder. "From your records, I don't have any reason to believe that you were fleeing the scene of a crime."

"No, sir."

"Well, all right, then, Mr. Hutchins. Since we have verified that there was no practical reason for you to be driving your vehicle—a BMW, I believe it was?—over the speed limit determined by our lawmakers, I see no reason for the court to listen to a ten-page excuse."

"Objection," said Penn, standing up. Immediately, the bailiff took a step forward, his hand on his gun.

"Sir," said the judge. His voice was deep and loud now, his eyes bright with anger. "Have you been sworn in by the court?"

"No," said Penn.

"Then you have no right to speak. Sit down!"

Penn remained standing. With a flick of his head, the judge indicated to the guard that Penn was no longer welcome in his courtroom. Before he was escorted to the door, Penn put his hat back on. He gave Charles a thumbs-up, and then he was gone.

The judge shook his head and looked once more at his folder. In a weary voice, he said, "Charles, the court finds you guilty of exceeding the speed limit by almost ten miles per hour. Since you are a student in good standing at Kanuga Christian College, with no previous criminal record, I will recommend that the usual sentence be suspended, that you are only required to serve one week in jail, and that this term be arranged in accordance with your academic schedule, so that you don't miss any classes. I think spring break would be appropriate." He tapped his gavel again. "Court dismissed."

We found Penn outside, stubbing a cigarette out on the statue of Nathan Bedford Forrest. "You are in a position to free this country," he told Charles, who was crying. Miss Octavia found a tissue in her purse and gave it to him, but she remained standing straight and tall beside him, looking at no one, saying nothing.

"This speeding charge is an illicit conviction," Penn said.

236 • *Melanie Sumner*

"Penn is right, Charles," said Diane. "We're not done here. I think you might keep a journal while you are incarcerated and submit an article to the *Kanuga News and Observer*."

"You can fight this," said Penn. "Take it to a higher court. That whole circus in there was illegal."

Charles blew his nose and tried a joke. "I guess I could call it 'What I Did Over Spring Break.'"

"I know this is tough," said Diane, "but I think you need to write about your dad."

Miss Octavia frowned, but Diane missed that cue.

"This is a crossroads for you," Diane continued earnestly. "It's unfair, but it's a chance for you to examine the choices people make while in the grip of injustice—"

"Excuse me?" interrupted Miss Octavia. "Whose 'dad' is this in reference to?"

"I'm talking about Charles's father," said Diane.

"Then you are talking about my husband," said Miss Octavia. "And you are talking about a subject of which you know nothing."

Nervously, Diane fingered the buttons of her denim jacket. "Charles mentioned his father in a few essays he wrote for me this year."

Miss Octavia turned to her son. "What the hell is she talking about?"

"Let me explain, Mama," said Charles. "Don't get mad."

"Ain't nobody mad," said Miss Octavia.

"His writing has a lucidity and honesty that eludes most of my students," said Diane. "Some things he writes *are* disturbing, and I admire the courage—"

"Was I talking to you?" said Miss Octavia.

Diane took a step back. Charles sucked his cheeks in, let out a long breath, and said, "Mama, Ms. Montgomery-Thibodeau just wants us to stop writing what we think people want to hear and write what we need to say."

"Charles's writing has improved dramatically this year," said

Diane. "The students"—her voice faltered as Miss Octavia faced her with her arms crossed over her chest—"they are fascinated with his telling of experience. He's discovering his story."

"*His* story?" said Miss Octavia. By now, she had eaten her lipstick off, and one wedge of hair had come unsprayed. When she reached out and shook her finger in Diane's face, the rope of pearls swung across her bosom. "Charles's life isn't a story for your class, Ms. Montgomery-Thibodeau. My family isn't a *cause* for you to get behind so you can wave your flag and say, 'I helped those poor black people.'"

"Mama, she didn't mean it that way," Charles said, but Miss Octavia wasn't hearing arguments.

"Charles is *my* son!" she shouted. "This story is *our* story, and it is *private!*" With that, she turned and stomped away in her high heels, clutching her bag tightly under one arm.

Charles called Diane the next day, the day of Max's talent show, to thank her for coming to the trial. I could tell he was trying to apologize for Miss Octavia's wrath, because Diane kept saying into the phone, "Believe me, I understand how protective mothers can feel about their sons." She did not mention that she had bawled all the way home from the courthouse and then crawled into bed with a stack of my *Seventeen* magazines and a jar of peanut butter. She definitely does not have a thick filter.

On the other hand, maybe she did understand Miss Octavia's desire to protect her son. Diane had been mollycoddling Max since he woke us up that morning with the bugle call of "I can't go to the talent show! I'm sick!" She took his temperature, looked in his ears and down his throat, inquired about his poop, and diagnosed him with stage fright. He did the *I am a failure* routine before and after breakfast and again after school. He tried it again at dinner, but he couldn't get much bandwidth because Grandma was calling us every few minutes to remind us not to be late.

Although we were not late, Grandma and Papa had been wait-ing for thirty minutes when we arrived, so we *seemed* late. Even though the auditorium was still empty, Grandma had saved our seats by weaving her long orange scarf through the chairs.

"You didn't bring Penn," she said as we untied the scarf. "I thought he was supposed to help."

"He might be busy," said Diane.

"Busy?" said Grandma, narrowing her eyes suspiciously. "Where are the dogs?"

"They're in the car with the window down," said Diane.

"Who's going to bring the dogs backstage?" asked Papa.

"Henry! We were just talking about that. Penn is supposed to be here, and he's late."

"Penn?" he said.

"Yes, Penn," she said loudly. "Diane's man-friend. He's not her boyfriend, I guess. I don't know. She never tells us anything."

Diane ignored her. Pointedly.

"Well, if he's not here in ten minutes, it will be too late," said Grandma.

"Too late?" cried Max. "You mean I'm going to fail?" He was so nervous he had thrown up in the car, right after the dogs did. "I don't think I can do this," he said. "My stomach hurts."

"It's just nerves, honey," said Diane. "Take a deep breath. Remember what I taught you? Breathing in, I calm my body. Breathing out, I smile."

He breathed in, gasping, and then exhaled like he was trying to put a fire out. That's when I noticed his breath.

"Oh Lord," I said. "He's been eating the dog biscuits."

"I have not!" he cried, and clamped his mouth shut. There were crumbs in the corners of his mouth.

"You should feed him meat," said Grandma. "I'd eat dog bis-cuits too, if I had to be a vegetarian." Then she heaved her pocket-book onto her lap, put her glasses on, and dug around until she found two peppermints good for dog-biscuit breath.

"I'm walking Max backstage now," said Diane, taking Max by

the hand. You could see the commands she had written on his forearm: "Sit Stay Shake Roll Over," and a new one they had practiced, "Wobble." His pockets were stuffed with Pup-Peronis.

"Penn isn't coming," Grandma said, looking at her watch. To distract herself, she asked me about Billy.

"We broke up," I said. It felt weird saying it aloud.

Grandma wanted to know if Billy had found another girlfriend in Massachusetts.

"He wouldn't find one cuter than Aris," said Papa. "That's for sure." He made a face. Papa's opinion of males who seek the attention of females in his family isn't exactly low. It's neutral. It's a certain kind of neutral, though. One wrong move from the suitor, and Papa is ready with contempt and the satisfaction of being right in the first place. Papa is more complicated than he lets on.

Anders came over to say hello. He complimented Grandma on her scarf and shook hands with Papa, looking him directly in the eye and calling him "sir." He expressed an interest in Max's talent. For an instant, I saw Anders in a positive light, but then, when no one was looking, he planted his heel firmly into my toes, grinning his evil grin.

"You are depriving some village of an idiot," I told him before he dashed off to his seat.

"What a sweet boy," said Grandma. "Is that his father over there? He's a nice-looking man. That's the one whose wife ran off. I don't know what her problem was. I can't think of their names to save my life."

Just then, Penn appeared. He came in through the back door, wearing his *Best Nanny Ever* T-shirt and a woman on his arm. At the same time, Diane entered the auditorium from the stage door. They were like balls rolling toward us from different directions, a Penn-and-the-other-woman ball and a Diane ball. Grandma was excited. Her head turned toward Diane, back to Penn and his friend, back to Diane again, and finally to me.

"Who is that girl with him?" she asked, as if I should know.

From the podium, Mrs. Waller suggested that if everyone

would please take their seats, we might get started. Leaning over the back of Diane's chair, Penn whispered, "Bad news. The dogs are gone. The back hatch is open, and the crate is unzipped."

"Someone stole the dogs!" said Grandma. "Max is going to be heartbroken."

"Don't worry," said Penn. "I'll find them before he goes on."

"I'm Max's grandmother," Grandma said to the woman Penn had dragged in from God knows where. They did the southern-female handclasp. "What's your name?"

Her name was Cynthia. Grandma smiled at Cynthia, awaiting further clarification.

Before Cynthia could define her role in Penn's life, the lights dimmed, and the curtain rose. I was terrified that Max would be standing under a spotlight without his dogs, but it was just the principal, yammering on about how thankful he was for this talented bunch of third graders, their hardworking teachers, and, of course, the supportive families. He pointed out, as he always does, that here at Lavender Mountain Laboratory School, we *are* a family.

Across the room, Anders was trying to catch my attention. *I'm sorry about Billy,* he mouthed, then put his hand over his heart.

"I don't know who would have opened that car and let the dogs out," said Grandma.

Suddenly, it came to me. Anders! Anders Anderson did it! Excuse me for the purple prose, but sometimes you have to do it: A bitter bile of hatred rose in my throat, foreshadowing the anger that exploded from the clenched fist of my heart to shatter his leering, satanic visage like a CBU-59 Rockeye II bomb blasting a rotten egg that someone had balanced on a whipping post. I craned my neck to find that foot-stomping, dog-stealing, horny little bastard and shoot him the bird. A lady with big hair blocked my view.

While we were clapping for Hammond Golden's tae kwon do demonstration, Penn slipped out to look for the dogs. When he returned, he whispered, "No joy."

"Max is next!" I said.

Penn left again, to look for the dogs in the woods, and I settled reluctantly into my seat to listen to Madison Fuller's pained performance on the violin. Grandma took this opportunity to establish a rapport between Cynthia and Diane, who had been ignoring each other.

"Diane," she said, tapping her firmly on the shoulder. "Have you met Cynthia?" Diane and Cynthia fake smiled at each other. Raising her voice to be heard over the noise of Madison's bow raking across the violin strings, Grandma pointed out everything Cynthia and Diane had in common, which included living in Kanuga and knowing Penn.

Diane told Grandma to hush. While they grimaced at each other over Cynthia's head, Cynthia opened her purse and took out a small pink compact of lip gloss. She peered into the tiny mirror, holding her mouth open as she applied the gloss with a miniature brush. Then she smoothed her hair, which was perfectly coiffed.

In comparison, Diane looked a little rough. Her bun had already sprung a leak, and her face was gray with worry. I rummaged through her purse for a lipstick, but there was nothing besides a wallet, a phone, and a book of to-do lists.

"Max will be okay," I whispered. She nodded, biting her lip.

"How did you meet Penn?" Grandma asked Cynthia.

"We're neighbors," Cynthia whispered, blushing as she glanced warily at Diane. "His car broke down, so I gave him a ride."

Immediately, I texted Kate.

SKANK Alert!

Madison finished her solo. In the brief pause before the audience rose from their seats to clap, Grandma announced, "That girl needs a lesson." I tried not to imagine what kind of trick Max would make up on the spur of the moment, without the dogs, and how the audience might stand up and clap in the same terrible way.

Returning to the auditorium, Penn shook his head at us and

lifted his empty hands. When Cynthia whispered something to him, she put her hand on his knee! I wanted to tell her that Penn only touches dogs, but the curtain was rising on Max.

"And now," announced Mrs. Waller from the podium, pausing to shake the static out of the mic. "Now I would like to present our very own Max Thibodeau and his two dogs, Lucky and"—she looked down at the paper in her hand—"Hiro?" Pushing her glasses up on her nose, she tried again. "Hiroshima?" She cocked her head. "Did I get that right? Your dog's name is Hiroshima?" A ripple of laughter ran through the audience.

Max stood alone on the stage, looking down at his feet. The technician was moving the spotlight around him, hoping to find some dogs. At last, the light encircled just Max. Normally, Max seems like a big person because he's loud. Silent Max alone on a stage was a small boy. Although I had picked out a dashing outfit for him to wear for the performance, he'd ditched it in favor of navy blue pants and a black shirt, with the traditional dab of toothpaste over his heart.

Max said something inaudible.

"Uh-oh," said Grandma.

All around me, people were shifting in their seats, rustling their programs, clearing their throats. It was the kind of tension that would make Max scream, throw himself to the ground, and slam his head against the floor. My chest tightened. Beside me, Diane wasn't even breathing.

However, Mrs. Kierkegaard, our kindergarten teacher, had heard Max. She appeared onstage with a chair. After a whispered consultation with Max, she turned to the audience, tucked her hair behind one ear, and smiled with her pretty white teeth.

In her public announcement voice, she informed us that we were going to witness an unusual performance by Max Thibodeau. Moving the mic away from her face, she had another brief, whispered consultation with Max. While they conferred, he took his hands in and out of his pockets, scratched his head, and looked desperately at the ceiling, but she kept nodding her head and smiling. Finally, she straightened up and said into the mic, "Ladies and gentlemen, this is Max, one of my all-time favorite students. He is going to do something utterly, astonishingly wonderful." She said this with such authority that even Grandma was quiet. "What you are about to see might look easy, but believe me, it's not." She glanced at Max, and then back to us. "Max," she said, "is going to meditate."

Max sat in the chair. His feet hung several inches off the floor, and for a moment he didn't know what to do with his hands. Then he remembered how to hold them out in front of him in the shape of an egg. At first, there was some nervous shuffling in the audience. A baby whimpered.

"Someone needs to cut those bangs," said Grandma, but we shushed her. Max sat absolutely still as his spirit entered the egg shape in his hands. Under the spotlight, his round face became a white moon, all aglow. You could almost see inside of it. As we watched, somewhere deep inside of Max, the choppy waves of self met the hard world, and Max grew calm. How did this happen? The glow didn't surprise me as much as the sitting still.

I set the timer on my phone. One minute, one and a half minutes, two minutes. Max was still. Three minutes. I smelled the lip gloss of Cynthia. Three and a half minutes. In his chair on the stage, Max was a lighted sculpture. Four minutes . . .

"Henry," said Grandma, "I gave that camera to you. Where is it?"

Henry shook his head.

"Yes, I did too!" She rummaged through her purse. "Oh, here it is!"

She got a picture, but it just looks like a boy in a chair.

At the reception for the talent show, we had to stand in line to talk to Max. When we finally got close enough to touch him, Mrs. Kierkegaard stepped in front of us.

"Excuse me," she said, "but I have to tell this child how absolutely amazing he is." She put her hands on his shoulders, turning him to face her. "Max, you are absolutely amazing. In my twenty-seven years of teaching, I have never, EVER seen a child sit still and actually meditate for a talent show."

Nibbling on the edge of a cookie, Max looked up at her with the serenity of a cow.

"I raised him," said Grandma, edging in close. "I helped raise him."

Diane rolled her eyes, but before all claims of ownership were staked, Anders tugged on my arm.

"Do not touch me," I said. "Ever."

"Well, excuuuuse me. I only wanted to tell you that your *nanny* found your dogs."

"Oh, really? After *you* let them loose?"

"What are you talking about? I didn't touch your dogs."

"Um, excuse me," said Max.

"You did too! You opened the car and let them loose so Max wouldn't have a performance."

"Hello," said Max. "A word, please."

"Why would I do a mean thing like that?" Anders asked.

"Because you are a horrible person. I'm sure there is a more accurate word for you, but I am too mad to find it right now, and it doesn't matter because you are now officially out of my novel!"

"What?" Anders looked at me with wide eyes, his cheeks bright red. Angrily, he jammed a package into my hand. "No nuts," he said. "Because you are one." Then he ran out of the room.

"Chocolates!" cried Max. "Can I have one?"

"Throw them out," I said. "They're probably poisonous."

"Aris?"

"What is it, Max? I'm busy hating someone."

"Anders didn't let the dogs out." He offered me a dangerously charming smile.

"Max," I said sternly. "What did you do?"

"It was an accident! I swear! I was tired of waiting for Penn, so I went to the car to get them myself. Then I saw a deer. A huge one. I don't know *how* this happened, but while I was trying to grab Hiroshima's collar, Lucky sailed over my head. I'm not kidding. She was flying. Like a pterodactyl. We should probably put her in a dog show or something. Then, somehow—again, I don't know exactly *how*—Hiroshima knocked me to the ground and ran after Lucky." He pulled his shirtsleeve over his elbow and stuck it in my face. "See? I have a bruise right here. I may have broken my arm, actually."

I sighed, sounding just like Diane, and handed him the box of chocolates. He removed the lid, looked inside, and sniffed. "Can I have two?"

Grandma breezed by and said she was taking Papa home because he had an upset stomach.

"He's sick?" asked Diane, frowning.

"He's just feeling puny," said Grandma. "Too much excitement."

Before anything else could go wrong, Ms. Chu appeared, ghost-like in her flowing gray dress. In her whispery voice, she asked me to come to the library with her. "I have a book you might need," she said.

The library smelled of pine oil and books. It was silent except for the shutting of the heavy wooden door and the rustle of Ms. Chu's skirt. When she pulled the gold chain on the lamp, sending shadows across the wall, I sank into a red faux-leather chair in the reading nook.

"Long day?" she asked. I nodded. We sat for a few minutes, watching dust motes in the air. She asked me how the novel was coming.

"Almost done," I said.

"That's good. What did you discover?"

"Oh, you know. The usual stuff. Chaos versus order, woman versus nature, good versus evil, individual versus society, the evils of racism, the effects of capitalism on the individual, the fallacy of eternal love, loss of innocence, appearance versus reality, the circle of life—" I couldn't tell her the rest. She'd have to read it.

"Ah," she said.

"I took some cheap shots at my characters," I admitted, "and I almost kicked Anders out."

"I wouldn't exclude Anders," said Ms. Chu. "He's very sensitive." She folded her hands in her lap. "He's your mirror."

Oh joy, I thought, but I didn't say it. Looking around at the polished shelves, I imagined slipping between the covers of the books, feeling the bumps of words on the page, climbing each line like the rung of a ladder. That deep into a story, I might let go and fall forever.

"Ms. Chu?"

"Yes?"

"I don't know how to end the novel. I don't think I've lived long enough to know how things end." I thought of Joe, sliding across the black ice with his hands clenched on the steering wheel, his jaw set, blood pumping. Did he think, *That child molester Lafontaine gets to live, but I am jerked off the planet, leaving my wife a widow, my children orphans*? Or was it a relief to die? Does suffering ever end?

"Look at the beginning," said Ms. Chu. "The ending is usually there."

"So I make a circle?"

"No," she said. "A spiral. The ending returns to the beginning, but on a higher level." She padded over to her desk and returned with a worn copy of *Writer's Market*. "I've been waiting to give this to you, Aris. I think you're ready now." The inscription on the flyleaf read, *To my wife, Mandy, with love eternal—Douglas.*

When I stepped into the parking lot, I saw the silvery glint of Max's smooth rock sailing into the fishpond. Apparently, Anders had taught him how to skip rocks. His dad must have taught him.

You don't need a penis to skip a rock, but there are things that single mothers just don't stand around doing, and one of them is skipping rocks.

Diane had packed the dogs in the car and was leaning against the hood, saying goodbye to Penn. His head bent close to her face. She smiled up at him, the way she does. I swear it looked like they were going to kiss. Cynthia must have thought so too, because at that moment she hit the horn. It was a silver car, with a KEEP CALM AND GO SHOPPING bumper sticker. Strands of shiny pink beads hung from the rearview mirror.

"Hello, boys," I said as I approached the pond, shoring up more courage than I felt. The water was muddy from the rock throwing, with no fish in sight. When I leaned over to see if I could find a fish, Anders hurled a heavy rock that splashed water all over my chest.

"Oops," he said. "Wet T-shirt contest."

This is my mirror, Ms. Chu? "I *was* going to apologize," I said, wringing out my shirt.

"The dog escape was a misunderstanding," said Max. "I explained it to him. I told him you would put him back in the novel."

"What are you—my editor?"

"I'll write my own part and email it to you," said Anders.

"Also," said Max, "we need a car chase. We *really, really* need a car chase."

I looked at my little brother, grubby from toothpaste, dog biscuits, and chocolate, with mud up to his knees from wading in the pond. He made a guttural noise. Was this the same guy who had reached divine communion with the eternal spirit in front of a restless audience, less than an hour ago? In fact, we have had a car chase in this novel, a very short, rather slow one, more of a truck chase. I would never tell Max about it; he would worry his little head off. Every time we passed a logging truck, he'd pull out a gun app, which could cause problems.

Max's car chase happened like this. We were pulling out of the gates of Lavender Mountain Laboratory School, two cars behind Cynthia's car. Diane was a little tense. She was chewing two pieces of nicotine gum at the same time, and she gunned her engine at the red lights, which was unnecessary.

Suddenly, Max yelled, "Look! There they are! They're on the side of the road!"

Cynthia had pulled her car over to the shoulder. Penn was leaning into the open passenger door, apparently arguing with her. Suddenly, she reached out and slammed the door shut. Her tires spun on the gravel as she squealed back onto the highway.

Diane slowed down and opened the window. "Need a ride?"

"Little misunderstanding," Penn said as he slid into the seat.

"It happens," said Diane coolly. (Go, team Diane!)

She had just pulled back onto the road when Max yelled, "Cynthia is turning around! She's coming back! She's gaining on us! Gun it, Mom!"

"Somebody's interested," I said, with a significant look at Penn.

"And somebody ain't," he said.

"Anybody got any nails I could throw out the window?" asked Max.

"Get your head back in this car," said Diane.

"Tacks might work," he said, still hanging his head out the window.

"Windows up!" yelled Diane. Then she turned up the radio and stepped on the gas pedal. One of her favorite oldies was playing, "Bad Reputation" by Joan Jett. A little smile turned up the corners of her mouth.

Behind us, the pink beads swung wildly on Cynthia's rearview mirror, and Max wished aloud that he had a bomb.

"That's plan Zulu," said Penn, lapsing into the military alphabet code. "Just take this right by the Quik Mart, Diane, if you don't mind."

"The other thing we could do is get between two semis," Max said as we turned. "Then, when she's not looking, roll over in a ditch."

"Plan Yankee," said Penn.

"Hang on, everybody!" called Diane as we took another quick left into the parking lot of a warehouse.

"Oh no," said Max. "There she is again!"

"She caught the first turn," said Penn. "I don't think there's another way out of this parking lot. Y'all should let me out. I'll handle this."

"Nope," said Diane.

"I'm serious," said Penn. "This isn't a car chase."

"Yes, it is," said Max.

"You can't compete in today's contemporary fiction market without a car chase," I said.

"Diane?"

"You're with us, Penn. You always have been." Her eyes shined at him, and I felt a surge of hope. We were a team of four.

"Well, all right, then. Diane, I think we can squeeze between two Dumpsters back there. Back in, if you don't mind, and if she does find us, we'll accelerate onto the hood of her car and do a roof jump."

"I think you need to get a new battery for your truck," said Diane, backing in between the Dumpsters with her headlights off.

"Naw, I can fix it," said Penn.

Cynthia failed to see us hidden between two Dumpsters in the warehouse parking lot. Apparently, she gave up. Penn said she has a short attention span. Then, of course, we took Penn home.

It was a dark and foggy night with a smudge of moon in the sky when we pulled into the gravel driveway of the house where Penn lived with his mother, way out in the country. A dog ran out, barking at us until Penn got out of the car. "Walk me to the door?" he asked Diane.

"I'm coming!" called Max. "Wait for me!"

"You stay in the car," said Diane. I didn't wink or anything tacky like that, but I wanted to. A light came on in the upstairs window. I hoped to God the old person wouldn't come out. *Penn is old too,* I reassured myself. *At least middle-aged, like Diane. Surely they know how to do this.* I decided that the kiss/rejection that took place on our back porch the night Diane lost her job didn't count. Billy and I had gone through that stage early on in our relationship. *Wow! Yes, I'm attracted to you* [insert make-out scene] . . . *but now that I think about it, I can't do relationships.* As Diane had pointed out to me, Penn had a few dings. Who doesn't? We aren't talking about freshly minted human beings here. Penn and Diane have done a lot of living, and they have some things to work out. This might take a couple of camping trips, some meditation, and a hot bath for Diane.

"What's taking them so long?" asked Max as he craned his head over the seat to watch them. He tried to open his window, but the engine was turned off.

"They're falling in love," I said. "It takes a few minutes."

They had stopped by a garden hose. Penn was slowly rolling it up while the silhouette of Diane petted the dog.

Come on, come on, I thought, *forget about the hose. Kiss her!*

Write a Novel in Thirty Days! says that every love story is a story of frustration. As soon as the reader thinks the lovers will finally hook up—bam! Obstacle. Readers love to be tortured like this in love stories. It's sick, but what can a writer do? We just deliver the merchandise.

A light came on in the downstairs window. The dog ran to the door. Suddenly, Diane stepped closer to Penn. In the pale moonlight, she was a queen, standing tall (for her) and proud. Her hair was all out of the bun now, falling around her face. When her shoulders began to shake, I thought she might be sobbing, but she lifted her chin, and in the light from the window of the house, I could see her laughing. What was so funny? In one step, he was beside her, his arms encircling her waist. Her hands moved up his arms and then along his broad back as they kissed.

It went on for a while. Snogging, playing tonsil hockey, interfacing passionately with each other, making out, creating a field of physical obsession and focused arousal, Penn being Mack Daddy and Diane the Lady of the Night. I began to wonder if I might be having a little brother or sister. Where would it sleep? What would I name it?

Finally, an old woman stepped out on the porch and called, "Buddy? Is that you out there?"

On that dark, delicious drive home, while Max slept and Diane played love songs softly on the radio, I envisioned my new life with a complete set of parents. I'd wake up in the morning to the smell of bacon frying. I'd find Penn in the kitchen, wearing plaid flannel pajamas, flipping buttermilk pancakes. He'd become a lawyer or something, so Diane wouldn't have to be a maid. In the evenings, he'd fling the door open and call out, "Wasup, Lab rats?" Would we hug him?

He and Diane would kiss, husband and wife.

When people asked me about my dad, I wouldn't say, "He died." Instead, I'd say, "Oh, he's a lawyer. He springs innocent people." Because that's the kind of lawyer Penn would be. He'd represent people like Charles, after Miss Octavia stopped being mad at us. Quoting Eugene Debs in the courtroom, he'd revolutionize the South. After Penn changed things, we might not even mind living here. Should I call him my step-dad? Do you hyphenate that? There were so many details to work out. So many things to do. It was like Christmas.

FALLING ACTION

But words are things, and a small drop of ink,
Falling like dew, upon a thought, produces
That which makes thousands, perhaps millions,
think.

—Lord Byron[31]

According to *Write a Novel in Thirty Days!*, writers begin to have nightmares about their novels as they near the end. Mine started coming on Day 25. I dreamed that the book floated away in a sewer, that someone dropped my laptop in a bottomless mailbox, that Hiroshima ate the manuscript, page by page. My worst dream, of course, was about the critics.

They are sitting at a polished table in an office at the top of a tall building in New York City, with windows all around, although there is nothing to see but gray sky and other buildings. They are all thin, dressed in black, and verbally gifted. One of them sips from a glass of sweet iced tea with a bright green sprig of mint from Diane's garden. A woman wearing a tailored suit and a small gray hat with a squirrel tail holds my manuscript in her hands.

31   Lord Byron, I'm not getting a big head here. But who knows?

"It does seem to strain for attention," she says, "but there are moments—"

"Hasn't pedophilia been done this season?" asks a young Nigerian with a British accent. He nods to the corner where I stand butt naked, not knowing what to do with my hands.

"The question remains," says another woman, suddenly sitting up very straight, "how is she going to handle the grandparents?" They all look over at me.

Here's the missing sex scene. That's right, it's MISSING. We are on Day 26, with four days left to finish the novel, and no sex scene. Did Penn MacGuffin pull that lame excuse about not being ready to be in a relationship AGAIN? I mean, dude, wheelchair is waiting. No, of course not. My PMI was ready to bed and wed and be the new father of a bouncing 12.5-year-old girl and an eight-year-old whirling dervish. I'm sure of it.

Diane, however, decided she likes her independence.

"You are ruining my novel," I told her when she made this announcement at our Ad Hoc Thursday Night family meeting.

"You can't control everything, Aris," she said.

"I saw you kissing," said Max as he unwrapped a Dum Dum for his new collection. "In Penn's front yard, after the car chase." When he dropped the sucker on the floor, he quickly picked it up and licked it clean. "It was gross," he said.

"It was beautiful," I said. "The perfect prequel to an ideal sex life."

"Aris, really! Use your boundaries."

"The human brain is wired to follow patterns," I said. "I read about this in *Write a Novel in Thirty Days!* The reader doesn't just want to follow a plot; she *has* to do it. We have evolved into creatures who are programmed to connect the dots, and when we find a dot missing, we freak. My readers are sinking into a plot hole here. My thirty days are almost up, and I STILL DO NOT HAVE A FATHER."

"Also, Mom doesn't have a job," Max pointed out.

Diane picked up her clipboard and checked something off. I can't imagine what she just thought she had accomplished. She smiled patiently at us. "I know this is frustrating to you two," she said. "I know how much you like Penn, and I like him too. I like him a lot. He likes us—all three of us. In a way, he is a part of our family. However, he is not going to be my husband. He is not going to be your stepfather. No, Aris, I am not going to sleep with him."

"Ew," said Max.

"Penn and I have talked about this. He has still expressed some concerns about his ability to be in a mature relationship—Aris, I saw your little face in Max's window that night, so you probably heard our conversation. His marriage didn't work out, and he has some issues to resolve there. He's not ready to move on."

"But you kissed him AGAIN," I said.

"It was the car chase," said Max, shaking his head. "I'm sorry I ever mentioned it." He leaned back in his chair, tipping it off the front legs, then remembered that he would fall and bust his head, and came forward again.

"In a traditional family, children would not be grilling a parent about her romantic life," Diane said to no one in particular.

"We are not traditional," I reminded her, "and this is a family meeting, where we discuss whatever is on our minds."

"Right," said Diane. She took a deep breath. "I told Penn that I didn't want to be in a relationship."

"Why?" Max and I said at the same time.

"I like my independence," she said. She shrugged. "I like sleeping alone in my bed. I like making all the decisions about money, and everything else, by myself. I like farting freely and not having in-laws."

"A husband could work," said Max. "Then you could be a housewife and stay home with us."

"That is so fifties," I said.

"I do want to spend more time at home with you," said Diane. "My new job will allow me to work from home. I've been meditating about my purpose in the world, my role of service to the community. I'm still revising my mission statement, but I know that I want to be a full-time mom while helping people find space in their lives so they experience the present moment more deeply."

"Decluttering?" I asked.

"Yes, you can call it that. We'll start on the physical level, addressing the whole underlying issue of chaos to design a streamlined space and a calendar with elbowroom. Then we'll be free to move on to the tangle of issues represented by that clutter. We create the environment that reflects our mind, and the mind itself is an environment reflecting the metaphysical landscape of the universe. So we enter into the realm of spiritual consciousness."

"She's going to be a maid," I told Max.

Diane gave me a hurt look.

"What about our playhouse?" asked Max. "It's not finished. It's still a shed, mostly."

"Penn will finish it," said Diane. "He's still our PMI. Actually, I think Charles is going to help him. They seem to be friends now. Anyway, Charles said he would drop by tomorrow."

Max drew the empty sucker stick out of his mouth and examined it. "Two men in the backyard doesn't make a dad," he said.

At that moment, every single light bulb in the house blew out.

"Sometimes we go through a box of light bulbs a week," Diane explained to the electrician the next afternoon. Papa had brought him to the house. His name was Danny. He had a watermelon belly and wore stiff new overalls.

"You're spending a fortune on light bulbs," said Papa. "A light bulb should last six months or even a year. I hope you're not leaving lights on when you aren't using them. If you are, you're just throwing money away." When Papa imagines Diane throwing money away, he looks like he is in physical pain.

"Let me check your voltage meter," said Danny.

While he and Papa were checking the voltage meter on the side of the house, Charles knocked on the door.

"Come in, come in," said Diane, wiping her hands on her apron. "I was just making black bean brownies. Hiroshima, be quiet! You know Charles."

"Black bean brownies?"

"You can't even taste them," she said, which is true.

Charles leaned down to pet Hiroshima. Then he had to pet Lucky. Then Hiroshima again. Then Lucky. The dogs get insanely jealous of each other. When he stood back up, he towered over Diane. Even in jeans and a T-shirt, he looked like an important person.

Diane lit a candle and set it on the table beside the couch. It was daytime, but dark and gloomy. "Have a seat," she said.

"Did your electricity go out?"

"It's just the lights," said Diane. "The electrician is checking them now with my dad."

Her face was so pretty in the candlelight—I wished Penn was here to see her. He would change her mind. That's how it is supposed to happen. She says no. He says please, please, please. Then she says yes, and we live happily ever after.

"Any word from the court?" Diane asked Charles.

"Yes, ma'am," said Charles. "I've decided to do my time over our spring break, which starts in two days. Might as well get it over with. I wanted to come by and tell you in person."

"I wish the judge had let you read your statement at the trial," said Diane. "It was beautiful. With every manuscript, your writing grows more powerful."

"Thank you," said Charles. "I thought writing was going to get me out of trouble, but it's gotten me into trouble."

"Charles, I'm sorry about my part in this. If I led you to believe you could write yourself out of that jail sentence—it's because *I* believed it. It never occurred to me the judge wouldn't allow you to read your statement."

"We all have our blind spots," said Charles. "It's natural for an English teacher to expect people to read. Honestly, writing that statement helped me see the situation more clearly. And the free-write! If my mama ever saw that . . ." He shook his head, whistling softly. "I'm sorry she lashed out at you after the trial. She doesn't want to hear one word about my father. She doesn't want anybody to know about him. To Mama, what's in the family stays in the family."

Diane nodded. "Also, she's a mother. She wants to protect you, especially right now. You are in a vulnerable position, and she feels threatened by the idea that you are exposing secrets."

"Maybe she's right?"

Diane thought about this. "Secrets are heavy to carry, but they aren't armor. The act of revelation requires courage. Drawing on that courage in the continuous exercise of expression—that is what makes you strong."

"Ms. Montgomery-Thibodeau, I don't mean to disagree with you, but—"

"Please call me Diane. I'm not your teacher anymore."

"Diane—" He smiled nervously. "Diane, I agree that exercising courage makes you strong, but I'm not entirely comfortable writing personal things. Frankly, I don't see myself as a writer." Leaning toward her on the couch, he said, "You, on the other hand—I can envision a book with your name on it."

"I don't write anymore," said Diane.

"Don't teach, don't write. What do you do, if you don't mind my asking?"

"I'm breathing," said Diane. "It's harder than it looks."

Papa and the electrician came back in the house shaking their heads as they talked. When Diane introduced Charles to Papa as one of her students, a look of recognition flashed through his eyes, but he just said it was nice to meet him.

"Yep," Danny was saying as he turned a bulb over in his meaty hand. "See how this bulb has got thick filaments?" He passed it to

Papa like an egg. "You've got a name-brand bulb here. It shouldn't burn out so fast. Wiring is good. Switches good. Voltage at one-twenty, like it's supposed to be."

"Come over here, Diane," Papa said. "You need to learn about these things. I may not always be around to help you."

Just then, the timer on the oven went off, and Diane slipped off to put the brownies on the table.

Danny took a long look at Charles. "I seen you somewhere," he said.

Charles raised an eyebrow, then went to the bathroom to wash his hands.

Danny said in a quiet voice, almost to himself, "I seen him somewhere. Maybe in the paper . . ."

Papa looked straight at him and then continued to look at him with a pleasant expression on his face, letting it be known that in this circumstance, he was as deaf as a stone and only a fool would keep talking. He had a lot of practice doing this with Grandma.

"Papa," said Max, "come outside and see the playhouse we're making out of the shed. We're going to paint it purple with the paint Mom bought for the shutters. You don't mind if we paint the playhouse purple, do you? No one can see it from the street."

"That reminds me," said Diane. "Charles—Penn texted me and asked if you could pick up a couple of paint trays. He forgot to buy them at the store."

"I'll get them," said Charles, pulling his car keys out of his pocket. I think he was relieved to get away from Danny.

"Purple?" asked Papa as he followed me and Max out to the playhouse. "Where did you put the lawn mower?" he asked as he opened the door to his former shed. "You can't put the lawn mower in the garage. That thing has gasoline in it. Your house will blow up."

Max and I played dumb on the whereabouts of the lawn mower and the gardening tools.

"Who is doing this for y'all? Penn? Where is he?"

Again, we were helpless to respond. He walked around the shed, poking at the unfinished second story, my office. Despite himself, he was interested.

"How do you get up there?"

"Penn is building a ladder," I said. "And a dumbwaiter."

"A dumbwaiter?" Papa smiled. "Penn can do just about anything, can't he?" Then he frowned again. "He's got to build some kind of rail up there, or you'll fall off and break an arm. That's not safe."

"It's going to have walls on the second floor. That's my office."

"*And* a roof," added Max. "Maybe with a chimney."

"There's no chimney," I said. "We don't have a fireplace."

"Penn said *maybe*."

"You absolutely cannot build a fire in here," said Papa, agitated now. "Why, with the old gas fumes in this shed, the place would go up in smoke in two minutes. It might explode."

"We're not building a fireplace," I told Papa, patting him on the back to help him calm down. His face was bright red, and I could feel his heart pounding in his back.

"Your mother should have asked me permission before she did all this. I had no idea. How is she going to pay for it?"

"It's free," said Max.

"Nothing is free," said Papa. "I may not have learned much in eighty years, but I know that for sure. Nothing, absolutely nothing, is free." He started picking up scraps of wood on the ground. "Here's a nail," he said. He held it up, huffing. "Look at that sucker. Somebody would have stepped on that and gone to the hospital. I hope you all have had your tetanus shots. You have to keep up with those. If you get a rusty nail in your foot, and that thing gets infected . . ." He took a white, ironed handkerchief from his back pocket and wiped his brow before replacing it. He looked at the nail again, checking it for rust, then put it in his front pocket. "Y'all jumped headlong into this project without asking anybody," he said. "You have to plan something like this carefully. You can't do it pell-mell, leaving nails all over the ground, putting gasoline in the garage . . ."

Max started to cry. "Please don't take our playhouse away, Papa. Please. I'll pick up the nails on the ground. We don't have to paint it purple. We can paint it gray, or any color—your favorite color."

"What are you crying for?" Papa took the handkerchief back out of his pocket and unfolded it so he could wipe Max's eyes. "Here, now, stop that. I want you to have fun. I just want you to be safe. We don't want anybody going to the hospital, do we?" When he had settled Max down, he looked back at the house, sticking his tongue out of the corner of his mouth the way he does when he's concentrating. "I can't figure out what's going on with those light bulbs," he said. "That's a mystery."

Back in the kitchen, Danny stood on a ladder with a screwdriver in his fist, squinting into a socket.

"I'll tell you what," Danny said, climbing down the ladder. "This may sound funny, but I've seen it before." He stuck the screwdriver in his back pocket. "Y'all got a spirit in here."

Papa laughed, but Danny didn't join him.

"I'm serious," said Danny. "You can call it a ghost or a spirit or whatever you want. People say different things. From a scientific point of view, what you've got going on in this house is a pretty powerful electromagnetic field."

"Is that right,"[32] said Papa. It wasn't a question.

"Somebody around here is a conductor," said Danny. He looked at each of us with suspicion. "I knew a lady that had the same problem. All she had to do was walk into a room and the bulbs would pop. One after another."

"Isn't that something,"[33] said Papa.

---

32 In southern gentleman code, that means, "You're full of shit."
33 "You're still full of shit."

"Yes, sir. It got so bad with her that she'd head down the sidewalk and the streetlights would go out. One after another, as soon as she got under them."

"Imagine that,"[34] said Papa.

"Well, her family got to thinking she had an evil spirit in her—you know how they are over in Alabama. They had an exorcism. I don't know how you feel about snake churches, but that's where they carried her to have the evil spirit removed." Danny shook his head at the wonder of it all. "The way I see it," he continued, "if God went to the trouble to put a rattle on a poisonous snake, he's done his part. If you don't have the sense to leave it alone—"

"There's another one," said Max, pointing at the ceiling. "Another light bulb went out."

"Well, I'll be darned," said Papa, and Danny shook his head.

"My point being," said Danny, "this lady ultimately had to make a sacrifice."

"Did she kill a sheep?" asked Max.

"No, young man, she did not. She moved to Michigan. She paid a rent up there that you would not believe, and it was cold as the dickens. But she sold that house—that's my point. What you've got in here, whether you want to call it a ghost or whatnot, is extra energy. It's coming up around the current. It's kind of like a vibration, but not one that most people can feel. I don't see it going away anytime soon."

Papa wrote Danny a check, and he left. "Everybody has a story," he said as he opened a fresh box of light bulbs. Papa himself had never looked deeply into the subject of ghosts. His expertise was managing human beings in the world of business, and he was familiar with the wiles of electricians. All the same, he looked pale and tired.

"Why don't you stretch out on the couch?" suggested Diane, bringing him a glass of water. Papa said no, he was dirty from

34 See previous footnote.

working in the garage; he didn't want to mess up the couch. Then he did the strangest thing—he lay down on his back in the middle of the living room and took a ten-minute nap.

Shortly after Papa left, Penn came to the door. I swear, it was beginning to seem like we had a social life. Somebody in, somebody out—I have a deadline here, people! Novels don't write themselves. However, Penn was holding a sack in his hand, and that was interesting. Diane waved him into the house as she traipsed by the window. She wore sweat pants and a T-shirt with *ALASKA* printed in faded letters across the front. Definitely not a breakup outfit. Just as you end a chapter with the reader wanting more, you should end a relationship looking provocative. But maybe she didn't know this?

"I found something at the Salvy you might like," Penn said, handing me the sack.

"My mad bomber hat!" I shrieked. "You found it!"

"Look at that!" exclaimed Diane, popping back into the living room. "Is it the same one?"

"This is my hat," I confirmed as I pulled it onto my head. Rules be damned, I wrapped my arms around Penn.

"Now I'll have to take a bath," he said, but he was smiling.

Diane touched the hat on my head tenderly, as if it were alive. "I'm so sorry I tried to get rid of it. That was wrong. Penn, can I pay you for it?"

"Catch me another time," he said, looking at his feet.

I sent Diane a telepathic message: *This is the man you are discarding?*

He and Diane weren't totally ignoring each other that afternoon—just enough to seem like a real married couple. Mostly, he talked to Charles, who had some experience with drywall. As they worked on the playhouse, they debated the existence of God. Max trailed behind them, picking up nails. Diane and I remained available for consultation on the back porch, where we were finishing up the pan of brownies.

"So what exactly are the symptoms of writer's block?" I asked her. I had three days left to finish my novel, and there were unresolved issues.

Before she could answer, her cellphone rang. "Damn," she said, glancing at the caller ID. Into the phone, she said, "Hi, Mom. I'll have to call you back."

Suddenly, she stood up. Turning her back to me, she said, "What? When? He was just over here. Oh my God, no!"

Please not Papa, I prayed. *Don't take my Papa too.*

But I knew it was him, even before Diane turned off the phone and faced us.

"My father has had a stroke," she said.

I do not do hospital scenes. I appreciate the medical services so readily available to us in this country, especially to those who have medical insurance, but I hate hospitals. As soon as I find myself in the bowels of one, I look for the exit, which is usually hidden. When I encounter a hospital scene in a book, I skip right over it.

The only thing I will share here about Papa's stay in Room 311 is the picture he drew for the neurologist. The doctor asked him to draw a clock.

"What kind of clock?" asked Papa.

"Just a regular clockface," said the doctor, handing him a pad and pen. "Round, with numbers and hands. Whatever you like."

While Papa was drawing his clock, the doctor smiled at us. "State-of-the-art diagnostic technology," he said.

Here is Papa's clock.

I took a picture of it with my phone and sent it to Kate, explaining about the stroke, which the doctor called a "ministroke." Then I googled Salvador Dalí's painting *The Persistence of Memory*. That was it—that was the Alzheimer's clock! I sketched Dalí's clock and sent it to Kate.

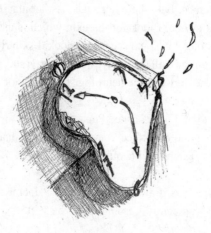

Kate texted back.

:0 He's in the 4th dimension!

At first, Papa was not fond of the fourth dimension. He kept asking for his checkbook, and he suspected Grandma of having an affair with one of the male nurses. He did well in physical therapy, however, referring to his young female therapist as "my trainer." He refused to draw any more clocks for doctors.

"I'm not an artist," he told them, and they sent him home.

The day before Charles went to jail, he came to see us. From the window, Max admired the BMW parked neatly in our driveway—he had decided to get one for himself when he was sixteen.

Suddenly, he yelled, "Miss Octavia is here!" We watched as Charles walked around to the passenger side of the car to open the door for his mother and then carried her packages to our front door.

"Well, my goodness!" said Diane, in her southern-hospitality voice. "This is a treat. You all come inside."

"Charles told me about your father's stroke," Miss Octavia said. "I'm so sorry. I fixed y'all a dinner—you probably can't even think about cooking right now. We won't stay long."

Did Miss Octavia know that Diane never thought about cooking? She must have, because when the bags were unloaded, we had a party on the table: fried chicken (huge platter—a henhouse massacre), a cold pink ham, creamy potato salad, coleslaw, corn on the cob, my favorite green bean casserole (with the French onion rings on top), and a three-story chocolate cake.

"We will certainly need some help eating this," said Diane. She called Grandma and Penn and told everyone to come over.

"How is your father?" asked Miss Octavia.

"He's recovering quickly. He had a TIA stroke, which is mild, but it has left some neurological damage that the doctors don't quite understand. The shock to his body may have triggered the onset of dementia."

"It's a deus ex machina," I said as I licked a finger that had accidently trailed along some chocolate frosting.

"Say what?" said Charles.

"Aris is writing a novel," explained Diane.

"I thought you were supposed to be finished with your novel today," said Max.

"I'm blocked, okay?"

"Fine by me," said Max. "I just thought this was the last day."

"It is day twenty-eight, actually. I have thirty days."

"It's not a leap year," he said.

"Leap year has nothing to do with my deadline!" I hissed, and then I had to leave the room. Writer's block is a serious matter. I put on my mad bomber hat. When I had it securely fastened, I felt calmer, but the block wouldn't budge. After her last review, Ms. Chu said that enough terrible things had happened in my novel—I did a good job with that—but now the characters needed to reflect. She wanted to see a scene with Aris and Max reflecting. I told her that aside from the anomaly at the talent show, Max doesn't stay still long enough to reflect. The rest of us are too busy with our new social life.

When Penn arrived, wearing a tool belt, Charles grinned with relief. "I was hoping we could finish up that drywall today," he said. "I hate to leave it for a week."

"I hope you men are going to sit down first and eat," said Miss Octavia.

"Penn doesn't eat," explained Max.

Miss Octavia paused with her knife over the ham and cocked her head at Penn. "Is something wrong with you?"

"Yes, ma'am," said Penn. He bowed his head humbly and then sashayed out the door.

Did I note an expression of longing on Diane's face as she watched his exit? What would happen when the playhouse was finished? Would he stop coming over? Miss Octavia looked at the retreating figure of Penn, at Max, who had followed him out with a chicken leg under his shirt, and then at Diane. She knew a love story when she saw one. I was hoping we might discuss this—now that it was just the women in the kitchen—but Diane had geared herself up for an apology.

"Octavia," she said as she poured herself a glass of tea, "I know that I offended you at Charles's trial."

Miss Octavia looked deeply into the coleslaw she was stirring.

"In my excitement over Charles's essays—they are so promising—I was insensitive to what their exposure might mean to his family, to you."

"My knees are talking to me," said Miss Octavia. "I think I'm gonna sit down here a minute." When she sat down at the table, the chair disappeared beneath her. She was wearing a white sweatshirt with *Praise Joy Church* on the front, and big red hoop earrings. "He showed me the essays last night," she said. "I read them all. I read them more than once. I read your comments, Diane—and yours as well, young lady."

When she looked at me with those purple eyes, I shrank two sizes. How did she know! Before Diane could come up with an intelligent explanation for letting a child grade her college students' essays, Miss Octavia resumed her speech.

"I see more than you think I do. Those essays—well, now I know why Charles stopped eating corn." With the back of her hand, she wiped a tear from her eye, and then another. "He's a good man. He shouldn't be going to jail—to jail!"

Diane handed her a napkin. She was trying to think of the right thing to say, but there was no right thing. Outside, all three hammers were going on the playhouse: bangetybang, from Penn, bangbangbang from Charles, and bangthudyelp from Max.

"I'm sorry," said Diane. "It's not fair."

Miss Octavia wiped her eyes carefully with the corners of the napkin and straightened her shoulders. When she spoke again, her voice rose above the sound of the hammers. "Who said life is fair?"

This was a rhetorical question; Diane and I kept our mouths shut.

"The Lord may be testing Charles now," said Miss Octavia, "but he won't give him more than he can handle. The Bible says, right there in the first Corinthians, God 'will not suffer you to be tempted above that ye are able; but will with the temptation also make a way to escape, that ye may be able to bear it.'"

"Penn's an atheist," I said.

"Is that right," said Miss Octavia. She took a sip of tea, studying Penn through the glass doors as if he were a zoo animal. "You have to believe in something," she said. "Even if it's nothing."

"I hope his beliefs won't be detrimental to Charles in any way," said Diane. "Penn likes Charles. He admires him. He wants to be his friend. Penn is—" she said, and stopped. "Well, he would hate to hear this, but he is more like Christ than most Christians."

Miss Octavia laughed then, showing the gold tooth at the back of her mouth. "Oh, Charles, he loves him an atheist. I believe this may be the Lord's work after all."

When I stepped out on the porch, Penn and Charles were having another go at converting each other.

"Okay," said Penn, leaning one arm against the railing. "You're saying God exists but can't be seen, like a radio wave. Actually, physicists have been able to detect radio waves by bouncing light off a vibrating nano-membrane, but I'll leave that point for a moment. Let's say that we cannot detect God because God doesn't want us to detect him. Why is he hiding?"

"So he can be revealed."

"Standard lock-tight," said Penn. "But the same could be said for leprechauns. So how is he revealed?"

"For example," said Charles, "through me. Through this discussion. You see, the soul is the vibrating nano-membrane in this case."

Penn smiled, took a cigarette from behind his ear, and lit it.

When I went inside, Grandma was coming through the front door. "Yoo-hoo!" she called. "Anybody home?"

"Where's Dad?" asked Diane.

"Oh, he's probably still getting out of the car. He's such a slow-poke."

"Mom!" cried Diane. "He has had a stroke! Don't leave him in the car!"

"Pshaw," said Grandma. "He's fine. They gave him a cane. He's just dawdling. Go out there and see about him."

When Diane darted out the door, Grandma turned to Miss Octavia. "You must be the friend that brought all this food."

"Yes, ma'am," said Miss Octavia. "I heard about your husband's stroke, and I thought y'all might need some refreshment."

I was nervous that Grandma would say something like, *Is that black boy out there in the yard your son? Is that the one that got arrested? That one in the paper?* Miss Octavia would have to slap her. In the ensuing chaos, it would come out that Diane was unemployed. Then what would happen?

As if she could guess what I was thinking, Grandma narrowed her eyes at me. "Why are you wearing that hat in the house? Take that thing off. I can't see your face."

"I can't," I said.

"Why not?"

"It's stuck on my head."

"Stubborn," said Grandma. "You're as stubborn as your mother and your grandfather."

"Let me get you something to eat," said Miss Octavia.

"Thank you," said Grandma. "I am just worn-out. Diane doesn't understand how hard this has been on me. Henry's not right in the head since that stroke. I have to do everything now. He leaves it all to me."

"Would you like some corn on the cob?" asked Miss Octavia.

"Yes, that would be fine—you don't have to wait on me. Oh, where did you get those beautiful ears of corn this time of year?"

"That comes from my mother's garden," said Miss Octavia. "I got in the habit of freezing them because my son, Charles, he loved corn on the cob. But after he got back from his duty in Afghanistan, he wouldn't touch it. These days, I can't get rid of it."

"I grew up on a farm," said Grandma. "My daddy grew corn." Her face softened, remembering a happier time in her life.

Grandma was gnawing into her second ear of corn when Diane and Papa came in.

"I took him around back to show him the playhouse," said Diane.

"It's fantastic," said Papa. "Y'all should go outside and see that thing. It's two stories high. There's a playroom on the first floor for Max, and an office on the second floor for Aris." He smiled at us. "Penn is even putting windows in. I'm going to give him some money for glass."

"What about the lawn mower?" asked Grandma. "You were worried about that. Where are they going to put the lawn mower with all that gasoline?"

"What lawn mower?" asked Papa.

"The lawn mower!" she shouted. "The one you bought for them. The one you use to mow their lawn, honey. You said it had to stay in the shed, and now they have turned the shed into something else. What is wrong with you?"

Papa shrugged. "I don't care where they put the lawn mower. It's their house."

"It's our house," said Grandma. "We own it. We paid for it. You were afraid Diane was going to set it on fire if the lawn mower was in the garage."

"That's crazy," said Papa.

"Crazy how? All you have to do is tell her. She doesn't listen to me."

"Why not?"

"Henry! Have you lost your mind?" She looked at me and Miss Octavia and then out in the yard at Penn and Charles and Max. "He's lost his mind," she said to all of us.

Papa came to the table with a plateful of chocolate cake and sat down.

"That's a sharp hat you're wearing, Aris," he said. "That looks like the hat your daddy used to wear, up in Alaska."

"Henry! What are you doing?" cried Grandma. "You can't eat all that cake. Put that back. That's for dessert."

Papa took a bite of cake. He licked his lips. "I can do whatever I want," he said, laughing. "This is the best chocolate cake I've ever had in my life." Then he stood up and looked through the French doors. "There he is. Look, Diane, he's building you a house. He needs to paint it, though. Don't we have some paint in the garage?"

He shuffled out to the garage and came back in a few minutes later with the can of purple paint. He said, "My! Wasn't that a pretty color."

After our guests had all left, except for Penn, I went outside. There was an eerie silence in the yard. Where was everyone? Even Max had disappeared. Looking around the empty backyard with the purple playhouse where a shed used to stand, I felt a moment of panic. Everything was changing. It was changing right before my eyes, faster than I could write it down. Diane was wrong. You could not "address the whole underlying issue of chaos to design a streamlined space." You could not move that fast. Maybe God could look at a heap of Legos and zap! But human beings? Any novelist can tell you that character study inevitably reveals some poor sucker hanging on by a thread.

"Diane!" I called. No answer.

"Hello!" I called. "Is anybody out here?" Penn and Max came around the corner of the house, where they had been washing out the paintbrushes.

"Where is Diane?"

"She's in there," Penn said, inclining his head toward the playhouse.

Diane was standing in the dwarf-sized door of the playhouse, looking out at us. The doorframe fit perfectly around her, like a picture frame, but the house was too small for her. She looked as though she could lift the entire building on her back and walk off like a turtle.

"There's still some work to do on your office, Aris," Penn said. "I don't have the right size board to fix that hole in the floor, but I have to leave now."

"No!" yelled Max. "Don't go!"

"I'll be back," said Penn. He pinched the red ember of his cigarette until it was out and placed it carefully behind his ear, saving it for later.

"Please stay," said Max. "Please. We haven't finished working."

"I'm done for today, buddy," said Penn.

"No!" I yelled at him.

"No? No what?"

"I have abandonment issues," I said.

"Plus, we like you," said Max.

Facing us, Penn said in a hoarse voice, "What did I say? I *said*, I'll be back."

I wanted to ask him when he would be back. I wanted to ask him all the questions you can't ask Penn. Penn, why do you do this, why don't you do that? Penn, my readers would like to know, Who do you love? Who will you touch? How will you live if you don't have any money? Are you lonesome, Penn? He looked at us with his silvery eyes shining beneath the faded brim of his cap, the closest thing to Jesus I'd ever seen. Then he turned, broad shoulders blocking my view, and was gone.

Two days later, we received a letter from Charles.

As I write this, my first letter from the Kanuga City jail,
I am aware of my subconscious desire to emulate the
greatness of a similar correspondence, Letter from the
Birmingham Jail, by the Reverend King. My little note
follows like a moth after an eagle in the great tradition
of black men writing from behind bars. However, unlike
the Reverend, and despite the spirited provocations of
my friend Penn MacGuffin, who has already visited me
here, I fight for no great political cause.

Ms. Montgomery-Thibodeau, Diane, you have read
some of the story of my childhood. You know the pain
I have suffered growing up in an impoverished home
dominated by a violent, ignorant father. You know, as
well, if you have read between the lines, my love for
that man and the despair I felt when I faced him in his
cage-for-life. For me to spend even one week in a jail
cell—like him—is an inexpressible horror.

And yet it is through suffering that we receive

grace. There is a small library here in a converted
storage room, and among the Harry Potter books
and gardening manuals, I have discovered Memories,
Dreams, Reflections, by Dr. Carl Jung. You talked about
Dr. Jung in our class, sharing his view that religion
is man's defense against God. With all due respect, as
a Christian, that didn't sit well with me at the time.
However, when I saw the author's photo on the back of
the book—an older man wearing his glasses pushed up
on his forehead, smiling with his eyes at the reader—I
knew I had found a friend.

Diane, as I confessed to you the other day, despite
the wonderful things I learned writing the essays you
assigned, I have no ambitions to become a writer. As
I read Memories, Dreams, Reflections, my decision
to join the ministry is confirmed, and I grow more
convinced with every line that I have found my next
teacher. Dr. Jung states that he never believed in God—
how could he believe in something that simply exists?
We do not say, "I believe in the sun." I am sure Penn
and I will go around the boxing ring with this one, and
I look forward to our next match! I do not judge my
friend Penn for his disbelief. I met several atheists while
I was stationed in Afghanistan. In fact, it was there,
where I earned the nickname "Preacher," that I first
felt my calling to serve the Lord. Carl Jung tells us that
he never experienced the absence of God anywhere on
earth except in the church. You can imagine how the
revelation affects me—I aspire to build the church he
would attend.

Please send my regards to your wonderful parents, to
the enchanting Aris, and to that fine young man Max.

Yours in Christ,
Charles

DENOUEMENT

"Have you thought of an ending?"

"Yes, several, and all are dark and unpleasant,"
said Frodo.

"Oh, that won't do!" said Bilbo. "Books ought to
have good endings. How would this do: and they all
settled down and lived together happily ever after?"

"It will do well, if it ever came to that," said Frodo.

"Ah!" said Sam. "And where will they live? That's
what I often wonder."

— J.R.R. Tolkien,
The Fellowship of the Ring

"I thought your novel was supposed to be finished," says Max,
looking over my shoulder as I type at the kitchen table.

"I'm wrapping it up," I tell him. Reading over my last chapter
is difficult with Max breathing in my ear, drumming his fingers on
the table. "Max," I remind him for the millionth time, "you're in
my personal space."

According to Wikipedia, personal space ranges from eighteen
inches to four feet. My bubble is right at four feet. As you probably
know by now, that distance is hard to find in our house. I haven't
used my under-the-bed office since I read "Greensleeves." I don't
even like to lie *on top* of my bed. In some weird way, it seems like

Mr. Lafontaine is under there, along with the red-haired driver of the logging truck, Grandma on her bad days, and now, Judge Burr Wiglett. They are all rolled up together, all those shadow selves, in one under-the-bed monster.

"Isn't Day 30 gone?" Max asks.

"This *is* Day 30. I have time."

"How much time?"

"Several hours."

"Three hours?"

"Stop it, Max! We have enough control freaks in this family." With my elbows resting on the table, I drop my head in my hands and imagine myself sobbing on Dr. Dhang's divan.

"Aris," says Max, pulling on my arm. "Are you okay? Why are your eyes closed? Are you sad? Are you falling asleep? Wake up, Aris." When I open my eyes, he says, "You can finish your novel in your office now. I nailed a small piece of wood over the hole in your floor so you won't fall through."

Outside, after taking a deep sniff of fresh wood shavings, I swivel both earmuffs of the mad bomber hat over my ears. It is getting cold. Ghost Daddy will have to communicate with me as best he can. After climbing the ladder to my new office, I haul my laptop up on the dumbwaiter and sit cross-legged on the floor. "God Is, God Isn't" has worn off both of my shoes, so I am back where I started. Or, perhaps, according to Ms. Chu, I have spiraled above that point? I look down, through the hole Max sawed in his ceiling, around the stick he nailed over it, into his Lego room below. As I gaze into the colorful piles of plastic—a Legos Big Bang—and face the task of ordering chaos into creation, I feel the shiver of God's madness.

On my screen, I tap out, *It's March 2 here in Kanuga, Georgia, that vale of soul making. As the sun sets into the clouds, the sky deepens into lavender. For a few minutes, the ragged netting of the trampoline looks like lace. All around the Orchard, laundry machines kick into gear, mingling the scents of detergent with paper-mill pollution and the first delicate perfumes of spring. The End.*[35]

Silently, I read it over to myself. Then I read it aloud. It sounds good, but somewhere in the back of my mind, Diane's voice minces the word *shirking*.

"Well, yes, you cleaned your room, but you were *shirking*," she would say. Marching into the room, she would find socks stuffed in desk drawers, dirty laundry mixed with clean, notebooks kicked under the bed—evidence of the moral failure of shirking.

To distract myself from the panic of my deadline, I check all social media sites. When I see Billy's face, my heart oh so briefly flutters one broken wing—I am almost over it. Sifting through my emails, I find an intriguing new message from Anders:

> plz dont forget to put me in yr novel ok? heres what I wrote for the part about me this is a good ending you can call me seth

> > *Seth drove up in his retrobuilt 1969 Mustang Fastback in Yellow Blaze with a fuel-injected 5.0-liter V8 generating 420 horsepower. Aris was waiting on the curb wearing a halter with her hair down.*
> >
> > *"Want a ride?" he asked her. He thought it would be fun to go swimming.*
> >
> > *"Okay," she said after a minute. She acted like she didn't like Seth all that much but maybe she did. Seth knew girls could be that way.*
> >
> > *"You are prettier close up than far away," Seth told her after they went swimming. She was wet all over. Her hair looked like long twisted ropes.*
> >
> > *"That's profound," she said. She was always mak-*

---

35 Diane told me never to end a story with "The End." She says that's juvenile. I agree completely, but this is a novel, not a story.

ing fun of things. Especially of Seth. He didn't care.
He loved her half to death.

Thanks, Anders. That was very helpful.

Finally—once an egg sucker, always an egg sucker—I check Diane's email. Her password has been "joegone1" ever since my dad died. I scroll through the ballyhoo: Lab parent meetings, organic food newsletters, a few pathetic Match.com cries for help. I am about to mark everything as unread and close out when I see the message from Miranda Delmar.

Dear Seller,
I assume the inclusion of your journal with the purchase of a used copy of *Gone with the Wind* was inadvertent, but I like your writing style. I hope you don't consider this intrusive (how did the journal get in the package?), but I was enthralled with the stories in the notebook. I'm an editor at *The New Yorker,* and I would be delighted to read a manuscript if you have one. It sounds like you might have a memoir.

Immediately, I text Kate:

my mom isn't a maid anymore she's a writer

There is so much to do! I will have to remove Diane's handwritten copy of "Greensleeves" from its hiding place under my bed and type it up for *The New Yorker*. Oh, the editing! Even though Diane is an English teacher, or was an English teacher, she makes a lot of mistakes trying to make everything perfect. Rewriting until feebleminded is one of the pitfalls of OCD. Then, of course, there is my own novel to finish. According to the clock on my screen, I have a good twenty minutes left before my deadline. I take another stab at the ending.

It's March 2 here in Kanuga, Georgia, that vale of soul making. As the sun sets into the clouds, the sky deepens into lavender. For a few minutes, the ragged netting of the trampoline looks like lace.

I read it over, erase it. Hogwash. Should I mention my novel when I write back to Ms. Miranda Delmar? According to *Write a Novel in Thirty Days!*, connections can't be overlooked. I don't want Diane to think I'm competing with her, but a memoir and a novel are quite different. My novel will probably be marketed as a coming-of-age story, a bildungsroman, even if I don't see it that way. Frankly, I don't grow up in this tale. I merely survive. Due to nuances of the fourth dimension and the fate of all fictional characters, I, Aristotle Thibodeau, am eternally 12.5 years old, give or take thirty days.

Diane, on the other hand—well, let me just say that I'm proud of her.

The End

ACKNOWLEDGMENTS

First, I would like to thank my A-team: Andrea Robinson at Vintage Books and Adriann Ranta and Allison Devereux at Wolf Literary Services. Adriann made savvy suggestions for this novel before sharing it with potential publishers. Her minute-to-minute updates kept me on a thrilling email watch. When Andrea took possession of the manuscript, I discovered an editor whose ebullient enthusiasm was matched with the relentless determination of a pro. We edited line by line in a correspondence so demanding and delightful that I saved it all. Meanwhile, Allison led a brilliant and successful campaign to sell foreign rights. To these three women, and all the people at Vintage and Wolf—thank you.

Before this novel met a paying audience, it rested in the hands of kind, wise friends. I am deeply grateful to my friend Shannon Ravenel for offering me spirited encouragement on early drafts. Shannon has read my work since I first began publishing and edited my two previous novels. As I hacked away at *How to Write a Novel* in a dusty, rented room shared with a few pigeons, Shannon's scintillating notes of praise kept me moving forward. I also want to thank my Friday Writers: Faith Shearin, Adrienne Su, Diana Rico, Tammy Powell, and Ray Atkins, who share their writing lives with me and accept my weekly reports. To my dear friend and reader

Pam Redden, thank you for your laughter, your eagle eye, and your unwavering faith. Finally, I would like to thank William P. Clifton for loaning my character, Penn, a couple of his best T-shirts.

Many years ago, when I first had the idea for *How to Write a Novel*, I envisioned a nonfiction book on the craft of fiction writing, inspired by my phenomenal mentor, the late Max Steele. With this in mind, I queried some of Max's other students, asking for their memories of Max's creative-writing class. I would like to thank Daphne Athas, Doris Betts, Will Blythe, Clyde Edgerton, Mimi Herman, Alane Mason, Rick Moody, Lawrence Naumoff, David Rowell, John Rowell, and Bland Simpson for contributing notes and photos about our teacher to the blog http://friendsofmaxsteele .blogspot.com. I am forever indebted to Max, who would probably be happy that I wrote a novel instead of that other thing.

In addition to the inspiration and hard work of mentors, editors, agents, friends, and peers, a writer needs space and time to write. For this, I would like to thank the National Endowment for the Arts and Kennesaw State University for grants that afforded me the time to work. My sister-in-law, Leslee Sumner, has kindly hosted me (and my entourage) on literary trips to NYC. I am also grateful to the late George Pullen, who rented me that dusty office with pigeons for an unbelievably cheap price with the promise of acknowledgment here. You're a good soul, George. As always, I am grateful for the support and inspiration of my parents.

Finally, without my two children, Zoë Page Marr and Sumner Rider Marr, this novel would never have happened. In addition to hourly inspiration, you have shown endurance and often tenderness in your forbearance toward a mom who writes. I would like to acknowledge Zoë (Z. P. Marr) for her illustrations in this book, and Rider for his generous offer to create the soundtrack when it becomes a movie.